"You won't believe what just happened..."

"Tami, what's going on?" Aiden asked, his brow furrowing as he joined her.

Tami took a deep breath and recounted the call with her mother, each detail making her stomach twist tighter. "She thinks *we're* engaged."

Aiden's eyes widened in surprise. "Engaged? *You and me?*"

She nodded. "She and Miss Lana figured that it must be you." Why had she told her mother about the surprise announcement?

She felt the heat of embarrassment rise to her cheeks. The pressure from her family to settle down was too much, and when she'd thought she was bringing Gary home, she'd been thrilled... and relieved. A holiday free from her mother's matchmaking attempts. Now Gary was out of the picture and her mother thought she was marrying Aiden. "I didn't mean for any of this to happen!" Tami exclaimed.

"It's fine," he assured her. "We can straighten it out. Explain that it's a misunderstanding."

Tami eyed him. "About that... What if...we don't say anything right away? What if we pretended to be engaged for the holidays?"

Dear Reader,

There's something truly special about the holiday season—the glow of twinkling lights, the warmth of family gatherings, and the little traditions that make Christmas unforgettable. One of my favorites is making peppermint bark, a simple yet meaningful treat that always brings loved ones together.

Fiancé Under the Mistletoe is a heartwarming holiday story set on Polk Island, where Christmas has a way of turning the unexpected into something magical. Tami Adams never imagined she'd be posing as Aiden Worthington's fiancée, but what starts as a simple arrangement soon stirs emotions neither of them expected. As the island comes alive with festive cheer, Tami and Aiden must decide if their pretend engagement is just for the holidays—or something much more.

So, grab some peppermint bark, cozy up by the fire and get ready to experience the magic of Christmas on Polk Island.

Thank you for your support!

Jacquelin Thomas

FIANCÉ UNDER THE MISTLETOE

JACQUELIN THOMAS

If you purchased this book without a cover you should be aware that this book is stolen property. It was reported as "unsold and destroyed" to the publisher, and neither the author nor the publisher has received any payment for this "stripped book."

Recycling programs for this product may not exist in your area.

ISBN-13: 978-1-335-46024-0

Fiancé Under the Mistletoe

Copyright © 2025 by Jacquelin Thomas

All rights reserved. No part of this book may be used or reproduced in any manner whatsoever without written permission.

Without limiting the author's and publisher's exclusive rights, any unauthorized use of this publication to train generative artificial intelligence (AI) technologies is expressly prohibited.

This is a work of fiction. Names, characters, places and incidents are either the product of the author's imagination or are used fictitiously. Any resemblance to actual persons, living or dead, businesses, companies, events or locales is entirely coincidental.

For questions and comments about the quality of this book, please contact us at CustomerService@Harlequin.com.

TM and ® are trademarks of Harlequin Enterprises ULC.

Harlequin Enterprises ULC
22 Adelaide St. West, 41st Floor
Toronto, Ontario M5H 4E3, Canada
www.Harlequin.com

HarperCollins Publishers
Macken House, 39/40 Mayor Street Upper,
Dublin 1, D01 C9W8, Ireland
www.HarperCollins.com

Printed in U.S.A.

Jacquelin Thomas is an award-winning, bestselling author with more than fifty-five books in print. When not writing, she is busy catching up on her reading, attending sporting events and spoiling her grandchildren. Jacquelin and her family live in North Carolina.

Books by Jacquelin Thomas

Harlequin Heartwarming

Polk Island

A Family for the Firefighter
Her Hometown Hero
Her Marine Hero
His Partnership Proposal
Twins for the Holidays

Love Inspired Suspense

Sorority Cold Case

Love Inspired Cold Case

Evidence Uncovered
Cold Case Deceit

Love Inspired The Protectors

Vigilante Justice

Visit the Author Profile page
at Harlequin.com for more titles.

For Bernard

My love, my rock, my greatest blessing. Through every chapter of life, you have been my unwavering support, my safest place and my greatest love story. Your belief in me, your endless encouragement and the way you stand by my side mean more than words can ever express.

Thank you for loving me, for making me laugh and for always reminding me that I am never alone. This journey wouldn't be the same without you.

CHAPTER ONE

THE TRAIN'S RHYTHMIC hum filled the cabin as Tami Adams stared out at the scenic landscape speeding past her window. The early December chill seemed to seep through the glass, a stark reminder of how far she was from the warmer, tranquil shores of Polk Island, just across the bridge from Charleston, South Carolina. Charlotte loomed ahead, its bustling chaos a sharp contrast to the serenity she called home.

This trip wasn't supposed to feel so heavy. Tami had imagined arriving in the city filled with excitement, ready to celebrate her friend Jessica's wedding and kick off the holidays with joy. Just two days ago, she had envisioned introducing her boyfriend to her family during their Christmas-tree decorating party, believing it to be the perfect setting to announce their engagement—or what she thought would be their engagement. Instead, Gary had shattered her carefully crafted plans, leaving her blindsided and heartbroken when he'd revealed he was marrying someone else.

At thirty-three, Tami thought she was past the

kind of heartbreak that left one questioning everything. Yet here she was, clutching the leather straps of her tote like a lifeline as disappointment pressed down on her. She knew she should focus on the here and now—Jessica's wedding was meant to be a celebration of love and friendship—but Tami's broken heart made it impossible to feel truly present. A part of her wished she'd stayed on Polk Island, wrapped in the familiar comfort of home, avoiding the emotional minefield ahead.

As the train slowed to a stop, Tami braced herself for the cold and chaos waiting on the platform. With trembling hands and a resolve that felt more like survival than strength, she stepped into the bustling station, her tote clutched tightly against her side. The frigid air bit at Tami's cheeks as she quickly exited the building and flagged down a cab, eager to escape the clamor.

Once in a taxi, the vehicle ate up the miles as the Queen City rose before her, its skyline shimmering in the late afternoon sun. Bathed in golden light, the towering buildings and lively streets were nothing short of breathtaking, but Tami's mind was too preoccupied to fully appreciate the view. She sank deeper into her seat, the warmth of the taxi doing little to thaw the heaviness in her chest.

By the time the driver pulled up to her hotel, Tami's nerves were already frayed. She handed him a few bills, stepped out, and stared up at the imposing hotel before her. Taking a steadying breath, she reminded herself that this trip wasn't just about enduring—it was about showing up, even when it hurt. With that thought, she walked through the glass entrance.

Tami hurriedly checked into her room, aware that Friday evening in the city wouldn't pause for her.

Moments later, she exited the elevator and made her way briskly to her door, eager to refresh herself and shed the fatigue of travel.

As she changed into a simple yet elegant navy-blue dress, her reflection in the mirror revealed a duality she knew all too well. On the surface, she appeared confident and composed, every detail meticulously in place. But beneath the polished exterior was a constant battle with social anxiety disorder—a relentless inner voice that magnified every glance, every conversation, and every interaction into something potentially catastrophic.

For Tami, social anxiety wasn't just a fleeting nervousness. It was a persistent nuisance that made gatherings feel like a performance, where every move could be scrutinized. The anticipation of walking into a room full of people was enough to set her pulse racing and her thoughts spiraling. Yet with practiced determination, Tami adjusted her necklace, smoothed the fabric of her dress, and forced a steadying breath. Tonight, she told herself, she would not let the anxiety win.

She absently spun the outer band of her fidget ring, the smooth motion grounding her restless thoughts. The simple design, with its freely rotating band, was meant to calm nerves, though now it barely took the edge off. She hoped the wedding weekend in Charlotte would provide a chance to relax and enjoy herself without the persistent burden of her mother's matchmaking schemes.

Rachel Rose Adams had made it her life's mission to find her daughter a suitable husband. Tami couldn't remember a time when her mother wasn't trying to set her up with an eligible bachelor. It was draining, and the constant pressure had worn on her over the years.

While Polk Island was her hometown, it was also where she felt the weight of her mother's expectations the most. This trip to Charlotte was a long-awaited escape.

Rachel Rose's relentless matchmaking had not only strained their relationship but had also made Tami hyperaware of how others perceived her. She knew that many people in her small town judged her based on her mother's actions, seeing her as the desperate daughter of an overbearing woman rather than the independent, accomplished woman she was. Which only added to the social anxiety that had taken root in her life, making her feel even more isolated.

Tami had gone to great lengths to keep her struggles with social anxiety hidden—not just from her family, but especially from her best friend, Aiden Worthington. She was determined that he never find out. The thought of him seeing her as anything less than strong and self-assured filled her with dread. After everything that happened with Gary, the last thing she wanted was to appear fragile or like someone who needed saving. Her friendship with Aiden meant everything, and she couldn't risk anything—least of all the truth about her disorder—disrupting the easy, comforting bond they shared. As she finished getting ready, Tami took a deep breath, trying to steady herself. Tonight she would have to push through the anxiety, pretend everything was fine, and enjoy the wedding. But she couldn't shake the feeling that she was barely holding it all together.

Tami took one last look at herself in the mirror, smoothing the fabric of her dress and adjusting her necklace's clasp, then running fingers through her short hair to fluff up the tiny curls. She looked fine, but her nerves made her fidgety. She hadn't expected to go to Jessica's wedding alone. Initially, she thought Gary would be with her...

She'd managed to keep her composure throughout the week, deflecting Jessica's inquiries about why Gary wasn't coming. However, when she'd finally opened up to Aiden, her resolve crumbled. It had all just come pouring out.

Aiden hadn't hesitated. *You're not going alone. I got you*, he'd said, his voice steady, like it was the most obvious thing in the world. As if it wasn't a favor but simply what he did.

Now, staring at her phone, she reread his latest message. I'm near the hotel. Be there in two minutes.

Tami exhaled, but the breath felt thin. Her fingers trembled as she grabbed her clutch and coat, then she made her way to the elevator.

The ride down felt longer than usual, each second stretching, pressing in on her. Her heart pounded—not because of Aiden, never because of him. He was the one person who didn't make her anxious. No, it was the thought of the wedding, of navigating a crowded ballroom filled with laughter and love, of slipping into polite conversations while pretending she wasn't unraveling inside.

She had imagined tonight so differently. With Gary. A warm hand in hers, looking at her the way Jessica's fiancé looked at her. Tami and Gary had dated for almost a year—long enough for her to start believing he might be the one. Gary had this polished charm, the kind that turned heads when he walked into a room. Tall, broad-shouldered, with an easy smile and a crisp wardrobe to match, he knew how to say all the right things.

In the beginning, he made her feel seen. But he never fully understood her need for space. At times, he called her "too sensitive," accused her of being "high maintenance" when she needed time to recharge. When he'd dumped her—via text, no less—she began picking up the pieces of a heart she hadn't realized she'd handed over so completely.

So no, tonight wouldn't look like the picture she once painted in her mind. Instead, she'd be walking in alone—except she *wasn't* alone. Aiden had made sure of that.

Still, as the elevator doors slid open to the lobby, that old familiar weight settled in. The quiet dread of being seen yet unseen. Of being too much and not enough all at once.

And then, she spotted him.

He walked confidently through the entrance, clad in a navy-blue tailored suit that perfectly set off his deep brown skin. Standing at an imposing six foot three, Aiden naturally drew attention with his broad shoulders and athletic frame, making wearing even the most sophisticated suit appear effortless. His well-maintained dark dreadlocks framed his face, highlighting the strong lines of his jaw. His well-groomed mustache and beard lent him an air of sophistication, combining a sense of order with a welcoming presence. Aiden's steady, knowing brown eyes immediately met hers, and just like that, the tension coiled within her chest began to relax. His warm smile—familiar and reassuring—was genuine, meant solely for her. Tami let out a breath, feeling the pressure of tonight lighten slightly.

She gave him a playful grin. "Looking sharp, Aiden."

She couldn't help but notice how well his navy suit coordinated with her dress. It was an unplanned yet perfect coincidence.

"Thanks," he replied, his eyes sparkling with humor. "You're looking good yourself. Ready to head over to the venue?"

They fell into step, but Aiden soon cast a searching glance her way. "So...how are you holding up? Really?"

Tami hesitated, feeling the depth of his question. She'd kept her pain buried for days, but his steady gaze was like a crack in her armor. "I feel like such a fool," she admitted. "I really thought... I thought he was the one. I thought Gary and I had something special."

His brow tightened, and Aiden pulled her gently to the side, away from the other guests. "You believed in him, and he led you on. That's on him, not you."

Her throat clenched, and she looked down, fingers trembling as she clutched her purse. "Gary never once mentioned marriage, but I thought he was deeply in love with me," she whispered, shock and betrayal filling her as she remembered.

She was in Charleston a couple of weeks ago to pick up a gift for Mama. When she left the boutique, she saw Gary enter the jewelry store across the street. Curiosity got the better of her, and she'd followed him inside, where he was browsing engagement rings. Tears formed in her eyes as she recalled how in that moment, she'd assumed he was planning to propose. Excited by the thought, she'd told her family that she'd be bringing someone special home for Christmas and hinted at a big announcement.

"It turns out he was seeing someone else the whole time. Apparently, that's why he spent so much time in Savannah. He plans to marry her. He had the nerve to tell me that it was a hard decision for him because he cared for both of us..." Staring down at her hands, she added, "He was basically saying that I didn't make the cut."

Aiden's jaw tensed, his gaze darkening. "That guy never deserved you, Tami. It's his loss."

"I should've listened to you," she murmured, her voice barely a whisper. "You saw through Gary from the start, but I just—I didn't want to believe it." She'd wanted so badly for Gary to be different. For *her* story to be different. Not another cautionary tale about ignoring the signs.

"I'm so glad I kept our relationship to myself. Outside of you...nobody else knew anything about him. It was easy to keep our relationship quiet since he lived in Mount Pleasant. I wasted a whole year on him."

Aiden's gaze softened as he rested a hand on her arm. "Hey, don't blame yourself for trusting someone. That's not something to be ashamed of."

She looked up, meeting his steady gaze, finding comfort there. "I didn't want to introduce him to Mama until I was sure that we were headed toward marriage. I guess I made it easy for Gary to treat me like this."

"Try not to waste any more time thinking about him. He's not worth it," he said, his hand lingering on her arm for a moment. "Now, let's get to that wedding. Tonight we're going to have a great time celebrating Jessica and Rob."

She smiled, grateful he was here to help her get through tonight.

Tami and Aiden had been friends since middle school, bound together by an easy rhythm that had only strengthened over the years. They had both grown up on Polk Island, their lives weaving together like the tides on the shoreline of their hometown.

Although they were in the same sixth grade class, their friendship hadn't really started until the seventh grade when Aiden ended up sitting next to Tami in homeroom. He had always been easygoing, quick to make friends, but for some reason, he kept striking up conversations with *her*—the quiet girl who preferred books to crowds. From the moment they'd discovered their shared love of mysteries, they'd been inseparable. As time wore on, she found that Aiden was the first person to truly *see* her—not just the quiet girl with her nose in a book but someone worth knowing.

And in turn, Tami understood the sides of Aiden that others often missed—the way he carried responsibility on his shoulders even when he made everything look effortless, how he always looked out for the people he cared about.

Through awkward teenage years, first heartbreaks, and college classes, their friendship had never wavered. Even when life pulled them in different directions, the island always brought them back together. No matter what changed, Aiden was still *her person*. The one she could call when things fell apart. The one who showed up—like tonight—without hesitation.

Aiden assisted Tami with her coat, then escorted her to his vehicle, and held the door open for her.

She smiled. "You are always the perfect gentleman. I used to stand and wait for Gary to remember to open a door for me. Finally, I just gave up and opened my own doors."

Aiden shook his head. "I guess he was raised differently."

Tami nodded in agreement.

"Weren't you supposed to be a bridesmaid?" he asked. "I thought Jessica asked you."

"I declined," Tami responded. She prayed he wouldn't ask why.

The idea of standing in front of a crowd, knowing all eyes would be on her, was suffocating. The mere idea caused her heart to quicken and her palms to become clammy with apprehension. She had given Jessica an excuse, citing work and other obligations, but the real reason was something she couldn't bring herself to reveal—not even to Aiden.

They were soon en route to the venue.

"How was the train ride?" Aiden asked, glancing at her.

"Smooth," Tami replied. "I spent the whole time reading."

Aiden nodded, a small smile tugging at his lips.

After a fifteen-minute drive, the car slowed down as it neared the entrance of a building, a masterpiece of glass and stone, with signage that read *The Crystal Palace*.

"We're here," Aiden informed her.

Tami forced a tight smile, but deep inside she was battling against a wave of unease.

Aiden got out and walked around to open the door for her.

"Thank you," she murmured as she stepped out of the vehicle.

When they entered the venue, Tami's breath caught in her throat at the breathtaking sight before her. The vaulted ceilings sparkled with crystal chandeliers that cast a warm glow over the marble floors. Delicate floral arrangements adorned every surface, their subtle fragrance adding to the dreamlike atmosphere. Every detail, from the gold-accented banisters to the cascading drapes framing the massive floor-to-ceiling windows, seemed meticulously designed to perfection.

It was evident that no expense had been spared in creating this enchanted wonderland. Her mother, a well-known wedding planner on Polk Island, would certainly approve.

As she made her way into the ceremony room, Tami could feel the buzz of excitement and joy in the air, drawing her deeper into the alluring atmosphere. This was more than just a venue; it was a celebration, a dreamlike setting where treasured memories would be made forever.

The ceremony was beautiful and emotional, leaving Tami with tears in her eyes—not just joy for Jessica and Rob but something heavier, something she wasn't ready to unpack in the middle of the wedding. She had *thought* this time would be different. She'd thought this holiday season would be different.

For once, she'd have a date to the Christmas Ball who wasn't chosen by her mother, a date she actually *wanted* to bring. She had been looking forward to it—imagining how it would feel to walk into the Grand Ballroom on Gary's arm, to have someone there *for her*, to finally silence the well-meaning but exhausting questions from her family about when she'd find someone special.

But all of that had shattered when Gary dumped her. Just like that, her carefully held hopes had crumbled, leaving behind the familiar ache of disappointment. And now instead of anticipating a magical night, she was dreading going home single *again*. The thought of facing her mother's pitying looks, the whispered speculation from family friends made her stomach twist with unease.

She swallowed hard, blinking away the sting of fresh tears as the guests began to rise for the recessional.

She might have to face Christmas alone, but at least tonight she had Aiden. He'd stepped in without hesitation, offering to be her plus-one tonight, but even his steady presence couldn't erase the gnawing anxiety in her chest. Because no matter how much she told herself it didn't matter, that she was fine on her own…deep down, she had wanted *this* to work. She had wanted Gary to be different.

But he wasn't. And now she had to figure out how to pretend it didn't hurt.

When the ceremony was over, guests were gently steered toward the adjoining ballroom, a grand spectacle of elegance and opulence, for the reception.

Each table was adorned with lavish floral arrangements that seemed to have been plucked straight from an artist's imagination. The vibrant colors danced under the soft glow of the chandeliers, casting a kaleidoscope of hues onto the crisp white tablecloths.

She and Aiden found their designated seats, their names elegantly scripted on small ivory cards. She appreciated that her friend had managed to take off Gary's name and substitute it with Aiden's.

As they settled into the plush velvet chairs, she took a moment to absorb the lively hum of conversations around them. The room was filled with an infectious energy; laughter echoed off the high ceilings and the clinking of champagne glasses punctuated the air with a celebratory note.

And then, amid the excited buzz, there was a sudden hush. A collective intake of breath swept through the room as everyone turned to look at the doors that had just swung open. It was time for the bride and groom to make their grand entrance into their own fairytale reception.

As the couple swept in, the room erupted in applause. The music swelled, and the atmosphere shifted back to one of celebration. But Tami couldn't shake the sense of melancholy that lingered, nor could she ignore the way Aiden's smile, though genuine, didn't quite reach his eyes.

She took a moment to study her friend. Since his father's death nearly two years ago, Aiden didn't come home much. Living in Charlotte kept him busy away from their hometown, but she knew that wasn't the only reason. Being back on the island meant facing memories of his father everywhere he turned—the barbershop they used to go to, the old fishing docks where Angus Jr. taught him how to cast a line, the family that no longer felt the same without him in it. It was easier, maybe even necessary, for Aiden to keep some distance.

He wasn't completely withdrawn, but he had changed. Not as quick to pick up the phone, not as available for their usual record store hunts when he *was* home. Even when they did manage to spend time together, there were moments when she could see it—that fleeting shadow in his eyes, the weight of loss he carried but rarely spoke about.

And yet here Aiden was, showing up for *her*, even when his own grief was still an undercurrent beneath the surface. It made her heart ache in a way she didn't have words for.

All around them, the celebration was in full swing, laughter and music filling the grand expanse of the ballroom. After they finished eating, Tami and Aiden met their friends on the dance floor. A line was forming, and the lively beat of an old-school tune had the guests eagerly joining in.

As the evening wound down, Tami found herself reflecting on the night. She had kept her disorder in check, the tight grip of anxiety loosening its hold for a few precious hours. She had danced, laughed, and even allowed herself to be swept up in the energy of the celebration.

For the first time in a long while, she felt a sense of accomplishment—not because she had conquered her challenges, but because she had embraced the joy despite them.

When they were in the car heading back to her hotel, Tami studied Aiden's face and noticed the faint lines of exhaustion around his eyes. "How are you doing?"

"I'm fine," Aiden answered, but his tone lacked conviction.

Tami's expression softened. "It's okay if you're not," she said gently. "Losing a parent is never easy. My dad's been gone for twenty-five years, but there are times when it feels like his death just happened."

Aiden hesitated before giving a slight nod. "My father loved the holidays…especially Christmas. He was worse than a kid at times."

His eyes grew distant as he spoke, and Tami could see the sadness and grief lurking there. The holidays had always been a special time for Aiden's family, filled with love and togetherness. But with his father gone, there was an unfillable void.

She reached out and squeezed his hand in silent support. Sometimes words were not enough in the face of such profound loss. After a moment, Aiden composed himself, taking a deep breath. "I'm sure Shane will put a lot of thought into decorating the hotel," he said softly, his voice steadying at the mention of his brother. "Dad always wanted the tree in the lobby to be a showpiece, to echo everything Christmas represents."

Tami nodded, understanding the significance. Aiden's family owned a historic hotel in their hometown on Polk Island. The Christmas tree, a symbol of joy and family unity, now stood as a bittersweet reminder of what had been lost. She could see the pain in Aiden's eyes, the way it mingled with fond memories of happier times. It made her heart ache for him.

When they reached the hotel, Tami said, "Thank you for being my plus-one tonight, Aiden. It means a lot to me."

"Anytime," he replied, his smile warm and genuine. "I like Jessica and Rob. They're good people."

Tami's heart swelled with affection for him. "I'll see you in the morning," she said before exiting the vehicle.

She knew that once the weekend in Charlotte came to an end, she would have to return to the challenges awaiting her back on Polk Island: another holiday season alone, and her mother's relentless matchmaking. But for now, she was content to enjoy the next couple of days before the pressure of reality sank in.

SATURDAY MORNING, AIDEN pulled up in front of Tami's hotel, leaving the car idling as he texted her that he was outside. He'd picked up hot drinks and his favorite breakfast sandwiches to go. They'd eat while he gave her a tour of the city.

He watched as she stepped out a moment later, bundled against the winter chill, and offered him a small smile before climbing into the passenger seat. Her pixie-cut hair framed her face in tiny, delicate curls. Her skin, the rich, warm color of a new penny, glowed under the soft lights outside the hotel. Her familiar chocolate eyes flicked toward him.

"Good morning," he greeted.

"Morning," Tami replied, settling in and fastening her seat belt.

They drove through the heart of the city, the car engine humming steadily as Aiden pointed out landmarks and relayed anecdotes about life in Charlotte. The quiet streets carried them past towering skyscrapers, historic neighborhoods, and sprawling parks.

Tami stared out the window, taking in the sights, but her brow occasionally furrowed as if her thoughts were elsewhere.

He felt a twinge of anger resurface, thinking of Gary and the way he'd treated her. The hurt he had left behind was etched on her face, and Aiden hated that it lingered. In truth, he'd never liked any of the guys that Tami had dated, though he'd never dug deep into why.

It was just instinct—he cared for her and seeing her hurt like this weighed on him more than he wanted to admit. The bond they shared was unique, forged through years of trust and understanding. They had helped each other through so much—like when Aiden went through a medical crisis as a child and couldn't attend school for two weeks. During that time, Tami showed up every day, bringing his schoolwork and keeping him updated so he wouldn't fall behind. It meant the world to him.

Through it all, they had always been there for each other. Laughter, books, and music had been their shared language, a way to cut through the tension of life's challenges. Whether it was a goofy inside joke or a favorite song they both sang out of tune, those moments had always been their escape. Late-night talks had run until dawn more times than he could count—about everything, about nothing, and about the things they couldn't say to anyone else. They had built a fortress out of those conversations, and in their own way, they were stronger because of it.

He never had to think twice about being there for her, even now, when things were more complicated than either of them wanted to admit. That was what their friendship had always been about—being there for each other, through the toughest parts of life, without anything else ever complicating it.

"Hey," Aiden said softly, his voice cutting through the quiet. "You doing okay?"

Tami turned to him, her expression softening. "Yeah. Just…taking it all in. It's nice to have something to focus on instead of my troubles."

He nodded, offering a small smile. "Anytime."

By the time they reached the first stop—a scenic overlook of the city skyline—Aiden felt a sense of satisfaction as the tension in her features began to fade. He couldn't erase her past, but he could remind her of the beauty in the present, one moment at a time.

His grip tightened slightly on the steering wheel. "Gary's an idiot for not seeing what he had." His voice was rougher than he'd intended. "You deserve better than that. Always have."

She offered a small, appreciative smile. "Thank you, Aiden. I guess I just wanted it to be real, you know? Especially after telling my family that I'd be bringing someone home for Christmas… I can hear Mama now… *Tami, what did you do? You had to have done something for him to leave…*" She trailed off, her expression twisting with embarrassment. "I'm not looking forward to Christmas at all."

Aiden's heart tightened at her words. His own plans for the holidays—or rather, the lack of them—had been weighing on him too. Since his father's passing, Christmas felt like an uphill climb, a reminder of who was no longer there to share it. The holidays had always been a big deal at the family-owned Polk Island Hotel, where his grandfather had held grand celebrations and hosted the annual Christmas luncheon for employees and their families—a tradition that spanned two generations. But since his father's passing, the joy had gone out of the season.

His older brother Shane had stepped up to manage the hotel, but Aiden had always thought of the hotel as his father's legacy. Now it felt like the thing that kept their family tied to the past, reminding them of everything they'd lost. He missed his mother and his siblings more than he let on, but going back home this year seemed impossible.

"Speaking of family...have you reconsidered coming home for the holidays?" Tami asked.

He hesitated, knowing he was avoiding the inevitable conversation. "No," he answered softly. "I'm staying here this year. The holidays...they're too overwhelming right now. Feels like a hurdle I can't overcome."

Last Christmas, the first without Angus, hadn't been much of a celebration for the family. They were still steeped in grief, still reeling from the loss. It had been hard to find any joy amid the silence, and they'd even decided, as a family, to skip the luncheon for the employees and their families—a break from tradition that had felt necessary, though painful. Aiden had told himself it would be different this year. He knew an opportunity would be opening up with his company's Charleston location, but he hadn't bothered to put in for it. The thought of uprooting his life again, even to be closer to family, felt too much. He wasn't ready to face that pressure, to be part of the family dynamic while still carrying the weight of his father's absence. So, he had decided he would stay in Charlotte, keep a low profile. Here, surrounded by the distractions of work and the anonymity of the city, he could at least avoid the pressure of pretending everything was fine. He'd wanted to give himself the space to breathe without the constant reminders of what he'd lost. But as much as he tried to shut it out, he couldn't ignore the pull to be with his family.

He missed them—missed his mom's cooking, the way Shane always tried to lighten the mood with his jokes, even the quiet moments with his siblings that reminded him of the warmth they used to have. Yet every time he thought about going home, the grief loomed too large, too palpable. It was easier to stay away.

A shadow of sadness crossed Tami's face, as if she'd been studying him. "I'm sorry, Aiden. I know how difficult this must be for you. The first few years after my dad died…it was very hard on us."

He swallowed and nodded. "I remember that, which is why I knew you'd understand."

She leaned over and squeezed his hand. "Of course I do. Hey, I have an idea. Maybe I'll come up here and spend the holidays with you."

"You're more than welcome to, but I know how much you enjoy Christmas on the island and all its festivities. You don't want to miss that."

Tami's expression changed in an instant; her brow furrowed into a frown. "You also know my mother. After I tell her about my breakup with Gary, I won't be able to bear her embarrassing me with another one of her matchmaking schemes."

Aiden chuckled under his breath. "Maybe you should talk to her and set some firm boundaries. Let her know you don't want her help in finding a man."

Tami rolled her eyes, a faint smile appearing despite her frustration. "Right, as if that will work with Rachel Rose Adams. She's relentless."

He shrugged. "Regardless, it's worth a try. Be clear about your intentions, or she'll continue pushing."

Tami heaved a sigh, her shoulders drooping. "I know you're right, but I can't help feeling that she would just see it as a challenge. To her, I'm not complete unless I have someone in my life."

"You're strong. You'll figure out how to handle her." Aiden looked at her again, feeling overcome with protectiveness. "Tami," he spoke softly, "I know it's hard with your mom always pushing you to find someone, but you're enough just as you are. You have so much to offer, and any man would be lucky to be with you."

She met his gaze, surprise flickering across her face. "Thanks, Aiden. I appreciate that. But sometimes it feels like...like I'm not meeting expectations, you know?"

"Expectations can suffocate us," he replied earnestly. "But you only have to be true to yourself."

AFTER BRINGING HER back to the hotel to rest before dinner, Aiden promised to return in a couple of hours. Tami kicked off her shoes and sank onto the plush armchair, letting the quiet of the room settle around her.

The shrill ring of her phone broke the silence, and her stomach twisted with anxiety as she glanced at the caller ID. Her mother's name lit up the screen, and a familiar mix of dread and resignation washed over her. She hesitated, already bracing herself for what was coming.

With a deep breath, she answered. "Hi, Mama." Tami forced cheerfulness into her voice, though it felt strained.

"Sweetheart, I just got off the phone with Lana Blanchard, and we've figured out the identity of your fiancé. The hint about an announcement—and this trip to Charlotte—was all the clue we needed."

Tami blinked in disbelief, her heart caught in a tug-of-war between relief and dread. She hadn't meant to be so vague when she mentioned a "big announcement," but Rachel Rose was nothing if not impeccably perceptive.

As a seasoned wedding planner, her mother had spent years stitching together the fragments of lovers' secrets, hearing the softest hints of change, and noting every tiny, trembling cue.

Tami had always been intentional about keeping her life as private. Yet once again, her mother had pieced everything together.

Tami felt a mix of embarrassment and uncertainty. "Mama, what are you talking about?"

Rachel Rose's voice bubbled with excitement, each word coming faster than the last. "Oh, darling, I know exactly what this is about. You called me over a week ago to say you were bringing someone special to spend the holidays with the family, and you mentioned a huge announcement! It's all starting to make sense now."

Tami's stomach dropped, her heart racing. She still wasn't sure what her mother had pieced together.

Rachel Rose laughed softly, the sound full of knowing amusement. "Darling, let's be honest… Jessica's wedding isn't the only reason you're in Charlotte. It's all falling into place now. It couldn't be clearer."

Tami felt a lump form in her throat. Her mind raced back to the call she'd made over a week ago—how she'd been so excited to share that she was bringing someone home for the holidays, how she'd hinted at something big without giving away too much. She hadn't expected her mother to put it all together so quickly. But she should've known Rachel Rose wouldn't be fooled by her vagueness.

Her mother had heard the quiet excitement in her voice, the way Tami had spoken about him—as if, for the first time in a long while, things were looking up.

And now? Now everything had crumbled.

"I'm thrilled about it," Rachel Rose continued, her voice full of joy. "Lana and I both agree that he's perfect for you. I can't wait to tell my friends…"

Tami's heart sank. Of course Lana knew. If her mother had figured it out, then she'd wasted no time sharing the news with her best friend. Which meant it wouldn't be long before the whole of Polk Island knew. And when the truth came out—that Gary was already engaged to someone else—Tami would once again be the topic of whispers and pitying looks over holiday dinner.

She swallowed hard. "Mama, hold on… I need to tell y—"

"Oh, sweetheart, stop being so secretive," Rachel Rose cut her off, undeterred. "I've noticed how happy you've been this past year. All those trips you were taking. I *knew* something was going on. I can't believe my baby girl is finally getting married!"

Tami squeezed her eyes shut. She should have known this would happen. Rachel Rose had been relentless for years, always trying to push her toward marriage. Every holiday, every family gathering, it was the same exhausting routine. The probing questions. The disappointed sighs. And worst of all—the blind dates.

There was the lawyer from Charleston who'd spent the entire dinner bragging about his latest high-profile case, barely asking her a single question. The doctor from Atlanta, who, while undeniably handsome, had checked his phone so many times she was convinced he had another date lined up that same night. And the real estate developer? He had launched into an unsolicited pitch about "investment opportunities" before their appetizers had even arrived.

Rachel Rose had set each of them up with confidence, insisting *this one* would be different, that *this one* could be the man to sweep her off her feet. Each time, Tami accepted and then walked away feeling more exhausted than before.

And now, because she'd dared to sound hopeful about someone, her mother had latched on with full force.

"You know how much I've been waiting for this day," Rachel Rose continued. "I just *knew* something was brewing between you and Aiden."

"Aiden?"

Tami's stomach twisted, her pulse kicking up. She could hardly get the name past her lips.

"You're marrying a Worthington, darling. This is so wonderful," Rachel Rose gushed, completely missing the panic in her daughter's voice.

"M-Mama…"

"Sweetheart, you don't need to hide it from me any longer. As far as I'm concerned, this is a match made in heaven. You and Aiden will be the talk of Polk Island this holiday season."

Tami's breath caught. The shock of it, the sheer absurdity, had her momentarily frozen.

But beneath the disbelief, something else stirred—something dangerously close to consideration.

Aiden and her? *A couple?* They weren't dating. They had never dated.

But her mother's words had planted a seed.

Maybe…maybe pretending—just for a little while—could be the solution. The perfect way to keep her mother off her back, to avoid the endless matchmaking attempts.

Her mother already believed it. And really, was it so unbelievable? She'd visited Aiden in Charlotte several times in the past year. And hadn't she caught a few curious looks from their friends when they were together?

Tami knew she should correct her mother, shut this down before it went any further. But the truth lodged in her throat, tangled with exhaustion and something she didn't want to name.

Rachel Rose was still talking, already dreaming up wedding plans in her head. "Oh, I just *knew* it would be Aiden. I told Lana, didn't I? That man has always had a soft spot for you. And after everything he's been through…it just makes sense.

I've never seen you so happy, sweetheart. This is exactly what I prayed for."

Tami gripped the phone tighter, her stomach twisting.

Maybe it wouldn't hurt to let her mother believe it—for now. Just for the holidays.

The thought sent a flicker of relief through her, but guilt followed close behind. Because no matter how much this solved for her, there was one glaring problem.

Aiden.

Her throat tightened as the realization sank in. She wouldn't just be weaving a harmless little lie. She'd be pulling Aiden into it, too.

"M-Mama," she finally said, her voice quieter, more subdued. "I'm not—we're not—"

"Sweetheart, don't worry. You and Aiden deserve this moment," Rachel Rose gushed, too caught up in her own excitement to hear Tami. "I'll take care of everything. Don't you worry about a thing. We'll make it official when you're ready."

Tami closed her eyes, her heart heavy with the unspoken truth. *Maybe it isn't such a bad idea after all.*

"Lana already knows…she helped me figure this out," Rachel Rose stated. "But I'll hold off telling anyone else until you and Aiden make your announcement."

"Miss Lana is not capable of keeping a secret. You know that."

Rachel Rose chuckled. "I'll do my best to keep her quiet, dear, but you know how journalists are—they have a knack for sniffing out secrets. I have to go but just want you to know that this is the best Christmas gift you could ever give me."

Once the call ended, Tami sank back against the seat, feeling the burden of her mother's expectations pressing down on her. She had painted herself into a corner, and now she had to come up with a solution.

An image of Aiden floated into her mind, and suddenly it struck her—a wild, desperate plan. She needed to find him, and fast.

Tami's mind raced as she thought of Aiden. He had been her best friend for years, always there to support her through thick and thin. The idea that he might help her out of this situation, though absurd, suddenly felt like her only option.

Without a moment's hesitation, she grabbed her phone and sent him a quick text.

Need to talk to you ASAP. Come to hotel. Urgent.

A flurry of emotions washed over her as she left her room to wait downstairs for him, anxiety clawing at her insides.

Within fifteen minutes, Tami spotted Aiden striding toward the hotel entrance. His tall frame moved with an air of confidence, effortlessly parting the bustling crowd. His locs swayed with each purposeful step.

He spotted her immediately and waved, his expression shifting from concern to curiosity as he approached her.

"Tami, what's going on?" Aiden asked, his brow furrowed with worry as he joined her in the hotel lobby.

She gestured for him to follow her to a quieter corner, where they could talk without being overheard. "You won't believe what just happened," she said, her voice trembling slightly.

She took a deep breath and recounted the call with her mother, each detail making her stomach twist tighter. "She thinks *we're* engaged."

Aiden's eyes widened in surprise. "Engaged? *You and me?*"

She nodded. "She and Miss Lana figured that it must be you."

"You're talking about Miss Blanchard? The editor of *The Polk Island News*?"

Tami nodded. "And you know that she isn't the editor of a newspaper for nothing."

He crossed his arms, trying to process the sudden twist in the narrative.

"What if your family hears about this?"

Aiden shrugged in nonchalance. "It's easy enough to explain."

"I didn't mean for any of this to happen," Tami

exclaimed, feeling the heat of embarrassment rise to her cheeks.

"It's fine," he assured her. "We can straighten it out, explain that it's a misunderstanding."

Tami eyed him. "About that… What if…we don't say anything right away?" The suggestion hung in the air, heavy with desperation. "What if we pretended to be engaged for the holidays?"

CHAPTER TWO

AIDEN STARED AT Tami in disbelief as the warm, velvety strains of Al Green's "Let's Stay Together" drifted from the hotel bar. The soft, romantic melody clashed sharply with the surreal request she had just made.

"Run that by me again," he said, as he sat down in a plush armchair. His brow furrowed deeply as his hand drifted to the back of his neck, rubbing absently—a nervous habit that always surfaced when life threw him something unexpected.

Tami stood across from him, arms crossed tightly over her chest, her athletic frame practically vibrating with a mix of determination and unease. She shifted her weight from one foot to the other, clearly bracing herself. "I need you to pretend to be my fiancé. Just for the holidays," she said, the words rushing out as if quicker delivery might somehow make them easier to swallow.

Aiden blinked, unsure if he'd misheard her. "Tami…" He let out a long breath, shaking his head. "You realize how insane that sounds, right?"

She huffed, rolling her eyes, but her nervous

fingers fidgeted with the hem of her sweater. "I know, but my mom is relentless. If I show up with a fiancé for the holidays, she'll back off."

"Your fake fiancé," he clarified, his voice tinged with disbelief.

"Yes," she said firmly, though the slight tremor in her voice gave her away. "Look, I wouldn't ask if I had any other options, but I don't. You're… well, you're perfect for this."

Aiden leaned forward, resting his elbows on his knees as he searched her face. "You really think this is the answer?"

She hesitated for a moment before nodding. "It's the only way to get through the season without her constant meddling. I just need a few days of peace, Aiden. Please."

He sighed, her plea settling heavily on his shoulders. He couldn't deny that there was desperation in her voice, a vulnerability she rarely let anyone see.

Before he could respond, a cluster of hotel guests bustled past, and Tami glanced around the crowded lobby, her expression tight.

"This isn't the best place to have this conversation," she said, her tone softening. "Let's go upstairs. I'll explain everything."

Aiden hesitated but finally stood, stuffing his hands into his pockets as he followed her to the elevator. The ride up to her room was quiet, and once inside, Tami gestured toward the small sitting area by the window.

"Okay," she said, taking a deep breath. "Here's the deal…we're talking about Rachel Rose…" She sighed softly. "She's convinced I'm incapable of finding a man because I don't let her help. She tries matchmaking, hinting, or outright lecturing me on why I'm still single. And every year I'm expected to grin and bear it."

He tilted his head, his confusion giving way to cautious understanding. "So, you're thinking that the fiancé act will throw her off?"

"Yes," Tami said, pacing the room. "If I walk in with you, it'll buy me some breathing room. She'll see that I don't need her meddling to be happy."

Aiden watched her, noticing the tension in her shoulders and the tightness in her voice. She wasn't just irritated—she was exhausted.

"Tami," he said carefully, "you're putting a lot of pressure on yourself. Why not just tell her to back off?"

She stopped pacing and looked at him, her arms falling to her sides. "Because I've tried that, and it doesn't work. She's my mom. I love her, but I can't spend another holiday looking and feeling like a failure in her eyes."

The vulnerability in her words hit him like a punch to the gut. He rubbed the back of his neck again, glancing at her. "And you really think me pretending to be your fiancé will help?"

"Yes," she said, her voice firm. "You're everything she thinks I need in a partner—smart, successful, charming. If I walk in with you, she'll finally leave me alone."

Aiden thought back to the handful of stories Tami had shared about her mother's relentless matchmaking. There was the lawyer who had shown up late to their date, then spent the entire evening regaling her with courtroom war stories, as if she were a juror he needed to impress. And there had been others like him.

It had always sounded amusing from afar, the way Tami would roll her eyes and laugh as she recounted her mother's latest attempt to pair her off. But now, looking at her—the tension in her jaw, the way she gripped her phone like it might betray her at any second—he realized it wasn't just an annoying quirk. This was a genuine source of stress, a constant pressure bearing down on her, holiday after holiday.

And now, somehow, *he* was part of the story.

"You really want me to go along with this?" he asked, running a hand through his locs.

She nodded, her gaze imploring. "Just for the holidays. We'll tell everyone after New Year's that we broke it off or something. For once, I can have a peaceful Christmas."

Aiden stared at her, his thoughts racing. He hadn't planned on going home to the island this year. Too many memories of his father, the weight of his absence during the holidays still too fresh. And yet…here was Tami, looking as though the world might collapse if he said no.

"Tami," he started, then paused, unsure how to phrase what he was thinking. "Pretending to be engaged—it's not exactly a small thing."

"I know," she said quickly. "But you don't understand how much this would mean to me, Aiden. I honestly can't handle another Christmas of awkward dinners with some guy my mother picked out for me."

He hated seeing her like this—so anxious. "You realize this could blow up in our faces, right? If Rachel Rose figures out that we're lying…"

"She won't," she interrupted, her tone firm. "She has no reason to. And we're close enough that it wouldn't even seem weird. Everyone knows we've been friends forever."

Aiden tilted his head. "So, you really want to do this?"

"Yeah. Like I told you…she already thinks we're involved."

"Tami," he said, his voice softer now. "It's just Rachel Rose being—well, Rachel Rose…"

Her gaze dropped to her hands, and for a long moment, she didn't speak. When she finally did, her voice was barely above a whisper. "But it's not just her. It's everyone. Every year I'm reminded that I'm the only one who hasn't…figured it out. My sisters have their perfect lives, their perfect husbands, and I'm still…alone. Gary even chose someone he thought was a better option."

Aiden hadn't realized how deeply this weighed on her. He'd always seen Tami as strong, independent, and completely in control. But now, he saw the cracks in her armor—the vulnerability she rarely let anyone see. "You're not alone. You've got me."

Her lips curved into a small, hesitant smile. "Which is exactly why you're perfect for this."

He groaned, shaking his head. "You're really not giving me much of a choice here, are you?"

Tami grinned, the first genuine smile he'd seen from her since his arrival. "Not really."

Aiden leaned back, staring up at the ceiling. He hadn't planned on going home this year. The thought of spending Christmas on the island without his dad still felt like too much. He wasn't ready for the traditions, the reminders, the empty seat at the table. But this? Pretending to be Tami's devoted fiancé? That might give him an easy out.

If everyone believed they were a couple, no one would expect him to participate in the usual family traditions—not in the same way, at least. He could see his family but sidestep the painful moments—plus it would give his family something else to focus on. Maybe this arrangement wasn't such a bad idea after all.

"Fine," he said finally, dragging the word out. "I'll do it."

"Really?"

Her face lit up, and for a moment, Aiden felt like he'd just handed her the moon.

"Yes, really," he said, holding up a hand to stop her from hugging him. "But on one condition."

Her smile faltered. "What?"

"You owe me," he said, pointing at her. "Big time. And not just chili-level big. I mean full-on, I-get-to-call-in-favors-for-months big."

She laughed, a sound that filled the room and eased some of the tension. "Deal."

Aiden shook his head, a wry smile on his face. "I can't believe I'm doing this."

"*Believe it*," Tami said, standing up. "And start practicing your 'adoring fiancé' face. We're going to need it."

As she headed for the bathroom, Aiden called after her. "This better not involve matching pajamas."

She glanced back, her grin mischievous. "No promises."

When the door closed behind her, Aiden leaned back on the couch, staring at the ceiling. One thing was for sure—this Christmas would be different.

What had he just gotten himself into?

The drive home to Polk Island was both familiar and foreign to Aiden. The steady hum of the highway beneath the car was a comforting rhythm, but his grip on the steering wheel told a different story. His hands flexed and tightened, betraying the tension that knotted his shoulders and twisted his gut. They'd been driving for nearly three hours, but the closer he got to their hometown, the more a familiar unease settled over him.

Aiden had made the decision to return, and though it wasn't one he had taken lightly, it was the right choice. As lead project manager, he had the flexibility to work remotely on his projects, managing his team from anywhere. But something about being back on the island—where his father's absence loomed so large—felt both like a return to comfort and a confrontation with his grief.

He sighed, his gaze flickering to the passenger seat where Tami sat. It felt right somehow, driving back with her. The holidays had always meant family, warmth, and the unmistakable sound of Angus Jr., booming out carols far too early in the season. Christmas had been his father's favorite time of the year. Thanksgiving was a close second, but Christmas? That was magic in their house.

Aiden had made peace with spending the holidays in Charlotte—just him, a pile of takeout menus, and his record player spinning old-school R&B. He'd even imagined which albums he'd play: Donny Hathaway's *This Christmas* and a Nat King Cole compilation to get him through December. It wasn't tradition, not really, but at least it wouldn't be a reminder of everything he'd lost.

Only helping Tami through a crisis could've changed his mind.

"So," he began, pushing thoughts of the holidays away, giving her his full attention, "tell me everything I need to know to play the part of your perfect fiancé."

Tami removed her shoes and propped her sock-clad feet up on the dashboard.

"I guess we're really engaged now," he teased, his tone light as he glanced pointedly at her feet. "Is this what I signed up for?"

"I signed *you* up for this, remember?" she replied with a small, self-conscious smile. "And you said yes."

"I did," he said, softening his gaze. "And I meant it. Relax, Tami. We're a team now."

She sank into her seat, her shoulders sagging with relief. "You don't know what this means to me," she murmured. "It's more than pretending. You've given me space to breathe."

Aiden furrowed his brow. "You don't owe anyone an explanation for your life," he said firmly. "But if this helps you find peace, I'm all in."

Tami blinked, appearing to hold back tears, and his heart went out to her. "This is going to be the first holiday in years I'm actually looking forward to."

He smiled gently, but as he refocused on the road, he wished he could say the same.

Every year his whole family would come together for the holidays—Madelyn, his mother, would make sure of that, gathering the family around the dinner table, no matter the weather. The chairs would be pulled up, the house would be filled with the sounds of their laughter, and Angus Jr. would lead them in their ritual of sharing memories of Christmases past. This year it would be different. Aiden knew it, and the thought of walking into the house, empty of his father, felt like a weight he could barely bear.

Christmas had always been his father's time to shine. He didn't just decorate; he transformed the house into a holiday wonderland. Lights draped every window, wreaths adorned every door, and the scents of cinnamon and pine seemed to linger in the air no matter where you stood. It wasn't just about the decorations, though. Angus Jr. had a way of making the season feel sacred, grounding every twinkle of a light and every bite of his famous gingerbread cookies in the joy of family and the miracle of Christ's birth.

And now, without him, Aiden wasn't sure what Christmas was supposed to mean.

Tami's gaze drifted to the car radio, where soft R&B played in the background. "Speaking of things to look forward to, you missed the holiday parade after Thanksgiving," she said, a hint of teasing in her voice. "It's become kind of a tradition…going with you. It wasn't the same this year."

Aiden gave a slight nod. He had decided to stay in Charlotte for Thanksgiving, telling everyone he had work deadlines. "Did I miss anything good?"

"Only the best part of the season," she replied, feigning indignation. "The high school band, the floats, Santa…"

"I'll make it up to you," he promised. "How about we go to the Christmas-tree lighting? My treat."

Tami's smile softened. "I'd like that."

The ache in his chest grew heavier as he thought again about the holidays without his dad, about walking into that house, seeing his empty chair in the living room and the other at the head of the table. His mother would do her best to keep the traditions alive, and his siblings would rally to help. But none of it would feel right. There would be a gaping hole in every laugh, every prayer, every moment.

Aiden's jaw tightened as he turned off the highway onto the familiar stretch of road that led to Polk Island. The trees lining the road were barren now, their limbs stretching toward the overcast sky like skeletal hands. The sight felt fitting somehow, a reflection of the emptiness he carried inside.

He glanced at the passenger seat again, almost expecting to see his dad sitting there instead of Tami, ready to crack a joke about Aiden's "city driving" or bring up the time he'd stubbornly taught him how to parallel park.

Aiden blinked rapidly, willing the tears away before Tami noticed. He wasn't ready for this. But he couldn't turn back now. His family was waiting for him, even if it would never be the same.

As the familiar sight of the island's coastline came into view, Aiden tightened his grip on the steering wheel. He came for one reason only. Because Tami had asked him for a favor. A big one.

Pretend to be her fiancé.

Aiden looked at her profile, studying her as she swayed to the soft music, the corners of his mouth twitching upward in a reluctant smile. It was absurd—ridiculous, even. And yet he'd said yes. He hadn't been able to say no when she'd looked at him with those wide, anxious eyes, practically radiating desperation. It wasn't like Tami to panic, and that was what had tipped the scales for him.

He could manage a few days of pretending if it meant giving her some peace of mind. The awkward act, the inevitable questions, the knowing glances from her intrusive mother—he had dealt with more challenging situations for friends. Nonetheless, a hint of doubt sneaked in. What if this little act sparked expectations? What if someone—her mother, in particular—grabbed onto the idea and took it further? Could this lie potentially cause more harm than good? He pushed the thought away. This wasn't about long-term consequences.

Not yet.

For now, it was about being there for Tami in any way she needed.

But going back to Polk Island—that was another beast entirely.

The island was home, yes, but it was also a minefield of memories he wasn't sure he wanted to navigate. The past few years had been hard enough, and Christmas without Dad still felt like a hollowed-out version of what it used to be.

He rolled his shoulders, trying to shake off the weight pressing down on him. *Focus. This isn't about you. This is about helping Tami.*

He knew her mother's annual fundraiser would be on her mind. Rachel Rose threw the Christmas Ball, a lavish local event, at his family's hotel every year, and it was the party of the season.

"How are you feeling about the ball?" he asked.

She shrugged. "I'd rather stay home but my mother would have a fit," Tami replied. "Plus, it's for a good cause."

Aiden glanced at the dashboard clock. He'd be dropping her off at her town house soon, then on to his mom's after. The bridge to the island was only a few miles ahead, the stretch of road that always felt like a line between the world he'd built for himself and the one he'd left behind.

"How are you doing with all this?" Tami's soft voice asked. "Tell me how you're feeling."

"How I'm feeling?" He smirked with nonchalance, even though he was nervous. "Like I'm about to walk into a Hallmark movie, but the kind where everything goes horribly wrong."

Tami groaned. "Don't say that. It's going to be fine. My family loves you, remember?"

"That's because they don't know what a terrible fake fiancé I'm going to be," he said, only half-joking.

But the truth was he wasn't sure if he could be any kind of fiancé—fake or otherwise. Losing his dad had left him feeling hollow in ways he still couldn't fully grasp. He'd immersed himself in work, keeping his days overflowing, his nights occupied, desperately trying to avoid the silence that crept in when he paused long enough to feel it. Love, relationships, commitment—those seemed like they belonged to another version of him, a person he no longer recognized.

Love demanded something from a person—hope, vulnerability, the willingness to give yourself completely to another. Aiden doubted he had any of that left. His dad had been the cornerstone of their family, the one who made everything feel stable and certain. Without him, Aiden felt unanchored, like he was aimlessly drifting through life without purpose. Yet a part of him yearned for connection, for the familiarity of being part of something meaningful.

If he didn't even feel like himself, how could he offer anything genuine to someone else? Any woman he was with deserved more than just half a man, more than someone merely going through the motions. Yet Aiden couldn't shake the desire to try, to see if he could find himself again in the process.

So no, he wasn't worried about being a terrible fake fiancé. He was worried that pretending would be too easy—because maybe he wasn't faking as much as he thought. Maybe the act of pretending could reveal parts of himself he thought were lost forever.

Tami sighed. "You'll be great. Just stick to the plan, and we'll get through this."

Aiden didn't respond right away. He could hear the tension in her voice, the slight edge that told him she was still nervous despite her best efforts to hide it.

"Hey, I was kidding," he said after a moment. "We've got this, Tami. No one's going to suspect a thing."

"Thanks," she said softly. "I mean it, Aiden." She shifted in her seat to face him. "I really appreciate this."

"Yeah, yeah," he said, his tone light. "You make sure I get some of your mom's sweet-potato pie."

Tami laughed, and the sound eased some of the tightness in his chest. "Deal. I'll make sure she saves you an extra slice."

"Good," he said. "Now, stop worrying." He turned onto her street, and the car was silent as he pulled up to her town house and stopped the car. After he'd helped her bring her bags inside, he turned to leave. "I'll see you soon. I spoke to my mom, so dinner is six thirty at my mom's house."

"Okay," she said. "Drive safe."

Aiden let out a breath as he walked to the car and started it, his gaze fixed on the road ahead. He pulled out of her driveway and drove down Main Street toward his mother's house.

It hadn't changed much since he'd last been here. The same small-town charm, the same weathered storefronts, the same stretch of beach that always seemed to beckon him no matter the season.

As he drove through the streets, memories flickered at the edges of his mind—Christmas mornings with his siblings, the sound of his dad's voice reading *'Twas the Night Before Christmas*.

Aiden eased off the gas as he approached his childhood home, a sprawling two-story house with a yard full of memories. He parked under the massive oak tree that had provided shade for countless family gatherings, but tonight its branches seemed to weigh heavily on his heart. This was where he'd grown up, but without his father, it felt empty and lifeless.

As he stepped out of the car, his gaze fell upon the garden that lined the stone pathway. The once vivid Free Spirit roses, which in spring and summer exploded in a fiery peach color, now stood bare, their thorny stems stark against the December chill. These roses were more than just decorative; they symbolized the enduring love between his parents—his father had chosen them for Madelyn's wedding bouquet many years ago.

"They'll bloom again," Aiden whispered, his voice heavy with emotion. Though stripped of their splendor, the roses still held life beneath the surface, a quiet promise of renewal. The memory of Angus Jr.'s booming laughter and warm embraces surged forward, a bittersweet warmth spreading through him despite the cold.

Aiden sat in the driver's seat, gripping the wheel tightly as he took a deep breath. He hesitated before finally getting out of the car and walking toward the front door. As he approached, the door swung open, revealing his mother, who greeted him with a warm smile.

"Aiden!" Madelyn exclaimed, pulling him into a tight embrace. "I'm so glad you changed your mind about coming home. This is the best present you could ever give me."

"Hey, Mom," he replied softly, his voice filled with emotion.

Madelyn was in her mid-fifties, with elegant salt-and-pepper hair that framed her face in soft waves. Her warm caramel complexion, kissed with a touch of honey, gave her a natural glow, and she carried herself with a quiet confidence that made makeup feel unnecessary. She was beautiful in that timeless way—graceful, grounded, and effortlessly striking.

She pulled back to study him with her sharp

brown eyes that always seemed to see right through him. "It's good to have you home for Christmas," she said, her smile masking something he couldn't quite decipher.

"It's good to be here," he lied, returning her smile.

As Aiden stepped inside, the warmth and familiarity of the house embraced him. Laughter and conversation echoed from the living room, where his siblings were gathered. Aiden entered the space, his gaze taking in his family scattered throughout.

Kenyon, the eldest, stood near the fireplace, his commanding presence as steady as ever. Shane, the second oldest, was laughing with his wife of six months, Alison—known to everyone as Ace, her infectious energy matching Shane's easygoing charm. London, their poised and confident sister, was deep in conversation with Micah, the youngest brother. Nearby, London's daughter Bella, still a little girl with wide eyes and an inquisitive nature, tugged at her mother's sleeve, eager to be a part of the conversation. Finally, there was Cia, the baby of the family, her bright smile lighting up the room as she flitted between conversations. Being fourth in the sibling lineup put him in the middle, and Aiden quietly observed the dynamics of the family he loved dearly.

Their welcoming smiles and open arms drew him in, and for a fleeting moment, Aiden allowed himself to relax.

Tami glanced around her kitchen, a contented smile tugging at her lips. She was home. After a weekend in Charlotte—dodging traffic, weaving through crowded sidewalks, and feeling like she was always in a rush—being back on Polk Island felt like a breath of fresh air.

She'd already brought her bags upstairs and unpacked, eager to settle back in. Now, as she stood at the counter, grabbing a mug to make tea, she let herself take in the familiar warmth of her space. The sight of driving up to her little townhome—its blue siding and black shutters standing strong against the lush island greenery—never failed to bring her a sense of peace.

One of the things she loved most about living here was the convenience. Her townhome was within walking distance of the high school where she worked, and often she preferred to make the short trek on foot. Walking gave her time to clear her head before the school day began, allowing her to center herself and ease into the routine. It also helped her with her social anxiety. The quiet walk through the peaceful streets of Polk Island in the early morning offered a buffer from the noise of the world, providing a safe space where she could gather her thoughts without the overwhelming pressure of interacting with others.

In the afternoons, the walk helped her decompress, shifting her focus away from the chaos of the school day and allowing her to transition into a calmer state. The rhythm of her steps felt grounding, a much-needed reprieve from the social energy she had to expend at work. Here, life moved at a slower pace—one that allowed her to feel more in control and less anxious, something she never took for granted.

Tami put the kettle on, then leaned against the cool countertop, feeling a mix of determination and apprehension about the weeks to come. Her role as a school psychologist demanded poise and confidence—qualities she had learned to project, even on days when her social anxiety disorder threatened to undo her.

Even now, with the holiday break just around the corner, she continued reporting to the school as usual, showing up for her students with a practiced calm and an encouraging smile. To her students, she tried to be a guiding star, a calm presence and an empathetic listening ear, helping them navigate the turbulent seas of adolescence. She tried to be their steady anchor, gently steering them toward hope and self-assurance. But here, in the quiet of this kitchen, the storm she kept at bay surfaced—whispers of doubt that she wasn't enough, that her own fears disqualified her from being the support they needed.

Tami closed her eyes and took a deep breath and exhaled slowly, grounding herself in the familiar routine. The sound of the water boiling became a meditative rhythm. Her mind shifted, as it often did in these moments, to the other source of her unease: her mother.

Rachel Rose's relentless matchmaking turned every family gathering into an endurance test. Her thinly veiled disappointment at Tami's single status lingered in every comment, every glance.

As if thinking of the woman had conjured her, Tami heard the unmistakable sound of the front door opening, without so much as a knock, and the familiar scent of lavender and vanilla greeted her in the kitchen moments later.

"Tami...you're back..."

Rachel Rose's voice rang through the house, a blend of excitement and determination that set Tami's nerves on edge. Her mother swept in like a whirlwind, her floral shawl over her pantsuit fluttering as she moved. "I thought I'd pop by to see you if you were here yet."

Tami suppressed a groan, suddenly regretting that she'd given her mother a key to her home. She wished she'd had a little while longer to gather her thoughts alone before facing her family, yet she turned to her mother. "Hi, Mama."

Rachel Rose clasped her hands together, her grin widening. "Oh, Tami, this is everything I've ever wanted for you. And Aiden...he's such a good man. Hardworking, respectable, comes from a good family. Oh, *I'm over the moon.*"

Tami felt her face heat up. She had expected her mother to be thrilled, but this level of enthusiasm was already teetering on overwhelming. "Mama, please don't start telling everyone about this," she said. "Aiden and I want to enjoy just being newly engaged. We'd like to make the announcement ourselves."

Rachel Rose waved her hand dismissively. "Nonsense... An engagement should be shared. Have you thought about where you'll get married? Of course, the Polk Island Hotel would be perfect. It's such a beautiful venue—not to mention that it's owned by Aiden's family...but then again there's that new space—"

Tami's head spun. "Mama, we haven't even set a date yet," she interrupted. "Can you slow down a bit? You should be focusing on the Christmas Ball. Before I left, you were complaining that two of the volunteers quit."

"I've got that under control," Rachel Rose countered. "Why slow down when everything's falling into place so perfectly? You know that you're not getting any younger, Tami. And neither is Aiden, for that matter. I'm sure you two will be wanting to start a family as soon as possible. Besides, the holidays are such a romantic time for a wedding. Oh, I just had a wonderful idea. Engagement photos...we could do a Christmas theme. Red-and-gold decorations, poinsettias everywhere, and maybe even a little snow machine for—"

"Mama," Tami interrupted, her voice sharper than she intended. She could feel the familiar tightening in her chest as the weight of her mother's expectations pressed down on her. She paused, taking a deep breath, trying to calm the storm of emotions swirling inside.

Her mother's excitement was understandable—Rachel Rose always wanted the best for Tami, but sometimes it felt more like control than care. It had been like this for years: matchmaking, nudging, and subtly orchestrating her life in ways that made Tami feel like she couldn't take a breath without someone else's plan for her.

"I do appreciate your excitement, truly," Tami continued, forcing the words out with a calmness she didn't fully feel. "But Aiden and I...we need to take our time to sort things out. We're not rushing into anything."

She glanced at her mother, already imagining the fallout if Rachel Rose started telling everyone about their "engagement." If her mother began planning parties or announcing it to the rest of the family—spreading the news to the entire island or, worse, her entire social circle—it would be a mess. The last thing she wanted was for people to start whispering, asking questions or speculating about something that wasn't even real.

Tami ran a hand through her hair, feeling the tension building. It wasn't just about this ruse anymore. It was about every subtle expectation, every conversation that felt like a tug at the strings of her life. She loved her mother, but sometimes it felt like her plans were just a little too suffocating. It was hard enough being the only one of her siblings who hadn't figured it out yet in the romance department, but with all this added pressure, Tami couldn't help but wonder if she was setting herself up for even more heartache.

Still, she couldn't back down now. If Aiden was willing to play along, at least for a little while, maybe it would give her the space to breathe—without the constant feeling of being boxed in by everyone else's expectations.

"Will you let us announce this in our own time?" she asked.

Rachel Rose's smile faltered, but only for a moment. "Of course, darling. I understand. But you can't blame me for being excited. My baby girl is finally settling down, and with such a wonderful man."

Tami forced a smile, knowing that any further argument would only prolong the conversation. "I know, Mama. But please, let us handle this in our own way. Don't you tell a soul. Aiden and I want to be the ones to share our news."

Rachel Rose nodded, though Tami could see the gears still turning in her mother's mind. "All right, all right. I'll try to contain myself. But if you need any help—with anything at all—you just let me know, okay?"

"Okay," Tami said, hoping to end the conversation.

But Rachel Rose wasn't done. She perched on the edge of the couch, her eyes scanning the room. "Have you thought about a dress? Something simple but elegant, I think. And your wedding colors... Oh, what about navy and silver? Or maybe blush and champagne? Those would be stunning against the backdrop of the hotel..."

Tami's head throbbed. "Mama, please. Can we not do this right now?" she said gently. "I literally just got home."

Rachel Rose frowned, clearly disappointed but relenting. "Of course, darling. You must be exhausted from your trip. I'll leave you to rest." She smoothed her pantsuit and planted a kiss on Tami's cheek. "But we will talk more soon. This is such an exciting time, Tami. Don't let it pass you by."

She nodded, walking her mother to the door. "Good night, Mama."

"Good night, sweetheart. Love you..."

"Love you too," Tami replied, closing the door behind her mother with a sigh of relief. She leaned against it for a moment. This was going to be more difficult than she'd anticipated.

She crossed the room and sank onto the couch, her mind racing. How on earth was she going to keep this up? She pulled out her phone and opened her messages, scrolling until she found Aiden's name. Her fingers hovered over the keyboard before she finally typed out a message.

Mama came over and she's already planning the wedding. Suggested the hotel. Hoping she will keep quiet but doubtful.

She hit Send and leaned back, closing her eyes. The idea of facing her mother's enthusiasm alone was daunting, but at least she didn't have to deal with her alone.

Tami's phone vibrated almost immediately, displaying Aiden's response.

Don't worry. Together we'll find a solution.

A small grin formed on her face, momentarily easing the building stress. What had he said earlier? *Relax, Tami. We're a team now.* The word *team* had sent a ripple of warmth through her chest. For so long, she'd faced her challenges alone—her mother's scrutiny, the critical whispers of their tight-knit community, and her own relentless self-doubt. But with Aiden, even in pretense, she didn't feel so exposed.

She placed her phone down and gazed up at the ceiling, attempting to calm her swirling thoughts. This challenge was going to be more difficult than she had anticipated.

CHAPTER THREE

TAMI ADJUSTED THE silver pendant at her neck, her fingers trembling as she stood at the edge of the Worthingtons' driveway. The sounds of chatter and laughter spilled from the house, muffled by the door but unmistakably warm and inviting. Normally, she'd feel a rush of comfort at that sound. Tonight it only added to the storm of nerves swirling in her chest.

Her breathing was shallow, rapid. She felt a bead of sweat cling to her temple despite the cool evening air. The door seemed to loom in front of her like a vast, unbreachable wall. Tami's mind raced with a thousand fears, each more irrational than the last.

What if she said something wrong? What if Aiden's family saw through the lie? She'd known them most of her life. She didn't want them to think badly of her. Tami's fingers tightened around the pendant, pressing it to her skin as though she could anchor herself with the cool metal.

This was a mistake.

She swallowed, trying to steady her breathing.

In, out. In, out. Playing with her fidget ring, Tami focused on the rhythm, attempting to ignore the clench in her chest, the tightness in her throat, the rising panic that whispered she wouldn't be able to do this. It felt like her skin was too tight, like the world was closing in on her. But she knew she couldn't back out now. She had to keep going.

It wasn't just her mother's expectations—though that alone was enough to send her spiraling. No, it was the pressure of being seen, of being *present* that made her feel so raw. The idea of a crowd, of people staring, of being under the microscope in a room full of strangers... It made her want to shrink into herself, disappear into the floor.

She squeezed her eyes shut for a moment, trying to focus on the gentle rise and fall of her chest.

You can do this. Focus on the breath. You don't have to be perfect. Just keep breathing.

She counted slowly, just for herself—five seconds in, hold for three, then exhale for seven. She tried to let her shoulders drop with each exhale, the tightness in her muscles slowly releasing as the panic ebbed, if only slightly.

Aiden's voice reached her from behind, warm and steady. "Tami?"

She opened her eyes, startled by how close he was. He'd come out to meet her, standing just a few feet away. His presence, as calm as it was, was a small lifeline—he didn't make her feel like she was about to lose control. Instead, there was simply that familiar steadiness she could lean on.

"Ready?" he asked.

Tami wanted to say no. She wanted to turn around, make up some excuse, and go home, hide in the comfort of her own space.

Focus. Just focus on the now. One thing at a time. You can do this.

She nodded, offering a weak smile. "Yeah. Let's go."

He looked at her closely, his eyes narrowing slightly as if sensing the struggle. He didn't say anything, just reached out to gently brush his hand against the small of her back, a subtle gesture of support.

That simple touch sent a wave of warmth through her, grounding her in a way that was impossible to explain. The panic wasn't gone, but for a moment it softened, like the edges of a storm cloud losing its power. No one had ever been able to do that for her. Not even Gary. Especially not Gary.

He'd always kept a certain distance, emotionally unavailable even in the moments that should've brought them closer. Aiden somehow, without saying a word, reminded her she wasn't alone. Maybe she should've seen it then—what real support looked like. What it *felt* like.

He opened the door for her, and the sounds of

the gathering came rushing in, louder now. Her heart skipped, but she forced herself to step inside.

Her palms were clammy, but she wiped them on her jeans before stepping into the living room. There were so many faces, so many eyes. It felt like too much. She swallowed, the tightness in her throat returning.

In, out. In, out.

It would be a long night—first dinner with the Worthingtons followed by heading to her mother's house for her family's annual tree decorating. She needed to keep it together.

She looked at Aiden, trying to focus on him, on the way he stood beside her—his posture straight but not stiff, his presence calm. He was her anchor. She only had to focus on him, she reminded herself. Just stay with Aiden.

His mother, Madelyn, was the first to approach, arms wide as she greeted her with a warm hug. Tami tensed instinctively, her chest tightening again, but she let the hug happen, forced herself to breathe through it.

"It's so wonderful to see you," Madelyn said, stepping back with a smile that was kind but slightly knowing.

Tami's heart sank. *She already knows about the engagement.* A wave of anxiety prickled under her skin. Her mother never wasted any time in spreading the news, always eager to push things along, making the smallest thing feel like a grand event. She offered a shaky smile in return, trying to steady her nerves.

"Thank you for having me," she managed, though it barely sounded like her own voice. The words didn't feel as light-hearted as she'd hoped. Her mind raced with dozens of what-ifs—what if she messed this up? What if her mother told the entire town before they had a chance to back out? She and Aiden had agreed they'd break up after Christmas, tell everyone they were better off as friends. This was supposed to be temporary, just a ruse to get through the holiday madness without disappointing everyone. But what if it hurt their families? What if Aiden's family, Madelyn especially, got too attached, too invested? Tami couldn't bear the thought of hurting her.

She loved Aiden's family. Madelyn had always been warm and welcoming to her, and the thought of betraying that trust made her stomach twist. She had a lot of respect for the Worthingtons, and the idea that they might end up hurt because of something she'd executed just to appease her mother felt like a heavy weight.

Tami wondered if she was playing with fire.

"Everything okay?" Madelyn's voice snapped her back to the present, concern lacing her tone.

Tami smiled weakly, nodding. "Yeah, just... I'm fine."

But deep down, she wasn't so sure. The weight

of the lie they were about to tell felt heavier every second.

Pretending to be engaged to Aiden was reckless, even by her standards. Letting her mother's assumptions about their relationship go uncorrected was one thing—it was entirely another to amplify the lie to this level.

Tami exhaled sharply, shaking her head. No, she couldn't back out now.

Aiden gave her a subtle nudge. She straightened, forcing another smile.

"Let me take your jacket," he offered, his voice low but steady—the perfect partner in this ridiculous charade.

She took off her coat and handed it over, giving him a quick look of thanks before he disappeared to hang it up.

The room was already alive with chatter again, the Worthington siblings seemingly unfazed by her arrival. Shane was holding court in the corner, gesturing animatedly as he shared an incident that had taken place at the hotel earlier. Kenyon was laughing along while sipping a glass of wine. London was perched on the couch, bouncing her baby daughter on her knee as she laughed along with the conversation.

Micah was busy helping Cia set up a board game on the floor for a test of skills after dinner. Only Cia still lived at home with Madelyn, and her youthful energy filled the room as she teased Micah about his inability to figure out the rules.

It was almost easy to forget the deception simmering beneath the surface—until Madelyn turned back to Tami, that knowing smile still firmly in place.

"So," she said, linking her arm with Tami's and steering her toward the kitchen, "you and Aiden. Tell me everything."

Tami swallowed hard, her heart hammering against her ribs. This was it.

Showtime.

"Well," she began, glancing over her shoulder to see if Aiden was nearby. Thankfully, he was already following, his expression unreadable but his presence grounding. "It's kind of a funny story…"

"Oh, I love funny stories," Madelyn said, her eyes sparkling with delight.

Tami shot Aiden a helpless look as he stepped into the kitchen. He leaned casually against the counter, his arms crossing over his broad chest, and gave her a slight nod.

"Right," she said, clearing her throat. "Well, we wanted to wait until we were sure before telling anyone. You know, keep things…private."

Madelyn's brows lifted, her smile widening. "That's just like you. You've never liked people in your business."

"That's true," Aiden said smoothly, stepping

forward and resting a hand lightly on Tami's lower back.

The touch sent a spark up her spine, but she forced herself to focus on the story they'd agreed upon earlier.

"We didn't want to rush into anything," Aiden added, his tone measured. "But when Tami's mom started, uh..." He hesitated, looking at her for help.

"Started meddling," she supplied quickly.

His mother laughed, her shoulders shaking with amusement. "Oh, Rachel Rose always had a knack for that. Bless her heart."

"Right," Tami said, her nerves settling slightly as Madelyn's laughter filled the room.

"And now?" the older woman asked, her gaze flicking between the two of them.

Aiden smiled, the kind of easy, confident smile that made her wonder if he'd missed his calling as an actor. "Now we figured it's time to share the news. We'd hoped you would've heard it from us, but Tami and I are engaged."

Madelyn beamed before her gaze flickered to Tami's finger, where the absence of a ring didn't go unnoticed. Her brow furrowed for a moment, but her smile remained warm as she reached out to gently squeeze Tami's hand. "Well, I'm thrilled. Truly. And let me just say—you two make a wonderful couple."

Tami barely managed a polite laugh, her throat

tight. She could feel Madelyn's eyes lingering on her, the unspoken question hanging in the air.

Aiden stepped in, his voice steady and reassuring. "We're actually planning to design our own rings." He shot Tami a quick glance. They had rehearsed this. "We want them to be something really personal, something that represents where we are right now."

Madelyn's expression softened, though a flicker of curiosity crossed her face. "Design your own? I like that…"

"We just think it'll mean more," Aiden continued, cutting off the unspoken inquiry. "A reflection of us, not just a standard piece of jewelry."

Madelyn beamed at them one last time before disappearing into the living room, leaving them alone in the kitchen.

Tami exhaled loudly, leaning against the counter as the tension drained from her shoulders. "That was too close."

"You're overthinking it," Aiden said, pouring himself a glass of water from the pitcher on the counter. "She bought it."

"Of course she bought it," Tami said, shooting him a look. "You're annoyingly convincing."

He grinned over the rim of his glass. "Just doing my part."

Tami couldn't help the small smile tugging at her lips. "Well, let's hope your part doesn't include blowing our cover before the holidays are over."

"Not a chance," Aiden said, setting the glass down and leaning closer. "We've got this, Tami. Trust me."

She met his gaze, the sincerity in his eyes easing the last of her doubts. "Okay," she said softly.

"Okay," he echoed, his smile softening.

For the first time since this whole charade began, Tami felt a wave of confidence. They could do this. They could pull this off.

The evening unfolded cheerfully, and they waited until right before dessert to tell his siblings about the engagement.

Aiden cleared his throat, then stood up. "Tami and I are going to have to leave in a few, but before we go, there's something y'all should know."

All conversation came to a halt.

He reached over and took her hand in his own. "We're engaged."

The room went silent for a beat, the kind of stillness that made Tami's palms sweat.

She could feel the intensity of Aiden's family's surprise on her as they reacted to the news.

Kenyon, ever the steady eldest, raised an eyebrow, his gaze flicking between them. "Engaged, huh?" His voice was calm but edged with curiosity, as if he were taking inventory of the situation in real time.

"Wait—what?" Shane blurted, his fork clattering against his plate as he stared at them with wide eyes. "When did this happen?"

London, the most outwardly expressive of Aiden's siblings, broke into a grin. "No way! Are you serious?" She leaned forward, practically vibrating with excitement.

Micah smirked, crossing his arms over his chest. "Guess that explains why you've been acting all weird lately, Aiden."

And then there was Cia, the youngest, who squealed so loud it made everyone laugh. "Oh my gosh, I knew it! I knew there was something going on between you two."

The whole exchange felt surreal, a blur of laughter and teasing that Tami knew well from years of friendship with Aiden's family. Over time, she had grown closer to all of them, her bond with each sibling like an extension of her bond with Aiden himself. But it was Madelyn who had always made Tami feel most at home. The warmth of her home, the unspoken acceptance had always been a comfort—a stark contrast to Tami's own family dynamic, where her mother's unrelenting expectations often overshadowed anything resembling warmth.

She never expected it to get complicated. But now, standing here, surrounded by Aiden's family, pretending to be something she wasn't, she could feel the tension starting to creep in again. This ruse was a slippery slope, one that could easily get out of hand.

Aiden held up his palms, his smile confident

back at the warmly lit house before they both got into his car.

The evening had been an odd mix of joy and discomfort. Tami couldn't help but appreciate the ease with which Aiden had navigated the dinner with his family. She still had her doubts, but she was happy he'd agreed to this outlandish plan.

"I knew she couldn't hold water," Tami muttered with a wry smile. "Your mom didn't say it, but I could tell that she wasn't surprised by the news. My mother had already told her. Pretty sure she's told my sisters, too."

Nodding in agreement, Aiden chuckled. "I knew my mom wouldn't say anything until she spoke to us first."

Tami's smile faded slightly. The sooner they got through this, the better.

As they drove toward Rachel Rose's house to decorate the family tree, the streetlights outside blurred into streaks of yellow and white. Tami let her thoughts wander, her mind darting to her own family. Her sisters—Samantha and Naomi—were living proof of their mother's matchmaking prowess. Samantha had built a successful career as a real estate agent, helping clients find dream homes in the competitive Charlotte market. Her husband, Jake, was a rising star in the world of real estate development, making him the perfect match in terms of ambition and financial success.

Naomi, the middle child, had carved out her

but measured. "We wanted you guys to be the first to know."

Tami's heart raced. She wanted to smile, to play along, but it felt more like a mask than anything else.

As much as she loved Aiden's family, she was starting to feel the sting of what this would mean for her own relationships. The more she thought about it, the more she wondered: Would they ever forgive her once the inevitable breakup happened? And how would this affect her bond with Aiden, at the end of it all?

Tami stole a glance at Aiden, his easy smile a contrast to the turmoil swirling inside her. He was so confident, so sure this would work. She, on the other hand, wasn't sure about anything anymore.

TAMI ADJUSTED HER scarf as she stepped onto the sidewalk outside Aiden's family home. The crisp night air nipped at her cheeks, and she pulled her gloves tighter, the chill only adding to the swirling uncertainty in her chest. She turned to Aiden, who was loading the last of the leftovers Madelyn had insisted they take into the vehicle. His jawline was relaxed now, a marked improvement from his clenched jaw earlier this evening.

"Ready?" she asked, tugging her gloves tighter.

"Ready as I'll ever be," Aiden replied, his tone light but laced with genuine warmth. He glanced own path as an accountant in Charleston, managing high-profile accounts for a prestigious firm. Her husband, Randall, a highly respected plastic surgeon, provided them with the lavish lifestyle her mother wanted for her daughters. Both sisters had married well, and their lives were polished and enviable from the outside.

Unlike Samantha and Naomi, Tami hadn't been swept away by grand expectations. She'd carved her own path, stayed in the community she loved. The thought of being anyone's pawn—especially her mother's—never sat right with her.

As they pulled up to Rachel Rose's home, they were greeted by the festive glow of Christmas lights, and the unmistakable hum of holiday spirit filled the air. Inside, the house was warm, the familiar scent of pine and cinnamon drawing Tami in.

Rachel Rose ushered them in with a pleased smile. "Tami, Aiden, so glad you made it… And I must say, darling, you're looking absolutely radiant tonight."

Tami offered a tight smile, thankful her mother's attention was focused on her outfit rather than the absence of a ring on her finger—at least for the moment.

As they chatted, Rachel Rose's gaze inevitably drifted to Tami's hand. Her smile faltered just slightly before she leaned in, her curiosity piqued. "So, no ring yet?"

Tami inhaled, bracing herself, then glanced at Aiden.

"We're planning to design our own." Aiden gave their rehearsed explanation again, his voice steady as he nodded toward Tami. "We want something that's uniquely ours, something that reflects us, you know?"

Rachel Rose pursed her lips, as if holding back a dozen questions, before finally offering a small nod. "Of course. That sounds perfect. I can't wait to see what you come up with."

Tami wasn't fooled—her mother would bring this up again, but for now, she let the topic rest.

The rapid patter of little feet echoed down the hallway, followed by a dramatic gasp.

"Aunt Tami! Aiden! You're soooo late!"

Summer, Naomi's four-year-old daughter, appeared in the doorway, hands on her hips, her face scrunched in exaggerated disapproval. Her curls were slightly askew from playing, and the glittery unicorn on her T-shirt shimmered under the kitchen light. Tami bit back a smile; even at four, Summer had a presence that filled the room.

Aiden raised a brow. "Late? What'd we miss?"

Summer stomped up to him, shaking her head. "The cookies...we waited and waited, but then we had to start without you and Aunt Tami."

Aiden crouched to her level, feigning devastation. "You made cookies without me? That's betrayal."

She giggled. "Y'all should've been here. I even got to crack an egg."

Tami smirked, folding her arms. "Sounds like you had it under control."

With a proud nod, the little girl said, "Yep. And I saved you two cookies, but Uncle Jake said he's gonna eat them all."

Aiden let out an exaggerated gasp. "Jake would never…"

Summer leaned in, whispering conspiratorially, "He already ate four."

Naomi entered the room, shaking her head. "She's not wrong."

"Tami, I was completely shocked when Mama told me that you two were engaged," her sister Samantha said. "I always assumed your relationship was platonic."

"It changed a little over a year ago." Tami glanced over at Aiden, who nodded in agreement.

"I'm thrilled for you both," Naomi interjected.

"There's going to be another wedding…" Rachel Rose sang.

Tami laughed softly, her cheeks warming under the attention. "We're still figuring everything out but thank you. It means a lot to have your support."

Aiden slid an arm around her waist.

Obviously bored with the news of an engagement, Summer grabbed Aiden's hand, tugging him toward the living room. "Come on... You can still help decorate the tree."

He shot Tami a look. "I guess I've been summoned."

Tami grinned as she followed behind. For now, at least, the night was about family, about tradition.

As they pulled ornaments out of plastic bins, Rachel Rose's attention, predictably, shifted to wedding plans.

"Now, about this wedding," her mother began, perching on the armrest of the couch. "Have either of you given any thought to venues?"

"Mama," Tami interrupted, her tone firm but affectionate as she met her mother's expectant gaze. "Let's focus on the tree for now. Wedding talk can wait until the new year."

"But I've already started working—"

"I mean it, Mama. Aiden and I are serious about this." Pointing to the tree, she added, "Let's get to decorating."

Tami caught Aiden's gaze across the room. He was leaning against the couch, a small smile on his face as he mouthed, *We survived.*

She grinned back, warmth filling her chest. She felt like she could breathe, and she enjoyed herself as she helped pull out ornaments and hang them on the tree as she caught up with her family.

When they finished decorating, the Christmas tree shimmered.

Rachel Rose clapped her hands in glee. "It's stunning," she murmured. "I love this emerald-green-and-gold theme. *Just beautiful*."

Aiden agreed.

"All right, spill," Samantha said, narrowing her eyes playfully. "Who made the first move?"

"I did," Aiden said without hesitation, his grin crooked but proud. "What can I say? I'm a man who knows what he wants."

"That's right, you did," Tami teased, shooting him a mock stern look that made everyone laugh.

"Bold move," Randall said with a nod of approval. "But I think we all knew it was bound to happen eventually."

Naomi grinned. "Yeah, I've been waiting for this. I always thought there was something more to you and Tami just being friends."

The room was filled with warmth, years of inside jokes and deep bonds evident in every exchange. Despite their fib, Aiden had always been family, woven into the fabric of their lives long before tonight.

As the conversation carried on, Summer, who had been curled up on the sofa, let out a soft sigh, her eyelids drooping. She seemed to have been fighting sleep as long as she could, but the excitement of the night had finally won.

Naomi noticed first, her voice quieting as she said, "Looks like someone's down for the count."

Randall stood and carefully scooped his daughter into his arms, her small frame settling against him without protest. "I'll put her in one of the guest rooms."

Tami watched as he carried Summer down the hall, her niece's arms loosely draped around his neck. Aiden's fingers brushed against hers, a silent moment of understanding passing between them. They were both missing their fathers.

Naomi glanced at her watch. "We should probably wrap up soon. It's getting late, and I'm sure Tami and Aiden have plans."

Rachel Rose's eyes sparkled mischievously. "Or maybe they've got a wedding date to set?"

Tami let out a little sigh. "Mama…"

Her mother simply smiled, undeterred, but Tami chose not to engage. One day at a time, she reminded herself. *I can do this.*

CHAPTER FOUR

AIDEN RETURNED HOME after the tree-decorating party at Rachel Rose's house. He sat on the edge of the twin bed in his old bedroom, his elbows resting on his knees as he stared at the worn wooden floor. The room hadn't changed much since he'd left for college over a decade ago. Posters of sports legends still adorned the pale blue walls, and the shelves above his desk displayed dusty trophies from high school track meets. Yet the comforting nostalgia that usually accompanied his visits home felt absent tonight, replaced by a gnawing unease.

He let out a slow breath, feeling conflicted about the situation he was in. His family was still gathered downstairs at eleven thirty at night, laughing and catching up. The smell of fresh cookies drifted up the staircase, mingling with the faint notes of holiday music. Normally, nights like this would be the highlight of his visit. But not tonight.

Tonight he was a liar.

Aiden ran a hand through his hair, leaning back against the headboard. His mother had been ecstatic when he and Tami announced their engagement. But now that Tami was more than his best friend—at least in the eyes of his family—his mother's enthusiasm had reached new heights. He'd noticed it during dinner that evening.

The guilt twisted tighter. He'd never been one to lie to his family, let alone about something as monumental as marriage. Yet here he was, contemplating the ramifications of a deceit that grew more tangled after just one day in town. But he couldn't let Tami down.

They'd always been best friends, partners in crime since high school. He'd been there for her when she got braces, when she struggled through college applications, and when she passed her counseling exam. She'd been there for him when his father passed away, when work felt suffocating, and when he needed someone who understood him without asking too many questions.

The stakes were high. His family's trust, his mother's happiness. And yet despite the risks, he couldn't bring himself to step back. Being with Tami, even in this half-pretend way, felt better than he'd expected. He like helping her…and navigating this situation with their families made him realize just how comfortable he was with her.

A soft knock at the door startled Aiden out of his thoughts. Before he could respond, the door creaked open, and his sister, Cia, stepped inside, holding a steaming mug in her hands.

"Hey," she said softly. "Thought you might want

this. It's hot chocolate. It's what you used to bring me whenever I was sad."

"Thanks." Aiden offered a small smile as she handed him the mug. "Is it that obvious?"

"No, but I can tell because we're all feeling the same way." Cia perched herself on the edge of his bed, her sharp gaze sweeping over him.

He sighed. "It's just a lot."

She nodded. "Aiden, talk to me… What's going on?"

Cia had always been someone he could trust, someone who could handle the truth without judgment. But this wasn't just his truth. It was Tami's, too. And he couldn't betray her like that, not even to his sister.

"It's nothing," he said finally, forcing a smile. "Just the usual holiday chaos."

Cia didn't look convinced, but she let it go. Instead, her expression softened, and she looked around the room. "I guess it feels strange being back here."

Aiden nodded, the familiar sights and smells of his old bedroom stirring memories he wasn't sure he was ready to confront. "Yeah. It's like stepping into a time capsule."

"Daddy loved this time of year," she said quietly.

His chest tightened. "Yeah, he did. It was his favorite."

"Remember how he used to go all out with the

decorations?" she said, a small smile tugging at her lips. "He'd have us out there stringing lights for hours, even in the freezing cold."

"And then he'd bribe us with hot cocoa and those terrible Christmas carols he loved," Aiden added, chuckling softly.

Cia laughed, but the sound was tinged with sadness. "Terrible or not, I'd give anything to hear him sing them again."

Aiden nodded, the weight of their shared loss pressing heavily on his chest. "Me too."

They both fell silent for a moment, swept up in memories of their father.

"You know," Cia said, her voice soft, "we were lucky. Luella never got to meet her dad. But we had Angus Jr. He was there for everything—every recital, every game, even when we didn't want him to be. We never had to wonder if we were loved."

Luella was a cousin, estranged from her father, who was a Worthington. By the time she arrived on Polk Island, her father had passed away, leaving behind only stories and memories passed down by those who had known him. It had made them realize just how fortunate they were to have had their father by their side for as long as they did.

Aiden smiled, a bittersweet ache in his chest. "Yeah, we were lucky. And now Luella has us. I'm glad she's part of our family."

"She's amazing," Cia agreed. "And I'm really

enjoying helping her plan her wedding. She and Noah are perfect for each other."

Aiden chuckled. "I don't know how you manage it, juggling all the wedding stuff with everything else." His sister was an event planner at the family hotel and often helped with weddings held there.

"It's worth it," Cia said, her smile widening. "She deserves something beautiful." Her expression turned thoughtful. "We should do something special this year for Mom too," she said suddenly, her voice filled with determination. "She's been trying so hard to hold it together for us, but I know it's been hard on her without Dad."

Aiden nodded. "Yeah. She deserves something good. Something he'd be proud of."

"Maybe we could recreate one of his traditions," Cia suggested. "Like the Christmas Eve luncheon at the hotel. We didn't do it last year—it was too soon after his passing."

He smiled at the memory. "He and Granddad both loved doing that for the hotel employees. Dad would be Santa." His smile disappeared. "It's not going to be the same without him."

Cia agreed. "It's not, but it's a tradition started by Granddad. Dad kept it going after he passed away. I'm going to talk to Shane. It just might make this holiday feel like old times."

"Okay," Aiden said. "Let's do it just to honor Dad and our grandfather."

She reached out, squeezing his hand. "He'd

want us to, you know. To celebrate, not just for him but for us."

Aiden swallowed hard, the lump in his throat making it difficult to speak. "Yeah. He would."

They sat in silence, the quiet punctuated by the distant sounds of laughter and music from downstairs.

"You sure you're okay?" Cia asked eventually, her gaze searching his.

He hesitated, the urge to confide in her about the engagement ruse bubbling up again. But he couldn't do it—not without breaking Tami's trust.

"I'm fine," he said finally, his voice steady. "Just...trying to figure some things out."

Cia studied him for a moment before nodding. "Well, whatever it is, I'm here. You know that, right?"

"I know," he said, his voice soft.

She gave him a small smile before standing and picking up her mug. "I'm really happy for you. Tami is a sweetheart. I like her a lot."

Aiden stood up to follow her. "I'm glad you approve." Deep down, he felt a thread of guilt for his deception.

The holiday had just begun, yet he was more than ready for it to be over.

THE NEXT MORNING, Tami hummed quietly to herself as she moved around her cozy kitchen, the scent of freshly brewed coffee filling the air. Sunlight streamed through the window, painting warm golden streaks across her teal blue walls. She loved this time of day—the quiet mornings that allowed her to gather her thoughts before facing the world. Today, however, the world had other plans.

The shrill ring of her phone cut through the peaceful atmosphere, jolting her out of her rhythm. She glanced at the screen and sighed when she saw her mother's name flashing. It wasn't that she didn't love her mother; she adored Rachel Rose. But phone calls from her often carried an undertone of urgency that made Tami's stomach clench.

"Good morning, Mama," Tami answered, forcing cheerfulness into her voice as she stirred the pancake batter. "I have to leave shortly for school."

"Good morning, sweetheart!" Rachel Rose's voice bubbled through the line, full of energy and purpose. "How's my favorite psychologist doing this fine morning?"

Tami chuckled softly. "I'm fine. What about you?"

"Oh, I'm wonderful. Busy as always, you know. Listen, darling, I have a favor to ask. The keynote speaker for the Christmas brunch at the Women's Leadership Alliance fell ill this morning—terrible flu, poor thing—and they need someone to step in last minute."

Tami froze, her heart thudding in her chest. "Oh?" she said cautiously.

"Yes… I told them you'd be perfect. It's a small

talk, maybe twenty minutes or so, about overcoming obstacles and finding purpose. You could do it in your sleep."

"Mama…" Tami began, her pulse racing. She gripped the counter to steady herself. "I don't think I can."

"Of course you can. You're a psychologist, Tami. You empower people all the time."

"It's different," she said quickly, the words spilling out before she could stop them. "I know my students. Speaking to a crowd of strangers…it's…"

"Tami, it's a wonderful opportunity. And it's Christmas. It would mean so much to everyone there." Her mother's voice had softened, but disappointment seeped through.

Tami closed her eyes, gripping the phone tightly. The walls seemed to close in on her, the familiar knot forming in her chest. She took a deep breath, trying to steady herself. "I… I'm sorry, Mama. I have meetings and student appointments. I can't just cancel at the last minute." She wasn't a fan of public speaking either.

A pause. "Oh."

Rachel Rose's disappointment was palpable, even through the phone. "Well, I understand. I'll find someone else. But you really would've been wonderful."

"I'm sorry," Tami repeated, her voice barely above a whisper. "I have a busy day today and I'm not prepared."

"I understand."

They exchanged a few more pleasantries before ending the call. Tami set the phone down and sank into a chair at the kitchen table, her appetite gone. She stared at the half-mixed pancake batter and the coffee growing cold in her mug.

The frustration bubbled up before she could stop it. "Why can't I just be normal?" she muttered to herself.

She spent her days counseling students through their struggles, teaching them about mental health, coping strategies, and resilience. And yet here she was, paralyzed by the mere thought of speaking to a room full of people. The irony wasn't lost on her, and it stung.

Tami rubbed her temples, the weight of her own inadequacies pressing down on her. It wasn't just the fear of public speaking—it was the suffocating self-consciousness, the relentless fear of judgment, the way her heart raced, and her palms sweat at the thought of being the center of attention. It was the social anxiety disorder she'd been quietly battling for years, the thing she never spoke about to anyone. Not even Aiden.

Especially not Aiden.

The thought of him knowing made her chest tighten further. She didn't want his pity or anyone else's. She didn't want to be the broken one, the one who couldn't handle something as simple as a Christmas brunch.

Her mother's voice echoed in her mind, tinged with disappointment: *You'd be perfect.*

Tami shook her head, fighting the tears that threatened to spill. She'd tried to manage it on her own, convincing herself that she didn't need help. But lately, the cracks were starting to show. Maybe it was time to consider therapy…

The thought made her cringe. She could picture it now: sitting across from a stranger, laying her vulnerabilities bare. The humiliation of admitting that she couldn't fix herself.

How could she face her students, her colleagues, her family, if they knew?

Tami pushed the chair back abruptly and stood, then paced the small kitchen. She didn't know what to do. She wanted to get better, to live without this constant fear hanging over her. But the idea of seeking help felt like admitting defeat.

The pancakes remained unfinished, the coffee untouched. Tami stared out the window, watching the snow begin to fall. The world outside was calm and beautiful, a stark contrast to the storm raging inside her.

She exhaled shakily, pressing her hand to her chest.

One step at a time, she told herself. For now, she'd focus on making it through the day.

But deep down, she knew she couldn't keep running from this forever.

Rachel Rose stood in the Grand Ballroom of the Polk Island Hotel, her practiced gaze sweeping over the elegant tables adorned with fresh floral centerpieces and precisely folded napkins. The chandeliers cast a warm golden glow, reflecting off the polished silverware and crystal glasses. Everything was in place, just as it should be.

But it wasn't perfection that weighed on her mind. It was Tami.

Rachel Rose had envisioned this event—the Women's Legacy Luncheon—as a celebration of strength, resilience, and success. It was about honoring the women who had paved the way and those who were still shaping the future. After the original keynote had to cancel, in her mind, no one embodied that more than her youngest daughter.

Tami should have agreed to go up on that stage, sharing her story, inspiring others. But she had declined the invitation. Politely, of course. Always polite.

Rachel Rose sighed, adjusting a place card before stepping back. After her husband, Henry, died, she had taken her love for event planning and turned it into a business—out of necessity at first, but eventually, it became a passion. She never had to work when Henry was alive; he had provided a comfortable life. But comfort had crumbled beneath her when she was left a widow with three young daughters to raise alone. She had learned to be strong, to build something of her own. And yet no matter how much she accomplished, her success always felt hollow without Henry by her side.

Love, in the way she had once known it, felt like a closed door.

But that wasn't true for her daughters.

It had been a whirlwind of emotions when Tami confirmed her engagement to Aiden Worthington, her childhood friend. Rachel Rose smiled to herself, imagining her youngest daughter walking down the aisle.

She'd wasted no time mentally planning the wedding. But as much as she wanted to immerse herself in the excitement, a small part of her felt the twinge of loneliness that came with such milestones. It reminded her of all she'd done to get to this point.

Twenty-five years ago, she had been a young widow and single mom with no savings and a pension that barely covered the bills. Her husband's sudden death had been a wake-up call. She'd started as a sales associate at an upscale wedding boutique in Charleston, learning the industry while juggling her daughters' school schedules and her own grief.

It wasn't long before she realized she had a gift for working with brides. She had an eye for detail, a calming presence, and an innate ability to bring a bride's vision to life. Clients trusted her instincts, coworkers admired her work ethic, and her manager encouraged her to take on more responsibilities. Soon, she was helping with full wedding consultations—coordinating dresses, accessories, and even liaising with planners to ensure every detail was perfect.

Within two years, she had built a reputation for understanding exactly what brides needed, often anticipating their concerns before they voiced them. By year five, she had a loyal client base, steady referrals, and the confidence to branch out on her own.

Now, Rachel Rose Events was one of the most sought-after wedding planning services in the region—a testament to her resilience, hard work, and the love she poured into every celebration. She had built her business from the ground up, and she wasn't shy about reminding her daughters of the importance of financial independence. She never wanted them to face the struggles she had.

She pushed the thought aside, focusing instead on the reason she was here today. This luncheon was more than just an event—it was a message. A reminder to women, to her daughters, that they deserved to be seen and celebrated.

Tami included.

Rachel Rose still didn't understand why Tami resisted the spotlight. Naomi and Samantha thrived in it, much like she did.

But Tami? She lingered in the background, always supporting, always steady, but never stepping forward. Rachel Rose had hoped the opportunity to give the keynote address might give her that push. She'd have to ask Samantha instead.

"Mrs. Adams?"

She turned to see Cia approaching, a clipboard in hand. "The A/V team will be testing the sound system shortly."

"Perfect," Rachel Rose replied with a practiced smile. "Let's do a final check on the stage setup."

As they walked, she glanced around the room one more time. The setting was grand, and the event would flawless. She wished Tami hadn't declined.

Maybe she was pushing too hard. Maybe she didn't understand her daughter as well as she thought.

But she wasn't ready to give up on getting her daughter the recognition she deserved just yet.

AIDEN ENTERED THE restaurant near the lobby of the Polk Island Hotel with the casual confidence of someone who'd walked through the space all his life. He knew his brothers were already at the hotel restaurant, Southwinds, holding court as they always did. His steps slowed when he spotted Shane, Kenyon, and Micah gathered around a corner table near the large bay window.

Micah waved him over with exaggerated enthusiasm, his grin as wide as ever. "Aiden…took you long enough, man. We were starting to think you overslept."

He smirked, sliding into the empty chair beside Kenyon. "Unlike you, Micah, I don't spend my nights scrolling Instagram until three in the morning."

Shane chuckled, shaking his head as he reached for his coffee. "Don't let him fool you. He was probably up late, too, talking to Tami."

Aiden shot him a look, but his older brother's teasing grin softened the sting. "We didn't get off the phone until after midnight," he replied evenly, though the mention of her name caused an unfamiliar warmth to creep into his chest. "But that's nothing new. That's just what we do."

Kenyon arched a brow, his tone dry. "Uh-huh. Well, what I want to know is when did you and Tami decide to date. And *marriage*?"

Micah laughed. "Let the man breathe. He's practically glowing."

"Can we eat first?" Aiden asked, gesturing to the waitress hovering nearby. "Or is this going to be an interrogation over bacon and eggs?"

Shane raised his hands in mock surrender. "Fine, fine. We'll wait. But don't think you're getting out of it."

The waitress approached, her pad in hand, and took their orders.

Once she disappeared, the conversation resumed, though this time with a touch more seriousness.

"So," Shane began, his tone lighter but still pointed. "You ready for marriage, little brother?"

Aiden leaned back in his chair, crossing his arms. "Why are you asking me that like I'm twenty-three instead of thirty-three? I've been ready for a long time—it's just been a matter of finding the right person."

Shane's expression shifted, his teasing falling away as he nodded. "Fair enough."

As the words settled between them, Aiden felt their weight. He'd spoken them without hesitation, but the truth behind them was undeniable. He had always wanted a family—a real one, not just the patchwork of relationships he'd seen crumble over the years. The plan had seemed simple enough when they'd come up with it—a temporary solution to help Tami navigate her mother's constant pressure for her to settle down. They'd agreed to pretend, to wear the facade of a couple in love for the holidays, until her mom's matchmaking antics were laid to rest. Aiden could handle this. He could play the role of the loving fiancé, make the motions of planning a future they both knew wasn't real.

But guilt gnawed at him. Tami deserved real love—not a charade. She deserved a man who could offer her the kind of commitment she wanted, not just an illusion built on their past friendship. She deserved someone who could give her their whole heart, who could stand beside her and actually *want* to build a future with her. And the more he thought about it, the more he realized he wasn't that man.

He thought of everything she'd been through—her breakup, the heartbreak, the loneliness that had followed—and how she was still trying to hold it all together for the sake of her family. Aiden could help her with this situation. He could be the shield between her and her mom's relentless matchmaking attempts. He could pretend to be the perfect fiancé, keeping up appearances and buying them both some time. But that was all it was: a temporary fix.

Lying to his family felt like a betrayal. His family had always known him as someone who was genuine, someone who never shied away from the truth. Yet here he was, pretending for Tami's sake, and he couldn't back out now. Not with Tami depending on him to hold up his end of the bargain.

Micah's voice broke the silence. "Hey, you still with us?"

Aiden met his younger brother's gaze. "Huh…?"

"I was saying that you and Tami look good together."

Kenyon leaned forward, his elbows resting on the table. "Honestly, I always thought you'd be the first of us to settle down."

The waitress returned with their plates, and for a moment, the conversation paused as they dug into breakfast. But it wasn't long before Shane circled back.

"Dad would've been proud," he said quietly, his fork stilling over his eggs.

The mention of Angus Worthington Jr. brought a solemnity to the table, the kind of silence that wasn't uncomfortable but heavy with shared memories.

Aiden swallowed hard. "I think about him a lot," he admitted.

"We all do," Kenyon said softly. "It's like…no matter how much time passes, there's still that piece of us waiting for him to walk through the door and tell us everything's going to be okay."

Micah, who rarely let his emotions show, nodded. "Yeah. And it's not just the big moments. It's the little stuff. Like when I finally learned how to fix the sink last week and all I could think was how Dad would've laughed at me for not calling a plumber."

The brothers laughed, the sound tinged with bittersweet nostalgia.

Shane leaned back in his chair, his gaze distant. "You know, when Ace and I were planning the wedding, I kept picturing him standing next to me, telling me not to screw it up."

Aiden's chest tightened. "He'd have been proud of all of us," he said, his voice low but steady. "Not just for the big stuff, but for the way we've kept going. For being there for each other."

Kenyon reached across the table, his hand gripping Aiden's shoulder briefly. "And for you, man. For stepping up when we needed you most. When Dad died, you came home and jumped right in—helping with everything...helping wherever it was needed."

Aiden shook his head, his throat tightening. "We all stepped up."

"But you made sure we didn't fall apart," Shane said firmly.

He blinked against the sudden sting in his eyes. "I just did what he would've done."

"Exactly," Kenyon said with a small smile. "That's why he'd be proud."

He cleared his throat. "Oh, did Cia talk to you about reinstating the Christmas luncheon for the employees this year?" Aiden asked Shane.

He nodded. "Yeah, she did, and I think it's a good idea. It's what Dad would want."

They fell silent after that, their plates gradually emptying as the conversation turned to lighter topics—sports, work, Micah's latest attempt at dating. But the undercurrent of their father's memory lingered, a quiet presence that reminded them of the bond they shared.

As they stood to leave, Aiden felt an unspoken weight lift from his shoulders. He glanced at his brothers, their camaraderie a steadying force.

For all their teasing, they were his foundation—his proof that love, in all its messy and imperfect forms, was worth fighting for.

CHAPTER FIVE

THE AFTERNOON SUN cast a golden glow over the quiet, palm-lined neighborhood as Aiden's car hummed to a stop, its engine ticking in the mild December air. He'd spent the earlier part of the day grabbing lunch with his brothers, followed by a couple of productive hours meeting virtually with his team to provide high-level updates on a project. Working remotely had its perks—especially when it meant he could be here on the island.

The faint scent of the sea mingled with the earthy aroma of pinecones and the holly wreath adorning Tami's front door—a festive touch that sparkled under the delicate glimmer of fairy lights. Her town house, a charming dark blue structure with crisp white trim, exuded warmth and familiarity. Though only five miles from North Beach, it felt worlds away—a haven that was quintessentially Tami. Unassuming, inviting, and now alive with holiday cheer, it stirred a deep sense of comfort and anticipation within him.

Tami greeted him at the door, her smile warm and genuine. She wore a simple sweater and jeans, her short haircut in a chic pixie style that framed her face effortlessly. The sight of her, so effortlessly herself, tugged at something deep inside him.

"Come in," she said, stepping aside to let him through. "Lunch is almost ready."

The warm, comforting aroma of freshly baked bread filled the air, making his stomach rumble. The scent grew even more irresistible as he stepped into her kitchen, where the cozy atmosphere seemed to wrap around him like a welcome embrace.

Aiden noticed the table was already set with plates, silverware, and a pot of red poinsettias. "This smells amazing," he said, shrugging off his coat and draping it over a chair. "What's on the menu?"

"Just something simple," Tami replied, her cheeks coloring slightly. "Salmon, veggies, a salad, and homemade bread."

"Simple?" He chuckled. "You're spoiling me. What's the occasion?"

Tami's hand trembled slightly as she poured steaming hot water into a teapot, her gaze avoiding Aiden's curious stare. "Consider it another thank-you for all your help with the engagement charade," she said lightly, but he caught the flicker of unease in her eyes.

Aiden pulled out a chair for Tami and noticed the tension in her shoulders as she sat down. He decided to bring up the women's legion brunch, hoping to distract her from whatever was bothering her. "So, my mom attended the brunch earlier. She was really excited about the keynote speaker, until she heard that they canceled last minute. She said your sister did a great job though."

Tami's hand froze in midair, her fork poised over her plate. A shadow crossed her face before she let out a small sigh. "Yeah, I know. My mom asked me to step in as the replacement."

Aiden's eyebrows shot up in surprise. "Why didn't you do it?"

She hesitated, her gaze falling to her plate. "It was too last minute. There wasn't any time to really prepare anything."

He could see the disappointment in her eyes. "Your mom is upset, isn't she?"

Tami nodded slowly, still staring down at her plate. "She is, but you know public speaking isn't my thing."

"You mean because it makes you anxious?" Aiden asked gently.

"Yeah," she admitted with a small shrug. "The large crowd, the pressure, the spotlight…it's overwhelming for me. Remember how sick I got in high school after having to present an assignment?" When he nodded, she continued. "Well, I still get that way."

Aiden wanted to probe further, but he didn't push. She'd say more when she was ready. Instead, he focused on their meal and offered a reassuring smile. "Well, for what it's worth, I think you're a great speaker. The one time I heard you speak, you did a fantastic job, but I understand that you don't like it. And as for your mom...she loves you too much to stay mad for long," he said with a chuckle.

Tami's lips curved into a small smile. "Thanks, Aiden."

Once they had finished eating and tidied up, Aiden proposed an impromptu excursion. "Why don't we go surprise Luella at the boutique? I need to grab something for my mom while we're there." He was eager to see his cousin again. They had formed a close bond when they first met a few years ago, after Luella's father passed away.

Tami's eyes lit up. "That sounds perfect. Let me grab my coat."

Main Street was a perfect picture of Christmas charm, with small shops decked out in festive garlands and twinkling lights. Every doorway was adorned with boughs of holly, and wreaths with red ribbons graced the windows, catching the eye of everyone passing by. The gentle hum of holiday music filled the air as people hurried along, some carrying bags full of presents, while others paused to admire the seasonal displays.

Aiden couldn't help but smile at the cozy atmosphere—it was like a storybook small-town Christmas brought to life. In the midst of this charming scene stood a boutique owned by famous designer Renee Rothchild Bowman.

Luella managed the store, while Renee worked out of her Charleston offices. The boutique radiated elegance, from its expertly arranged window displays to its sophisticated interior decor.

Luella's face brightened the moment they stepped through the door. "Aiden! I had no idea you were back in town. And Tami…what a lovely surprise."

She pulled them into warm, welcoming hugs, her smile radiating genuine delight. Stepping back, she looked them over with a mix of curiosity and excitement. "So, what brings you two here?"

"I couldn't come home without visiting my favorite cousin," Aiden said with a grin. "Plus, I need a Christmas gift for my mom."

"And I'm looking for some inspiration for presents for my sisters," Tami added.

Luella's grin widened. "Well, you've come to the perfect place. Let me show you some of our latest treasures."

As she guided Tami toward a display of jewelry, Aiden wandered over to a shelf of scarves. His fingers brushed over the soft fabrics until he found one in a deep crimson hue that reminded him of his mother's favorite holiday decorations.

"What do you think?" he asked Luella, holding up the scarf.

"It's perfect," she said with a nod. "Aunt Madelyn will love it."

"These earrings are beautiful," Tami murmured, holding up a pair adorned with tiny pink pearls.

"There's a matching necklace. Would you like to see it?" Luella asked, joining her. "Makes a nice gift for a sister."

"Maybe," she said thoughtfully. "Or for me. Is that selfish?"

"Not at all," Luella said with a laugh. "Treat yourself, Tami. You deserve it."

As they browsed, Aiden found himself watching Tami more than the merchandise. She moved through the boutique with an ease that belied the tension she'd shown earlier. Here, among family and friends, she seemed lighter, freer.

After they completed their purchases, Luella accompanied them to the door. He had opted for the scarf, while Tami selected the pearl jewelry. "Thanks for stopping by," she said, hugging them once more. "It means a lot."

"Of course," Aiden said. "How's married life treating you?"

Luella's smile widened. "It's great. I've never met a man who loves me as much as Noah. I can't even put into words how much I love him."

"I'm so excited for you," Tami said. He knew she'd become close to his cousin since Luella moved to the island.

Aiden glanced at Tami and caught a flicker of something unreadable in her expression before she quickly masked it. Was it longing? Was she thinking about her breakup or her hopes of a real proposal this Christmas? It was brief but enough to spark his curiosity.

As they stepped outside, Tami turned to Aiden, her cheeks flushed from the cold. "I didn't mention the engagement," she admitted. "I know my mom will spread the word soon enough, so I figured we'll just deal with it as it comes."

He nodded in agreement.

"Thanks for suggesting this," Tami said. "It was nice to get out of the house."

"Anytime," Aiden said, his voice warm. He glanced at her, his heart swelling with a mix of emotions he couldn't quite untangle.

TAMI BUSIED HERSELF in the kitchen.

Two shopping bags were stacked neatly near the sofa, their contents peeking out as a testament to the productive—and surprisingly fun—afternoon Tami and Aiden had shared.

He was in the living room, flipping through her collection of vinyl records. His presence filled Tami's town house with an energy she simultaneously cherished and feared. It was so easy with him—too easy. And that scared her more than the idea of her secrets being exposed.

The truth was Tami had a lot of walls up, built

piece by piece over the years. It wasn't that she didn't trust Aiden—she did. But the way she'd trusted Gary with everything she had, only to have it all ripped out from under her left her terrified of being vulnerable again. That kind of pain was not something she was ready to risk. And Aiden, even though he was just pretending, was still close enough to break through.

Gary's betrayal hadn't just hurt; it had shaken her to her core. She'd never seen it coming, the way he'd just...discarded her. It made her question everything: her judgment, her ability to recognize what was real, and, worst of all, herself. Was she weak for not seeing it? Did she somehow deserve it? She didn't want Aiden—*anyone*—to think she was that person. She didn't want him to look at her and see someone who was easily fooled, someone whose heart could be broken so easily. She hated how small she felt, like the whole world could see the cracks Gary had left behind.

And here she was, pretending with Aiden, putting on a smile and playing the part of someone who had it all together. It felt like a balancing act. She trusted Aiden, yes, but the idea of letting him in more than that—the idea of him seeing her, all of her, including the parts she was still trying to protect—was terrifying. She couldn't do it. She couldn't let him see how fragile she really was.

And yet she felt so drawn to him. Too drawn to him as he'd helped her navigate the past few days.

That was what scared her. It wasn't the fake engagement. It wasn't the act. It was that *maybe*, just maybe, in the middle of all this, she'd start to feel something real again. And if she did, then what? What if she let him see her too clearly, like she had with Gary? What if he let her down too? No, she couldn't be that vulnerable, not now. Not when she was just starting to feel like she had control over her life again.

The irony didn't escape her. Aiden wasn't asking for anything more than what they'd agreed to. He wasn't pushing her for more feelings, more commitment, but the mere fact that he could see through her defenses made her heart race. She didn't want to be that open with him. Not yet. Not until she figured out how to guard her heart again.

"Hey, you've got some classics here," Aiden called out, holding up a sleeve. "Did you ever find that Marvin Gaye album you were searching for?"

"Not yet," Tami replied, setting two mugs on a tray along with a plate of cookies. "I've got my eye on a couple of auctions online. Hopefully, I'll snag one soon."

"Well, if anyone deserves it, it's you," he said, his grin so genuine it made her stomach flip. "Want me to put something on?"

"Sure. Something mellow," she suggested, balancing the tray as she walked into the living room.

He chuckled, setting the record down and choosing one she hadn't played in years. As the soft strains of Bill Withers filled the room, she placed the tray on the coffee table and sank onto the couch.

Aiden joined her, sitting closer than was strictly necessary but not close enough to make her move away.

Her nerves were buzzing, and it wasn't because of the music. She knew she needed to focus on the here and now, on enjoying the time with Aiden, but the encumbrance of her deception hung heavily over her. How long could she keep hiding the truth?

She found herself hyperaware of Aiden's every movement. The way he laughed at the jokes, the warmth of his arm brushing hers when he adjusted his position—it all felt magnified, overwhelming.

Tami tried to focus on the lyrics but her mind kept wandering. She thought about the way Aiden had smiled at her earlier in the boutique, how he'd looked so at ease browsing the scarves and jewelry. How easy it would have been to pretend that they were a real couple, shopping for gifts for their family.

She shook her head slightly, as if the motion could dislodge the thoughts swirling in her mind. But they refused to leave. The humiliating breakup with Gary had left her raw, exposed. She couldn't let herself go there. The last thing she ever wanted was to feel was that sense of humiliation again—the feeling of being discarded like she hadn't meant anything. It had taken every ounce of her strength to regain some semblance of confidence after Gary's betrayal.

She didn't trust herself right now. Her judgment was clouded. Her feelings were a mix of confusion and grief, and she wasn't sure which one she was clinging to more. The comfort that came from knowing Aiden was someone she could count on, someone who saw her not as a failure but as a person with strengths, with flaws, with everything in between.

She couldn't risk losing that. Losing Aiden's friendship would destroy her. It was the one thing in her life she could depend on, the one thing that didn't come with strings attached, the one constant that wasn't clouded by broken promises or betrayal.

"Tami, you okay?" Aiden's voice broke through her spiraling thoughts. She blinked, realizing she hadn't laughed at a particularly funny scene.

"Yeah," she said quickly, forcing a smile. "Just...distracted, I guess."

"You sure? You've been a little off today."

Her stomach twisted. She hated keeping things from him, but she couldn't tell him the truth. Not about her social anxiety, and certainly not about her sudden conflicted feelings for him. "I'm fine, Aiden. Really."

His expression showed doubt, but he gave a slight nod before focusing back on the movie.

Tami let out a soft breath, glad that Aiden didn't insist on discussing it further.

When the film ended, he stood up. "I should probably get going. Mom wants me to help her with the tree."

"What's on your agenda tomorrow afternoon?" Tami asked. "I don't have any plans after I leave school."

"We can hang out if you want."

She smiled. "I think everyone will expect us to spend a lot of time together since we're supposed to be a couple. After next Friday, I'll be on holiday break."

Tami walked him to the door.

As Aiden stepped out into the night, he turned back, his expression soft. "Hey, if you ever need to talk…about anything…"

She nodded, swallowing the lump in her throat, her heart heavy with unspoken words. "I know. Thanks, Aiden."

He smiled and walked to his car, leaving her standing in the doorway.

As the taillights of the vehicle disappeared into the distance, Tami closed the door and leaned against it, her chest tight with emotions she couldn't fully name.

She knew she needed to make a change, to find a way to face her fears and stop hiding from the people she cared about. But for now, all she could do was take it one step at a time—and hope that she didn't lose Aiden in the process.

AIDEN STEPPED INTO his old bedroom, the familiar creak of the wooden floorboards beneath his boots grounding him in a way that only this space could. The faint scent of lavender lingered, a reminder of his mother's meticulous care. He shut the door behind him.

The small shopping bag in his hand felt heavier than it should, its contents a carefully chosen gift for his mother. Aiden crossed the room swiftly, his gaze darting to the closet in the corner.

Pulling open the door, he spotted an empty space on the middle shelf, and he slid the bag in, nestling it between a dusty photo album and an old baseball glove. Satisfied it was well hidden, he closed the door with a quiet click, a faint smile playing on his lips.

The day with Tami lingered in his mind, her laughter still echoing in his ears as he took a steadying breath.

"Aiden?" His mother's voice floated up the stairs. "Can you go up to the attic and check for the crystal ornaments? I couldn't find them in the garage."

"Yes, Mom," he replied. Thoughts of Tami still lingered in his mind like an unwelcome guest.

Aiden left the bedroom and turned toward the

end of the hallway where the attic door was located.

He pushed it open; the familiar creak of the old wooden stairs greeted him as he climbed up. The attic, with its slanted ceiling and wooden beams, held decades of family history and memories. A cool breeze hit his face as he stepped inside, mixing with the faint scent of cedar and dust from forgotten seasons.

Moonlight poured through a small, round window at the far end of the space, casting a golden glow on rows of neatly labeled boxes and bins. It was clear that this was his father's domain—everything was arranged meticulously, from holiday decorations to stacks of magazines tied with twine. His father's precise handwriting marked each bin: *Christmas*, *Tools*, *Camping Gear*.

Aiden took a moment to take in the room before him, his eyes scanning over all the familiar objects. The sight of his father's old toolbox in the corner made his heart ache. It was scratched and worn, a symbol of years spent doing projects, repairs, and lessons passed down. He remembered his dad showing him how to fix a squeaky hinge using that very toolbox and how to take care of things so they would last.

He walked over to the row of Christmas bins, the floorboards softly creaking under his feet. Opening one up, he found tangled garlands and lights inside. Aiden smiled slightly as memories flooded back. His dad patiently untangling those lights while humming along to holiday music.

Christmas used to be his favorite time of year, not just because of the decorations but because of the way his father made it feel magical and meaningful. Now with Angus Jr. gone…it no longer felt the same.

Opening another bin, Aiden's fingers brushed against tissue paper carefully wrapped around delicate crystal ornaments. These were his father's pride and joy; they had been in the Worthington family for generations and were always saved for last on the tree, each one being placed with great care.

Standing there with the box in his hands, Aiden took in the sight of the attic once more.

His father's presence could still be felt in every corner—a gentle reminder of the man who had shaped him in so many ways.

He spoke softly to himself, the words flowing out before he even realized it. "I used to think it was funny when you said Tami and me were perfect together, Dad."

The memory floated back to him as though it had just happened. It was years ago, right after one of their usual backyard barbecues, his dad sitting across from him with that smile he reserved for moments of unexpected insight. *You know, son, you and Tami—you're both the missing pieces to each other's puzzle. It's obvious to me, but you'll see it when the time's right.*

A bitter laugh caught in Aiden's throat as he remembered that conversation. His chest tightened at the thought of his dad's death, the loss still fresh in his heart. That spark of life Aiden used to have, the one his dad had always believed in—so eager to move forward, to take chances, to embrace life with open arms—felt like it had gone out. It wasn't just his grief he was carrying; it was a sense of *stagnation*, a belief that maybe he wasn't meant to give anyone the full, undivided love his dad had always championed.

"You were always the optimist, Dad," Aiden murmured, leaning back against the couch, trying to picture the easy smile his father had always worn. He could almost hear him now, his voice gruff but warm, giving Aiden some half-joking advice: *You'll figure it out, son. You're not like me, but I know you'll find your way.*

But Aiden wasn't so sure. The spark was dim. The love he used to believe was out there—pure, full of possibility—felt harder to believe in these days. His dad's death had knocked something loose inside him. The urgency to move forward, to give someone his heart had faded. How could he offer something that deep, something so whole, when his own heart felt fractured? It had become easier to pretend things were fine, to hide behind the distractions of work, the occasional visit home, the fleeting moments where he told himself he was still capable of real connection.

Before he made his way down the stairs with the box of crystal ornaments, he couldn't help but take one last look around the attic. Though he still felt a pang of sadness at missing his father, there was also a warmth and sense of peace knowing that his memory would always be with him, a constant reminder of who he was and the family he wanted to build.

As Aiden stepped into the living room, Madelyn smiled and motioned towards the boxes in his arms. "You found them," she said, her eyes lighting up with joy. "I really thought we'd put them in the garage with the other Christmas stuff."

Aiden shrugged as he set the boxes down. "There's a bunch of decorations still in the attic," he said.

Madelyn's eyebrows shot up in surprise. "Really?"

He nodded and rubbed his hands together. "About four containers full."

Madelyn's face softened as she gazed at the box. "Your daddy loved Christmas," she said wistfully, her voice filled with memories. "He would buy decorations wherever he could find them. And don't let him discover a year-round Christmas store…"

Aiden chuckled, but inside he felt a pang of sadness for his late father's love for the holiday season. "Yeah, he was serious about Christmas," he said. "Said the tree wasn't right unless every ornament had its story and was in just the right spot."

Madelyn's gaze turned tender as she looked at her son. "He had a knack for making the ordinary feel extraordinary," she said softly, placing a hand on his shoulder.

Madelyn carefully pried open the lid, revealing layers of tissue paper wrapped around delicate ornaments. She reached for a glass angel, its shimmering wings catching the light.

"This one was his favorite," she murmured, her thumb brushing over the intricate details. "He always hung it at the top of the tree, said it needed the best view."

Aiden felt a lump form in his throat, his gaze fixed on the delicate ornament. He reached out a trembling hand to touch it, the cool glass sending shivers through his fingertips.

"He always said the holidays were about family and tradition," he said softly, a bittersweet smile tugging at his lips. "I miss him so much, especially during this time of year."

Madelyn placed a comforting hand on Aiden's shoulder, her touch warm and reassuring.

"I miss him too, but he's always with us, especially in moments like this."

Together, they carefully hung the ornament at the top of the tree, just as Angus Jr. used to do.

As they stood back to admire their handiwork,

a sense of peace settled over them. Surrounded by the beauty of the holiday season and the echoes of the past, Aiden and Madelyn found solace in each other's company, knowing that this beloved tradition would continue to live on, year after year.

CHAPTER SIX

THE POLK ISLAND CAFÉ buzzed with the familiar hum of clinking plates and soft chatter. Today, the holiday spirit was in full swing. Twinkling white lights draped across the windows, casting a cozy glow over the rustic wooden tables. Evergreen garlands lined the counter, their deep green accented by bright red bows, while the scent of cinnamon and fresh pine mingled with the rich aroma of freshly brewed coffee.

Upbeat holiday music played from the speakers, the cheerful melodies weaving through the café, adding to the festive energy. But Tami barely noticed the decorations or the music.

She stepped inside, her eyes scanning the room until it landed on her mother, waiting for her at a corner table. Rachel Rose was a vision of elegance as always, her posture regal despite the casual setting. Her crimson blouse set off her flawless complexion, and her pearls—always pearls—added a timeless sophistication to her look. Tami could tell from the slight tilt of her mother's head that she was already preparing for whatever subject she had brought Tami here to discuss. They'd had a wonderful day together on Sunday. She hoped her mother wouldn't do anything to taint that memory.

"Tami," Rachel Rose greeted warmly, rising from her seat to kiss her daughter's cheek. "You're punctual, as always. I like that."

"Hi, Mama." Tami smiled and settled into the chair across from her. She'd left school to have lunch with her mother.

"I'm sure you're excited having Aiden home."

Tami broke into a grin. "I am."

A waitress arrived almost immediately to take their drink orders, and Rachel Rose didn't miss a beat, requesting her usual Earl Grey tea. Tami opted for a lemonade, hoping the tartness would help steel her nerves.

Once the waitress disappeared, Rachel Rose turned her full attention to her daughter.

She leaned forward slightly, her sharp gaze settling on Tami. "I must admit I was surprised by your decision not to take on the keynote address at the brunch the other day."

And there it was—the reason for the lunch. Tami had been waiting for this conversation ever since she'd politely declined the invitation. She'd anticipated her mother's disappointment but facing it in person made the sting sharper.

"I know you were counting on me," she began, fiddling with the edge of her napkin. "I just... I didn't feel it was the right fit for me this time."

"The *right fit*?" Rachel Rose's tone held a touch of incredulity. "Tami, you're an incredible psychologist and an inspiring woman. You have every qualification to speak at that podium. Why would you let this opportunity pass you by?"

Tami hesitated, searching for the right words. "Mama, I've never been comfortable in the spotlight. You know that. Public speaking—it's Samantha's thing, not mine."

Rachel Rose's lips pressed together in a thoughtful line. "Samantha did do a wonderful job. I won't deny that. But Tami, this wasn't about comparing you to her. This was about celebrating your accomplishments and letting others see the remarkable woman you are."

Tami's chest tightened. "Samantha has always been gifted at speaking. She thrives in those moments. But me? I'd rather be in the background, making sure everything runs smoothly."

Her mother's expression softened, though the disappointment didn't entirely leave her eyes. "Dear, there's no shame in being humble, but sometimes you have to let the world see what you're capable of. You have so much to offer, and it's not just about standing behind others—it's about standing for yourself."

Tami swirled her lemonade around in the glass, the ice clinking against the sides with each movement. Then, as her mother's eyes gleamed with satisfaction, Tami's heart began to race.

"So," her mother said, setting down her teacup carefully, "let's talk about you and Aiden now that we've cleared things up about the keynote."

Tami's grip tightened on her glass, trying to keep her smile in place as she asked, "What about us?"

Her mother leaned forward eagerly, a mix of curiosity and delight on her face. "You and Aiden have always been close, but I didn't realize it had turned into something more. Why wouldn't you tell me?"

Tami felt a lump form in her throat as she forced another smile. "Well," she replied carefully, hoping her answer sounded convincing enough, "it wasn't just one moment. It was a gradual realization."

Her mother's eyes sparkled with joy as she clasped her hands together. "Oh, how romantic. It must have felt like you were blind all along and then suddenly, there he was."

Tami laughed uneasily, feeling guilty for leading her mother on. Her mother looked genuinely happy for her, and that touched her heart. "Something like that."

"Turns out you didn't need my help." Rachel Rose winked.

With the mention of her mother arranging dates for eligible bachelors, any guilt or hesitation vanished. Her fake engagement to Aiden was both a shield and a lie.

"I guess you can cancel the matchmaking service now," Tami said slyly. "Aiden beat you to it."

Her mother chuckled, her delight obvious. "I suppose he did. But I can't say I'm disappointed. He's a wonderful man—handsome, successful... I've always liked him."

Tami nodded along, but the situation weighed heavily on her mind. She knew she needed to sit down with Aiden and solidify their story before her mother's persistent questions unraveled their lie.

As the conversation shifted to more trivial topics, Tami couldn't help but feel a sense of relief when lunch finally ended, and her mother hugged her goodbye. But alongside that relief was a sense of determination.

She needed to make sure she and Aiden were always on the same page. No slip-ups, or their carefully constructed lie would come crashing down around them.

The quarterly family meeting had gone well, Aiden thought, as he and his mother left the conference room at the Polk Island Hotel. He felt a quiet sense of satisfaction, knowing the family business was thriving. He had attended these meetings virtually for most of the year, but being home for the holidays meant he could finally join in person.

Shane, his other siblings, and their cousin Oliver had gone over the latest numbers, reviewing occupancy rates, seasonal projections, and upcoming renovations. Everyone seemed pleased that the hotel's revenue continued to climb steadily. For a family venture built on hope and a shared vision, the progress felt personal.

Aiden had always played more of a supporting role, offering his expertise in project management and strategy whenever needed, but moments like this reminded him of the deeper connection he had to the place.

As they stepped into the bustling lobby, Madelyn looked up at him with a smile. "Why don't we grab some lunch before heading back? Northwinds is just upstairs."

Aiden nodded. "Sounds good."

The restaurant, the sister restaurant of Southwinds, offered a stunning view of the ocean, the waves sparkling under the winter sun. Aiden and Madelyn were seated near the window, where the scent of saltwater mingled faintly with the aromas of grilled seafood and freshly baked bread.

They ordered quickly, Aiden opting for a blackened-fish sandwich and Madelyn choosing a shrimp salad. As they waited, his mother's expression turned thoughtful. "It's so good to see everyone working together for the hotel. Your father would've loved this, you know."

Aiden managed a smile, though the mention of

his father tugged at his heart. "Yeah, he would've been proud. The hotel was his dream."

Madelyn's hand rested lightly on the table, her silver bracelet catching the light. "Speaking of dreams, have you and Tami started making plans for the wedding yet?"

The question hit Aiden squarely, but he kept his face neutral. Hiding the guilt was becoming second nature. "Not yet," he replied, his voice even. "Right now, we're just enjoying being engaged."

Madelyn's smile softened. "That's important. Don't let anyone rush you. It's your journey, after all."

He nodded, grateful for her understanding, but the weight of their deception pressed harder. He hated lying to his mother, yet he'd told himself it was necessary—especially with Rachel Rose's matchmaking tendencies.

Madelyn stirred her tea, her gaze distant for a moment. "You know," she said, her tone light, "Rachel Rose had quite the plans for Tami before you announced the engagement. She mentioned to me that she'd lined up two of the most eligible men she could find to be Tami's dates for the holiday social season."

Aiden chuckled despite himself, some of the guilt lifting. "Well, I guess I saved Tami from that."

Madelyn laughed. "You certainly did. She's lucky to have you—and you're lucky to have her."

Lucky wasn't the word Aiden would have chosen. The truth was he and Tami had stumbled into this charade more for convenience than anything else. Still, as he thought of Tami, he couldn't deny the ease of their friendship or the way her laughter had a knack for lightening his mood.

Madelyn leaned forward slightly, her curiosity unmistakable. "When did it happen? When did you realize you wanted to be more than friends?"

Aiden hesitated, choosing his words carefully. "It wasn't a single moment," he said, echoing the vague answer he and Tami had decided on should they be asked this. "It just...felt right."

Madelyn studied him for a moment, then nodded with a smile. "Sometimes the best things happen that way—quietly, without fanfare."

He returned her smile, faking an ease he didn't feel at the moment.

Their food arrived, and the conversation turned to lighter topics, the tension in Aiden's chest easing as they ate. By the time they finished their meal and headed back to the family home, he felt steadier, though the nagging thought of their fabricated engagement lingered.

Madelyn went upstairs to check on something, leaving Aiden alone in the quiet. He poured himself a glass of water and leaned against the counter, staring at the garland-wrapped banister of the staircase. The conversation at lunch, his mother's gentle probing, played over in his mind.

He set the glass down with a soft thud, running a hand through his locs.

When did it happen? His mother's question had seemed innocent enough, but it had felt like a spotlight on their fragile lie. They couldn't afford blunders, not when their families were so invested in their supposed romance.

Aiden sighed, his mind drifting to Tami. She was probably juggling her own share of awkward questions from Rachel Rose, who was undoubtedly buzzing with excitement over the engagement. He couldn't blame Tami for her mother's relentless matchmaking—it was the very reason they'd concocted this charade in the first place.

Aiden had thought the fake engagement would buy Tami some peace, but instead, it seemed to have added a new layer of complexity to her life. Aiden pulled out his phone and sent Tami a quick text:

We need to talk. Soon. About…everything. Let me know when you're free.

He stared at the screen for a moment before sliding the phone back into his pocket. He wasn't sure how Tami felt about the engagement lately—whether she still saw it as the convenient solution they'd agreed upon or if their lie had started to take its toll on her too.

He couldn't deny that there were moments

when the fake engagement felt…natural. Comfortable, even. He and Tami had always had an easy rhythm, a connection that didn't need words. He thought again of the day they'd gone Christmas shopping together. But that same ease made the lie feel more precarious, as if they were walking a tightrope between reality and pretense.

Aiden felt a mix of emotions swirling within him—guilt over the lie, gratitude for his mother's unwavering support, and a growing determination to see the charade through without hurting anyone.

THE PARK WAS quieter than Tami had expected for a weekday afternoon, but the holiday season still made its presence known. Twinkling lights had been wrapped around lampposts, and a towering Christmas tree stood near the pavilion, its ornaments catching the soft afternoon sun. The scent of cinnamon and cocoa drifted from a festive food truck parked near the entrance, where a line of bundled-up families waited for their turn to order steaming drinks.

Nearby, children built Christmas-themed sandcastles in a designated play area, shaping them into festive cottages and decorating them with seashells in place of ornaments. The occasional squeal of laughter or sharp cry of frustration pierced the otherwise serene atmosphere as a gust of wind carried the distant sound of holiday music playing from a speaker near the vendor stalls.

Trees swayed gently, their bare branches casting delicate, shifting shadows across the ground. Aiden sat beside her on the weathered bench, his shoulders hunched as he stared off toward the playground. His expression was unreadable, but Tami could sense his thoughts weighed on him.

The silence between them wasn't uncomfortable—but it was heavy.

Tami wrapped her jacket tighter around herself, the crisp air biting at her cheeks. "You ever think we're just bad at this?" she asked finally, her voice barely louder than the rustling palm leaves.

Aiden turned to her, a brow arched. "Bad at what?"

"This." She gestured vaguely, as though trying to encompass everything in the space around them. "Life. Relationships. Pretending we've got it all together."

He let out a short, humorless laugh. "More often than I'd like to admit."

She glanced sideways at him, her lips curving into a small smile. "It's a little comforting, actually. Knowing I'm not the only one drowning in guilt and second-guessing every decision."

Aiden leaned back, his gaze drifting to the playground where a group of children chased each other around the jungle gym. "I feel like I'm constantly waiting for someone to figure it out," he said, his voice quieter now. "That I don't have it together. That I'm just...faking it until it falls apart."

Tami nodded slowly. "Me too. Every time I smile and pretend I'm fine, I wonder if anyone can see through it. It's exhausting."

They fell into silence again, watching as a little boy tried to climb up the slide while his friends laughed and cheered him on.

"I used to think I'd have it all figured out by now," Tami said suddenly, feeling regret bubble up. "Career, love, family. Kids."

Aiden nodded. "Same here. I thought by thirty I'd have a house, a wife, a couple of kids running around. Instead, it's just me, a job I'm good at but don't love, and an apartment that feels too big most days."

Tami looked at him, her expression softening, though uncertainty lingered in her eyes. "You'll get there, Aiden. You're...you're good at this whole life thing, even if you don't think you are. You're steady. Reliable. You'd make a great husband and an even better dad."

Aiden smiled faintly, the corners of his eyes crinkling. "Thanks, T. But what about you? You're smart, funny, gorgeous. You've got a good heart. Any guy would be lucky to have you."

She shrugged, her gaze fixed on the playground, grappling with her own fears. "I don't know. Maybe. But sometimes it feels like I'm running out of time. Like...what if I don't find the right guy? What if I never get married? What if

I never have kids? And what if that's okay, but I just can't accept it?"

Aiden hesitated, then leaned forward, resting his elbows on his knees. "You'll find someone. You just haven't met him yet."

Tami shook her head, a bitter laugh escaping her lips. "What if I don't? What if I end up alone? No husband, no kids, just…me and my cats?" Her voice wavered between fear and defiance.

Aiden smirked. "You don't even have a cat."

"Exactly." Her response was a blend of self-mockery and longing. "I'm not even prepared for that cliché," she quipped, a small grin tugging at her lips, though her heart felt heavy with uncertainty despite the melancholy she felt. They both fell silent again, their thoughts heavier now. Children's laughter rang out across the park, and Tami's eyes followed a little girl who was carefully building a sandcastle.

"I've thought about it, you know," she said after a moment.

"Thought about what?" Aiden asked, glancing at her.

"Having a child… London's a wonderful mother. I'm not saying I'd do it tomorrow, but if the right guy doesn't come along… I don't want to miss out on being a mom."

Aiden was quiet for a moment, his expression unreadable. "You'd be a great mom," he said finally.

She smiled at him, grateful for the sincerity in his voice. "Thanks. That means a lot."

Aiden leaned back, crossing his arms. "Well, if you're still single in a couple of years and you decide you want a kid...let me know."

Tami turned to him, startled. "What?"

He shrugged, his expression casual but his tone serious. "I mean it. If we're both still single and you want a kid, we can marry for real. No strings attached."

Tami blinked, trying to process what he'd just said. Then, unexpectedly, she burst into laughter.

Aiden joined in, shaking his head. "What? I'm serious."

"I know you are," she said. "That's what makes it so funny."

The thought lingered as they sat in comfortable silence, watching the children play. Maybe she didn't have it all figured out, but she didn't have to. Not yet.

CHAPTER SEVEN

THE MORNING SUNLIGHT poured through the floor-to-ceiling windows of Rachel Rose's office, spilling across the polished hardwood floors. The space exuded elegance and romance, a reflection of her twenty-plus years in the business of making dream celebrations come true. Soft cream-colored walls were adorned with framed photographs of breathtaking wedding venues, past clients beaming in their bridal attire, and magazine features showcasing her expertise. A large desk made of dark cherrywood sat near the back of the room, flanked by tall bookshelves filled with event planning guides, color swatches, floral arrangement catalogs, and an array of tasteful decor items—vases, ribbon spools, and framed pictures showcasing her three daughters at various milestones.

A fresh bouquet of white lilies—her favorite—stood in a vase on the corner of the desk, filling the room with a delicate fragrance. Behind her desk, a vision board hung on the wall, pinned with ideas for future events, color palettes and venue sketches. Among them, a collection of wedding inspirations for Tami stood out—a subtle but undeniable reminder of Rachel Rose's ongoing mission to see her last unmarried daughter walk down the aisle.

Rachel Rose leaned back in her leather chair, scrolling through her laptop. On the screen were pages of wedding dresses—elegant ball gowns, chic sheath designs, and romantic A-line styles. Her eyes narrowed as she bookmarked another contender, a strapless satin dress with a sweetheart neckline that she thought would highlight Tami's slender figure.

A light knock on the open office door pulled her attention from the screen.

Rachel Rose looked up to see her middle daughter stepping in. Naomi, with her sharp cheekbones and the confident poise of someone who always knew her own mind, was dressed in a tailored navy blazer and black trousers. Her brown eyes sparkled as she entered and surveyed her mother's screen.

"Mom," Naomi said, arching an eyebrow, "I hope those are for one of your clients and not for Tami."

Rachel Rose clicked her laptop shut, a sheepish smile spreading across her face. "I was just… browsing. It's exciting, Naomi. Your sister is getting married."

"She hasn't even set a date yet," she pointed out, perching on the edge of the desk. "And you're already planning the wedding like it's happening next month."

Rachel Rose folded her hands on the desk, tilting her head in mock offense. "A mother can dream, can't she? Besides, I want to help her avoid stress. Wedding planning can be overwhelming."

Naomi's expression softened, but her tone remained firm. "Mom, listen. I know you mean well, but you have to let Tami do this her way. She needs space. You're excited, but if you start pushing, she's going to feel pressured."

Rachel Rose leaned back, her enthusiasm fading slightly. "I don't mean to interfere. I just want her to have the best. You know how much I care about all of you being secure and settled."

Naomi nodded. "We know, Mom. And we appreciate it. But Tami's relationship with Aiden? That's hers to navigate. You taught us to stand on our own feet, remember? Let her take the lead on this—without feeling like she's got to match your timeline."

Rachel Rose's lips curved into a small smile. She reached out to pat Naomi's hand. "You're right."

"And you've done an amazing job building our future," Naomi said softly. "But let Tami come to you. She will if she wants your help."

Rachel Rose nodded slowly. She knew Naomi was right, but letting go was never easy. After her husband's death, she had poured everything into ensuring her daughters' success and stability. She wanted them to have everything she had to fight for. Still, she could see the wisdom in stepping back.

"Okay," she said with a sigh, lifting her hands in surrender. "I'll try to keep my enthusiasm in check. For now."

Naomi grinned, hopping off the desk. "That's all I'm asking. Now, how about I take you to lunch? My treat."

Rachel Rose stood and grabbed her purse. "You're on. But don't think that gets you out of helping me with the books this afternoon."

"Deal," Naomi said, looping her arm through her mother's.

As they stepped out of the office, Rachel Rose glanced back at her workspace, her heart swelling with pride. She had built this life from the ashes of tragedy, and while she still carried the weight of that loss, she knew she had given her daughters the tools to forge their own paths. Now it was time to trust her girls to use them.

Tami adjusted the last strand of twinkling lights on her artificial tree, her fingers brushing over the pine-scented ornaments she'd bought to make the town house feel more festive. The hum of holiday music played softly in the background, blending with the gentle rain pattering against the windows.

She stepped back to admire her work, hands on her hips, a faint smile tugging at her lips.

The tree wasn't extravagant, but it was hers—a symbol of independence and the traditions she was building for herself.

The knock at her door startled her out of her thoughts. Wiping her hands on her jeans, she crossed the living room, her socks sliding slightly on the hardwood floor.

When she opened the door, Aiden stood there, his hands tucked into the pockets of his coat. His easy smile didn't quite reach his eyes, a detail she didn't miss.

"Hey," she greeted, stepping aside to let him in. "You're just in time. I was starting to think you'd gotten lost."

Aiden chuckled, taking off his coat before hanging it on the rack by the door. "Traffic was a mess. Everyone's out doing last-minute shopping." His gaze shifted to the tree. "Looks nice in here. Cozy."

"Thanks. It's not much, but it does the job," she said, motioning for him to follow her into the living room. She picked up the remote to lower the music's volume. "You okay? You look…tired."

Aiden hesitated before answering, his posture stiffening slightly. "Yeah, just a lot on my mind. Mom's been…well, you know how she gets around Christmas. Everything must be perfect. And with

Dad gone…" He trailed off, his jaw tightening as he glanced away.

Tami's heart ached at the pain she saw flicker across his face. Stepping closer, she rested a hand on his arm, drawing his attention back to her.

"You don't have to do this alone, you know," she said softly. "If it's too much, if you need a break, say the word. We can get out of here for a while. Anywhere you want to go—just you and me."

Aiden's eyes softened, gratitude mingling with something deeper. He reached up to cover her hand with his, the warmth of his touch grounding her. "I appreciate that. Really. But I'm not running from this."

Tami nodded. "I get that. And I know you probably would've stayed away this Christmas if I hadn't asked you to help me out of a jam. So… thank you. Just promise me you'll take care of yourself too. You can't pour from an empty cup, Aiden."

He smiled faintly, a trace of his usual charm breaking through. "I'll try. And thanks for being my backup plan, just in case."

"Always," she said, squeezing his arm before letting her hand fall away. She stepped back toward the kitchen. "You want something to drink? I've got cider, hot chocolate, and…let's see…water. Very exciting choices, I know."

Aiden laughed, the sound lighter than before. "Hot chocolate sounds good."

Tami set to work preparing two mugs and heating the milk, her movements practiced but unhurried. As she stirred the cocoa powder into the milk, she glanced over at Aiden, who had settled onto the couch, his long frame stretching across the cushions. He looked more at ease now, the tension in his shoulders easing as he watched the flickering lights on her tree. But she knew him well enough to know the tension was still there.

She handed him a mug and sat beside him. "Want to talk about it?"

He took a sip of the hot cocoa, his hands cradling the mug as if drawing warmth from it. "It's just been a lot. Trying to keep up with work, helping Mom around the house… I don't know. It feels like I'm trying to fill shoes that are too big for me."

Tami's brow furrowed as she listened. "No one expects you to replace your dad, Aiden. Least of all your mom. She's just trying to hold on to the traditions that make her feel close to him."

"I know that," he said, his voice barely above a whisper. "But it doesn't make it any easier."

"No, it doesn't," Tami agreed. She hesitated, then added, "I've been thinking about my own mom lately. We're overdue for a conversation about…well, a lot of things. But I've decided to wait until after the holidays. I don't want to stir up anything when everyone's already juggling so much."

Aiden's gaze sharpened. "What kind of conversation?"

Tami sighed, curling her legs beneath her on the couch. "It's about the way she's always trying to control everything, especially when it comes to me. I know she means well, but it's exhausting. And I'm tired of pretending it doesn't bother me."

"Sounds like a tough one," Aiden said, his tone empathetic. "But you'll handle it. You're one of the strongest people I know."

Tami's cheeks warmed at the compliment, but she didn't shy away from his gaze. There was something steady and unshakable in the way he looked at her—like he genuinely believed she could handle anything. His faith in her sent a flutter through her chest, unexpected and a little disarming. It made her feel seen...and wanted.

"I just hope I can find the right words when the time comes."

"You will," he assured her. "And if you need someone to practice on, I'm here."

She laughed softly, the sound easing some of the tension that had settled in her.

"I'll keep that in mind."

Tami felt a deep sense of gratitude for Aiden's presence, for the way he made her feel seen and understood. Lately, that connection had started to mean more to her than she was ready to admit—more than friendship, maybe. She didn't want to lose that, especially now when it felt like they were both navigating uncharted waters…and her heart was starting to drift in a direction she hadn't planned.

She couldn't solve all of Aiden's struggles or fix her own family dynamics overnight, but she could be present. And sometimes that was enough.

Rachel Rose was practically glowing as she navigated the scenic drive to Polk Island's latest wedding venue, a charming estate nestled near the shoreline. It used to be a bed-and-breakfast that hosted weddings on occasion—Rachel had accompanied a bride here once, back when it was still flying under the radar. Since then it had been transformed into a fully-fledged wedding venue and was quickly climbing the ranks as one of the island's top destinations. It could be a lovely setting for Tami and Aiden's wedding.

Christmas decorations adorned the streets, and the salty tang of the ocean breeze wafted through the air, mixing with the scent of pine and cinnamon.

She couldn't suppress the thrill bubbling inside her—Tami was finally engaged. Rachel Rose had always dreamed of this moment, not just for the joy of seeing her daughter in a beautiful white dress but because it symbolized something deeper. Security. Stability. A future built on love and partnership. After raising three daughters on her own, she had longed for each of them to find someone to stand beside them, to cherish and protect them in ways she hadn't been able to after their father had passed. For years, she had watched Tami focus on her career, brush off matchmaking attempts, and insist she wasn't in a rush. Rachel Rose had told herself to be patient, to trust that her daughter knew what she was doing. But now, with the engagement announced, it felt like a dream realized—a promise that her daughter wouldn't have to face life's challenges alone.

More than anything, she wanted Tami to be happy, to feel loved, and to know the security of a partnership that could weather life's storms. This moment wasn't just about a wedding; it was about the life that would follow. And Rachel Rose was determined to do everything she could to make sure her daughter had the perfect start. Beginning with a perfect wedding day.

While the Worthington family's Polk Island Hotel, with its Grand Ballroom and breathtaking views, seemed like the ideal location for the celebration, Rachel Rose believed in doing her due diligence. Today's trip to this newer venue was just to cover all her bases—and to be thorough, as any good planner would.

While Naomi's words the other day were still on her mind, Rachel Rose couldn't help herself; planning Tami's wedding felt like a dream come true. As a wedding planner, it was second nature to envision every detail, and she was determined to create a perfect day for her daughter. She had never had that for herself—her own wedding had been a rushed affair, and Tami's father's death had left little room for the fantasy she'd once imagined. Now, with Tami's engagement, Rachel was eager to make up for it, to give her daughter the perfect celebration she deserved.

But there was more to it—Rachel wanted to ensure Tami's happiness, and in her mind, that meant securing the details. She needed everything to go smoothly, to avoid the stress and chaos she'd faced in her own life.

As she turned onto the estate's gravel driveway, the sprawling property of Seaside Haven came into view.

The main building was a stately structure with wraparound porches and tall windows, framed by oak trees draped with Spanish moss. The surrounding gardens were impeccably maintained, even in the winter, with pathways that wound toward the ocean beyond.

"Well, this is promising," Rachel Rose murmured to herself as she parked and stepped out of her car. Dressed in a tailored crimson coat and black leather boots, she felt ready to tackle the day. She had an eye for elegance, and if this venue didn't meet her standards, she'd know it within moments.

The front door opened before she could reach it, and a tall man stepped out to greet her. He was striking, with salt-and-pepper hair, warm hazel eyes, and a charismatic smile. His presence carried an easy confidence, the kind that came with years of experience.

"Ms. Adams," he said, extending his hand. "I recognize you from your ads. Welcome to Seaside Haven. I'm Daniel Sterling, the owner."

"Rachel Rose," she replied, shaking his hand. His grip was firm but not overpowering. "We actually met briefly the last time I was here. You were on your way out to a meeting, but you left me in great hands. Beth was wonderful." Rachel Rose recalled touring the venue previously with a bride, in which she'd learned ownership had changed and Daniel had bought the place. Touring a second time with her daughter in mind would be different. "Thank you for meeting with me today on such short notice."

"It's my pleasure," he said. "I understand you're planning a wedding for your daughter?"

"Yes. She's just gotten engaged," Rachel Rose said, unable to hide her pride. "I want her day to be absolutely perfect."

Daniel's smile widened. "Congratulations. That's a wonderful milestone. Will she be joining us?"

"Not this time. Beth told me last time that you were planning some renovations, so I thought I'd come take a look."

He smiled. "Let me show you around—we'll make sure it's everything you're envisioning."

Rachel Rose followed him inside, her eyes immediately drawn to the vaulted ceilings and the wide-open space of the main hall. The polished wood floors gleamed, and the large windows offered stunning views of the ocean. It was clear that this venue had been designed with events in mind.

"The main hall can seat up to five hundred guests," Daniel explained as they walked. "We also have a smaller space for more intimate gatherings. And if you're considering an outdoor ceremony, our gardens are quite popular, even in the cooler months."

Rachel Rose listened attentively, taking mental notes. The venue was beautiful, no doubt, but her heart still leaned toward the Polk Island Hotel. Tradition mattered to her, and the Worthington family had a history on the island that felt deeply intertwined with her own. Still, she appreciated Daniel's willingness to showcase his property.

They stepped into the garden, where a pergola adorned with twinkling lights overlooked the water. Rachel Rose imagined it decorated with flowers and greenery, the perfect setting for a romantic ceremony.

"It's lovely," she admitted, turning to him. "You've created something truly special here."

"Thank you," he said, his tone sincere. "I wanted this place to feel like an escape, a sanctuary where people can celebrate life's most important moments."

Rachel Rose studied Daniel with a discerning eye. There was something disarming about him—something that set him apart from the typical smooth-talking businessman. He didn't carry the usual air of salesmanship; instead, there was an authenticity in his demeanor. His interest seemed to go beyond securing a deal. It felt like he genuinely wanted to ensure that people had memorable, meaningful experiences at the venue.

"And how long have you owned Seaside Haven?" she asked as they strolled back toward the main building. "I didn't know that Alice Wallace had sold it until last year. I thought one of her children was running it."

"About two years now," he said. "I moved to Polk Island after retiring from my first career. This was a passion project that turned into something more. With the recent renovations, we plan to put our stamp in the wedding business."

She nodded. "And what was your first career?"

"Architecture," he said with a grin. "I designed commercial buildings for decades. Eventually, I decided it was time to design something more personal."

Rachel Rose nodded again, impressed. "Well, you've certainly done a fine job."

"Coming from someone with your reputation, that's high praise," Daniel said. She couldn't help but notice the warmth in his voice, the way it seemed to wrap around her like a soft blanket. "I've heard about the events you've organized over the years. You have quite the eye for detail."

Rachel Rose waved a dismissive hand, though she couldn't help but smile. "I just like things done right."

"Clearly," he said, his gaze lingering on her. "And speaking of doing things right, I'd be delighted to host your daughter's wedding here if you decide this is the place."

His words were smooth and confident, but it was the way he spoke—slow and deliberate—that made her pause. His eyes, a deep shade of green, caught the light, and for a moment, she couldn't quite look away. They were warm, expressive eyes that seemed to see right through her, drawing her in.

She cleared her throat. "Thank you, Daniel. I'll certainly keep it in mind."

As she followed him through the venue, the faint scent of his cologne—woodsy yet fresh—lingered in the air, subtle but captivating. It was the kind of scent that made her inhale just a little deeper, almost unconsciously. The first time she met Daniel, she'd brushed aside the flicker of something she'd felt. He'd been charming then, but she was focused on her client, and the attraction had felt unimportant—just a fleeting moment.

Today, though, it was different. Something was

stirring inside her. As they returned to the main hall, Daniel handed her a folder filled with details about the venue's packages. She glanced down at the paper, her mind still preoccupied with him. Her heart quickened for the briefest second as he smiled and bid her goodbye. The spark she'd felt before—the one she had dismissed—was still there. She tried to push it away, but it lingered.

This visit wasn't about her though; it was about Tami. She tried to regain her focus. But even as she walked away, the feeling stayed with her.

Back in her car, Rachel Rose took a moment to collect her thoughts. Seaside Haven was undeniably beautiful, and Daniel Sterling was undeniably charming. But her instincts told her that the Worthingtons' hotel was the right choice for Tami's wedding. Tradition, history, and family connections mattered more than novelty.

Her phone buzzed on the passenger seat, and she glanced at the screen. It was a text from Samantha, asking how the venue visit had gone. Rachel Rose typed a quick reply before starting the car and heading home.

As she drove, her mind wandered to Tami. Her youngest daughter's engagement to Aiden Worthington felt like a triumph—not because Rachel Rose had orchestrated it, but because she knew how deeply the two cared for each other.

She imagined Tami walking down the aisle, radiant and confident, with Aiden waiting for her at the altar. The thought brought a lump to her throat. Tami deserved a love story as beautiful as her sisters, and Rachel Rose was determined to give her the wedding of her dreams.

By the time she reached home, Rachel Rose had made up her mind. She would call Cia tomorrow to discuss booking the Polk Island Hotel. And as for Daniel Sterling…well, perhaps she'd find another reason to visit Seaside Haven. After all, there was no harm in keeping her options open.

CHAPTER EIGHT

TAMI LEANED AGAINST her kitchen counter, watching the morning light filter through the blinds. She'd spent the last hour fielding a whirlwind of texts from her mother.

Rachel Rose, the Wedding Planner Extraordinaire, Tami thought wryly, scrolling through yet another message laden with exclamation marks and links to floral arrangements. Her mother had seamlessly transitioned from matchmaking into wedding planning, and Tami was starting to suspect that both roles were two sides of the same coin: control.

Tami's phone buzzed again.

This time it was a photo of an elaborate floral arch, complete with cascading roses and twinkling fairy lights. Below it, her mother had added Wouldn't this be stunning at the Polk Island Hotel? It's so romantic!!!

Tami groaned and set the phone down before it pulled her into another spiral.

"There isn't going to be a wedding," she muttered.

Her phone buzzed again. She ignored it, opting instead to pour herself another cup of coffee. The rich aroma filled the room, grounding her. She took a deep breath and reminded herself why she'd agreed to this in the first place.

She'd have to remind her mother again that they weren't planning anything until the new year. But would Rachel Rose listen this time? Would she give her that space to breathe? Tami wasn't sure, but the pressure of maintaining the lie had become heavier as the holidays approached. She felt more trapped than ever.

By mid-morning, Rachel Rose arrived unannounced, her presence filling the space with an air of determination. She carried a large binder adorned with gold lettering that read *Rachel Rose Events*. It would be an impressive sight...if she were planning a real wedding.

"Darling!" Rachel Rose exclaimed, sweeping into the living room like a woman on a mission. "I've been brainstorming, and I just had to bring my ideas over. This is going to be the most beautiful wedding Polk Island has ever seen."

Tami plastered on a smile and gestured for her mother to sit. "Mom, don't you think it's a little early to be planning? We haven't even picked a date."

"Exactly why we need to get started," Rachel Rose said, flipping open the binder to a page filled with swatches of fabric. "The Worthingtons' hotel is lovely, of course, but I've been looking into other venues, just in case. Did you know there's a new event space on the island? I went there yesterday and did a walk-through. Seaside Haven is run by this charming man named Daniel. He's older but very handsome. Anyway, the facility has the most exquisite views of the water."

Tami barely suppressed an eye roll. She'd been looking at other venues? "Mom, Aiden's family owns one of the most renowned venues on the East Coast. I think we're covered."

Rachel Rose waved a hand dismissively. "Options, darling. It's always good to have options."

As her mother continued detailing Daniel's venue, Tami felt her frustration mounting. It wasn't just the wedding planning; it was the underlying assumption that Rachel Rose always knew best. That same assumption had led to countless blind dates and not-so-subtle hints about marriage over the years.

Tami's grip tightened on her coffee mug. She knew her mother meant well, but it was suffocating. And now, even her fabricated engagement wasn't enough to grant her autonomy.

Still, she listened patiently, serving her mother tea and catching up, and when her mother finally left, Tami sank onto the couch, exhausted. She'd been bombarded with so many ideas and suggestions that her head was spinning. Yet in the back of her mind, she couldn't help but hear the voice of guilt whispering, *She's just trying to make you happy.*

She sighed and reached for her phone, scrolling absently through messages. Aiden's name popped up, a reminder that she wasn't alone in this. She was meeting him for breakfast soon. They'd promised to have each other's backs, and so far, he'd been the perfect partner-in-deception.

Still, the stakes felt higher for her now. Being around Aiden so much had stirred feelings she'd long buried, feelings that made this charade infinitely more complicated.

As the day wore on, Tami's thoughts drifted to the upcoming Christmas ball. She'd been dreading it for weeks. Her mother's parties were legendary, filled with glittering lights, gourmet food, and, in the past, an endless parade of eligible bachelors who always seemed to find their way to Tami's side.

But this year, things were different. For once, there wouldn't be any awkward introductions or unsolicited matchmaking. Her engagement to Aiden had put a stop to all of that. Yet the thought of attending still filled her with unease.

She didn't want to go, but she knew she couldn't back out. Her mother would be devastated, and Tami couldn't bear the thought of causing her pain.

The doorbell rang, jolting her from her thoughts. Tami set her water bottle down and went to answer it. Aiden stood on the other side, a warm smile on his face.

"Ready for breakfast?" he asked, stepping inside.

"Almost," she said, closing the door behind him. "I just need to grab my coat."

As she reached for it, Aiden leaned against the wall, his gaze softening. "You okay? You look a little stressed."

Tami hesitated, then nodded. "Just my mom. She's in full wedding-planning mode." Her heart warmed at the realization that he always noticed when something was off, even when she tried to hide it.

Aiden chuckled. "Sounds about right. She's probably got the whole thing mapped out already."

"You have no idea," Tami muttered, slipping on her coat. "But it's fine. I'll survive."

He studied her for a moment, then said, "You know, if it gets to be too much, we can always call it off. The engagement, I mean. I don't want you to feel trapped."

Her heart clenched at the sincerity in his voice. "I'm fine. Really. This was my idea, remember? Besides, it's kind of nice not having to fend off every single guy my mom throws my way."

Aiden grinned. "Glad I can be of service."

They shared a laugh, the tension easing. For a moment, Tami allowed herself to bask in his presence, grateful for his steady support. He'd always been her rock, her confidant. And that was precisely what made her feelings for him so dangerous. She couldn't start falling for him—that wasn't part of their arrangement. He was her friend, and when this was over, they'd remain friends.

Breakfast at the cozy Polk Island Café was a welcome distraction. The scent of sizzling bacon filled the air.

They talked and laughed, the conversation flowing effortlessly as it always did. But as they sipped their juice and finished the last of their omelets, Tami's thoughts drifted back to her mother and the Christmas Ball looming on the horizon. She thought about it the whole drive home, where Aiden dropped her off.

"Are you sure you're up for this party?" he asked, as they stood at her front door together.

She shrugged. "It's not like I have a choice. My mom would be heartbroken if I didn't go."

"At least you've got me as your date," he said with a wink.

Tami's heart swelled with gratitude for the man by her side, his unwavering support a lifeline in the storm of her emotions.

A*iden stood in* the doorway of Tami's town house.

"At least you've got me as your date," he'd said, trying to keep things light. She laughed, and he leaned closer…and for a second he felt so drawn to her. His gaze shifted to her lips. He wanted to kiss her.

Being playful was his go-to defense mechanism. He'd learned years ago that humor and sarcasm were safer than vulnerability. But even as he said the words, he felt a gnawing tug in his chest. He cared about Tami. Had for a long time. He wasn't sure if it was the familiarity of their connection, the comfort they shared, or something else entirely, but for a split second, he wanted it to last forever. Tami's gaze held his for a moment before she turned away, ushering him inside.

He shifted on his feet, stepping further into the town house, the door clicking shut behind him.

Tami had already moved to the kitchen, bustling around, busying herself with something—perhaps trying to act like nothing had happened. He couldn't blame her. He'd probably do the same if he were in her shoes. Were her feelings as jumbled as his were right now?

He ran his hand through his hair, pacing just a little as the thoughts began to swirl. *Did that moment mean something?* It was hard to ignore the way his chest had tightened, how his heart had skipped when he'd gazed down at her. She'd been so close, her eyes soft, her smile gentle, and he'd felt something flicker deep inside him. Something that wasn't just the usual affection he had for her but more.

His stomach tightened at the thought. He had

been in enough situations to know how quickly things could be misread. A simple gesture, a brief kiss, could mean a lot of different things depending on the circumstances. He had been burned before, had let his emotions get the best of him, had allowed himself to believe in something that wasn't really there.

Tami was his friend. His best friend. He didn't want to risk that—didn't want to mess it up by overthinking something that could just be a fleeting moment.

But what if it wasn't just that?

He shook his head. *Focus, Aiden.* He had to pull himself together. It was so easy to get lost in the what-ifs—to start imagining things that weren't there. It was better not to read too much into it.

The kitchen was quiet now, save for the soft clink of dishes. Tami was still moving around, her back to him, and he found himself staring at her. She didn't seem like she was dwelling on the moment—she seemed fine, as if it hadn't affected her in the way it had affected him. He didn't know if that was a good thing or a bad thing.

Taking a deep breath, Aiden pushed himself away from the counter and walked over to where she was standing, her focus on the dishes in front of her. He reached out, lightly touching her shoulder, just enough to get her attention.

She turned, giving him a soft smile. "You okay?"

He met her gaze, trying to keep things light, trying to push away everything that was swirling in his mind. "Yeah, I'm good. Just…thinking."

"About what?" Her eyes searched his.

He hesitated for a moment, then shrugged. "Just…everything." He let out a short laugh, trying to make it sound casual. "The holidays, I guess. Our ruse."

Her expression softened, and for a second, he wondered if she saw right through his facade. But she just nodded, the smile still lingering on her lips.

"Well, the holidays do have a way of making us do crazy things," she said lightly. And yet he couldn't help but notice the flicker of something in her eyes. Was it guilt? Embarrassment? Or maybe just surprise at how the moment on her porch, that almost-kiss, had turned out? He couldn't tell, and he wasn't sure if he wanted to.

"I'm sure you'll forgive me for putting you through all this," she said with a small chuckle, as though trying to defuse the tension.

Aiden smiled back, but he knew it didn't quite reach his eyes. He was still reeling from the attraction he'd felt just now, still wondering if it was something he should brush off or something that could change everything. But right now, all he could do was nod, keeping his feelings hidden behind a mask of indifference.

"Of course," he said. "Happy to help. No harm done."

But deep down, a part of him couldn't help but wonder if this situation would lead to more harm than they'd bargained for.

On Friday, Rachel Rose adjusted her scarf as she stepped out of the restaurant where the Christmas Ball planning committee had just wrapped up their meeting. The cool air nipped at her cheeks, but her spirits were warm with satisfaction. Everything for the ball was coming together nicely. The decorations were finalized, the catering menu was exquisite, and the guest list was shaping up to be the talk of the island.

As she passed through the restaurant, a familiar voice called out, halting her in her tracks.

"Rachel Rose?"

She turned and found herself face-to-face with Daniel Sterling.

He was seated at a table near the window, a charming smile spreading across his face as he waved her over. Rachel Rose blinked, momentarily caught off guard. When they last saw each other, he had made an impression with his tall, confident frame, salt-and-pepper hair, and the easy charisma that seemed to follow him wherever he went.

"Daniel," she said, recovering quickly and making her way over to his table. "What a surprise."

"Not as much as seeing you here," he replied, standing to pull out a chair for her. "Join me for lunch?"

Rachel Rose hesitated, glancing at her watch. "I appreciate the offer, but I was just leaving. We had a planning meeting for the Christmas Ball that ended not too long ago."

His eyes lit up. "The famous Polk Island Christmas Ball? I've heard about it. Everyone says it's the event of the season."

"It is," she said with a touch of pride. "Are you planning to attend?"

"I wouldn't miss it," he said, gesturing for her to sit. "In fact, I'd like to be a sponsor. Seems like the kind of event that could use a little extra support."

Her interest piqued, Rachel Rose lowered herself into the chair. "That's very generous of you." She felt a small wave of guilt that they likely wouldn't host Tami and Aiden's wedding at his venue.

He chuckled. "I figure it's a good way to contribute to the community. Plus, I could use an excuse to break out my tuxedo."

She laughed lightly, impressed despite herself. "Well, in that case, I'll have to ensure you get all the details for sponsorship."

The waiter appeared, and Daniel ordered a hearty bowl of clam chowder and a slice of the restaurant's famous sourdough bread.

Rachel Rose declined to order, explaining she'd

already eaten at the meeting, but Daniel insisted she try the peppermint tea.

"Best on the island," he promised with a wink.

As they waited for the tea and his meal, she couldn't help but study him. Daniel Sterling carried himself with a quiet confidence that was undeniably appealing. He asked about the event, his questions thoughtful and genuine, and she found herself relaxing in his company.

"So, Polk Island must be a change for you... how are you liking it here?" she asked.

Daniel nodded, sipping his water. "I bought the business on a whim, really. After spending years in the corporate grind, I decided I needed a change of pace. Polk Island seemed like the perfect place to start fresh."

"And how are you finding it so far?"

"Peaceful," he said with a small smile. "But also vibrant. There's a sense of community here that I haven't experienced in a long time. It's refreshing."

Rachel Rose nodded. "It is a special place."

Their tea arrived, and she took a sip, finding the minty warmth unexpectedly soothing.

They enjoyed the view in silence. Daniel was halfway through his chowder when he leaned back in his chair, his expression turning curious. "What about you? Have you always lived here?"

"Yes," she said, her tone softening. "My late husband and I grew up on the island. Raised our daughters, grew our roots. I can't imagine living anywhere else."

Daniel's gaze was kind. "Your husband must have been quite a man."

"He was," she said simply. "And I was lucky to have him. We had a good life together."

"Do you think you'll ever…" He hesitated and seemed to be choosing his words carefully. "Find that kind of happiness again?"

Rachel Rose felt wistful. "I don't believe in lightning striking twice, Daniel. I already had my happily-ever-after. Now my focus is on ensuring my daughters find theirs."

He tilted his head, his eyes searching hers. "That's a noble sentiment, but don't you think you deserve happiness too?"

Her fingers tightened slightly around the handle of her teacup. "Happiness comes in many forms. Right now, mine is in helping people create their dream wedding, planning events like the Christmas Ball, and watching my daughters thrive."

Daniel nodded and didn't press the matter, instead steering the conversation toward lighter topics. They discussed the local businesses on the island, the unique charm of the community, and more of the upcoming ball.

Rachel Rose found herself enjoying the conversation more than she expected.

When Daniel finished his meal, he pulled out a checkbook, scribbling quickly before tearing off a check and handing it to her. "For the ball sponsorship," he said with a grin. "I hope it helps."

Rachel Rose glanced at the amount and blinked in surprise. "This is very generous, Daniel. Thank you."

"My pleasure," he said, standing and holding out a hand to help her up. "And if you ever need more sponsors—or just someone to talk to—you know where to find me."

She smiled, feeling a mix of gratitude and caution. "Thank you. I'll keep that in mind."

As she walked to her car, Rachel Rose's thoughts swirled. Daniel Sterling was charming, no doubt about it. But the idea of opening her heart again, of risking the pain of loss, that was something she couldn't imagine.

For now her focus would remain on her family and her community.

CHAPTER NINE

AIDEN ADJUSTED THE collar of his flannel shirt, feeling slightly out of place amid the festive chaos of the Polk Island Christmas market. The crisp winter air mixed with the sound of children's laughter and the scent of roasted chestnuts wafted through the square. He glanced over at Tami as she slipped her hands into her coat pockets, her red scarf a cheerful contrast against the sea of neutral winter coats around them and her sweater and boots effortlessly stylish. She looked beautiful.

As they made their way through the bustling crowd, Tami greeted familiar faces, her smile lighting up the square. Aiden watched her, admiring the way she moved so naturally through the locals, always smiling, always making people feel seen. But it didn't take long for him to notice the whispers. Subtle, but unmistakable—the way people's eyes lingered on them.

Word was definitely getting around, and Aiden realized with a sinking feeling that they hadn't even officially told anyone yet.

"Looks like your mom's been busy," he muttered under his breath, his gaze scanning the crowd.

Tami rolled her eyes, but there was a hint of a smile on her lips. "Yeah, I guess she couldn't help herself. Word spreads fast."

The pair continued moving through the stalls. Aiden wanted to say something more, to ask how she was feeling about the sudden attention, but Tami seemed determined to keep things light, chatting easily with the locals. He noticed a few pointed looks at her left hand once she took it out of her pocket to shop. Tami's smile, while warm, didn't quite reach her eyes, and Aiden couldn't help but wonder if she was just as uncomfortable with the attention as he was.

It wasn't that he didn't want to get married to her—he'd be lucky to have her. But this feeling, the weight of it all wasn't quite how he imagined things would go down. The casual nature of the market, the laid-back atmosphere was supposed to be a nice break from the questions about wedding planning from their mothers. But now it felt like the pressure was building, the engagement becoming more real than either of them were ready for.

"Guess we're the talk of the town now," Aiden said, his voice light but a little heavy with the realization that things were shifting faster than he expected.

"Guess so," Tami said quietly, offering him a quick glance before returning her attention to the market wares. There was a flicker of something in her expression, something Aiden couldn't quite place.

Despite all the market goods around them, it suddenly felt like they were the ones on display.

As they moved through the bustling Christmas market, he couldn't help but notice that Tami looked increasingly uncomfortable. Her gaze darted from face to face, always scanning the crowd, never fully settling. It wasn't like her to seem so…guarded. She'd always been so social, so present in the moment, but tonight there was something about her that felt distant, almost like she was playing a part.

Aiden had known Tami long enough to recognize when she was a little off. They'd been through enough together for him to know when something didn't feel quite right, but he couldn't pinpoint it. Maybe it was the crowd—Tami had never been the biggest fan of large, overwhelming spaces—but this felt different. The way she kept adjusting her scarf, the way she kept bunching her hands in her pockets as if she was seeking some kind of comfort, it all seemed a little more than just the usual nerves.

He brushed it off, telling himself it was probably just the pressure of the engagement being out in the open. Some people congratulated them or even asked about wedding plans. But as they walked past a booth, Tami's steps quickened, like she was trying to escape.

"Hey," he said quietly, nudging her with his elbow as they slowed to look at a display of handcrafted ornaments. "You okay?"

Tami flashed him a smile. "Yeah, I'm fine," she said a little too quickly, her voice a bit too bright. "Just…a lot of people, you know? Asking too many questions."

Aiden didn't press her, but deep down, he sensed that there was more to it than she was letting on. Something about tonight was wearing on her, and he couldn't figure out what it was.

He wished he could be the one to take it all away, to help her feel at ease, but she'd said she was fine and he knew better than to push. Still, as they continued to walk through the market, the nagging feeling that something wasn't right lingered in his mind.

LIGHT FILTERED THROUGH the blinds in Tami's laundry room, casting golden streaks across the counter and over the scattered laundry. The washing machine hummed softly, its steady rhythm almost hypnotic against the jumble of thoughts tumbling through her mind.

She leaned against the doorframe, arms crossed, staring blankly at the open laundry basket at her feet.

Last night at the Christmas market had been

great until her anxiety threatened to take over. The twinkling lights, the festive music, the laughter—suddenly, it all felt so much. And then, of course, there was Aiden. Pretending to be engaged to him, to step into a role that felt so far from reality, had been easier than she'd expected, but only in front of others.

The moment they'd entered the market, the crowds had swarmed around them. Everyone had seemed so thrilled for them—glancing, whispering, some even congratulating them—that she couldn't help but feel trapped in the spotlight. And as the night wore on, the weight of the attention became almost suffocating.

Tami had done her best to smile and nod, to keep the conversations flowing with ease. Trey and Gia Rothchild had been especially insistent, grinning ear to ear, their questions coming fast and curious.

Tami, when did this happen? We didn't know you two were a thing, Gia had asked, her eyes sparkling with excitement.

And Trey, as always, had been louder, slapping Aiden on the back with a booming *Congratulations, man...you've got yourself a keeper!*

In the midst of it all, Tami's chest had tightened. The more she smiled and nodded, the more the crowd seemed to close in on her. She found it hard to breathe, hard to focus. Her thoughts felt disconnected, racing from one worry to the next.

Am I doing this right? Is everyone buying it? Am I even convincing myself anymore?

She'd forced herself to laugh at the right times, to give polite responses, but inside, she felt like she was suffocating. She hadn't noticed it at first, but the anxiety had crept up on her like a shadow, pulling at the edges of her mind. The kind of anxiety she was so familiar with, the kind that had ruled so many social situations for years. She could handle small groups, sure. But in large, crowded places, her anxiety always found a way to make itself known. The more people approached, the tighter her chest felt.

Later that night, back at home, she'd sat on the edge of her bed, replaying the evening in her head, repeatedly. The constant hum of her own nervous energy had refused to fade, lingering like a stubborn echo. The social anxiety that she had always managed to control was now spilling over, and she couldn't just push it aside. *What is wrong with me? I should be fine. I've done this a hundred times before.*

She sighed deeply, reaching for the laundry basket and trying to shake the feeling. But it stayed with her, lingering in her chest.

I can't keep pretending like this isn't an issue.

Tami thought back to the moments when she had excused it over the years, told herself it was just nerves, or that she'd get used to it, but she wasn't getting better at it. If anything, it was getting harder to control. And last night had been a perfect storm of social anxiety and the pressure of pretending her relationship with Aiden was something it wasn't.

She set down the basket, grabbed her tablet, and began scrolling, her fingers hovering over search results about social anxiety treatment. *Evidence-based treatments for social anxiety disorder,* she typed into the search bar. She read through article after article, each one outlining various strategies. There were so many options, so many ways to address what she had long shrugged off as just part of who she was—despite receiving a formal diagnosis during her first year of college. Back then, she'd buried it beneath a full course load and the pressure to appear like she had it all together.

Now, as a licensed therapist, she knew better. She'd counseled students through similar struggles with care and compassion. But turning that same grace inward, admitting she might need help too—that felt like a huge step. One she wasn't sure she was ready to take.

I'm supposed to be the one helping others, she thought bitterly. *How can I expect my students to trust me if I can't even trust myself to ask for help?*

The irony was not lost on her. As a psychologist, she spent her days helping kids navigate their own challenges, their own fears and anxieties. She'd been there for them, helping them build coping strategies, teaching them the importance of seeking help when they needed it. But when it came to her own struggles, she couldn't seem to practice what she preached. She should be stronger than this. *Shouldn't I be able to handle this on my own?*

Tami closed her eyes for a moment, letting out a slow breath. She thought of her students, some of whom were wrestling with even greater battles, and the lessons she'd shared with them about self-care, about being kind to yourself, about reaching out when you needed help. How could she expect them to take her seriously if she couldn't take her own advice?

The idea of sitting in front of a therapist, opening up about her anxiety, felt terrifying. *What will they think of me? What if they think I'm weak for not having it all together?* But the more she thought about it, the more she realized that perhaps it wasn't about weakness. Maybe seeking help wasn't a sign of failure but a sign of strength. Maybe it was time to practice what she preached— not just for her own well-being but for the sake of those she helped every day.

It was time to stop ignoring the signs and to finally confront her anxiety head-on. With a final, determined exhale, she began searching for a therapist.

Aiden adjusted his grip on the oversized television box as he followed Shane through the front door of his and Ace's new home. The chill still clung to his coat, but the warmth of the house immediately enveloped him, offering a sense of comfort.

"Watch the doorway," Shane said, stepping into the family room. "Ace will have my head if we scratch her walls."

"I'm more worried about the tree," Aiden quipped, nodding toward the corner of the room where a majestic Christmas tree stood. Draped in shimmering silver-and-gold garlands and crowned with an elegant star, the tree dominated the room, commanding attention. Its base was surrounded by neatly wrapped gifts, with bows perfectly tied, each box a testament to Ace's meticulous nature.

"Careful, guys," Ace called from the kitchen, her tone light but with a hint of warning.

She appeared in the doorway, wiping her hands on a festive towel adorned with tiny reindeer. "If you knock over my tree, there'll be no cookies for either of you."

Shane rolled his eyes good-naturedly. "We'll be fine, babe. You're looking at two highly capable men here."

"Mmm-hmm," she said, arching an eyebrow before disappearing back into the kitchen. "Just remember—I've got eyes in the back of my head."

Aiden chuckled as he and Shane carefully maneuvered the television box toward the entertainment center. The family room was spacious yet inviting. A plush gray sectional anchored the space, piled high with soft throws in shades of cream and crimson. A stone fireplace framed by built-in shelves flickered with a welcoming fire, its mantle adorned with stockings and a garland of holly and twinkling lights. The aroma of cinnamon and fresh-baked cookies wafted from the kitchen, adding another layer of warmth to the scene.

"This is the perfect setup for the holidays," Aiden remarked, setting his end of the box down. He straightened and surveyed the room, admiring how well Shane and Ace had made it their own.

"Thanks," Shane said, crouching to open the box. "Ace has a real eye for this stuff. She's been planning the decor since July."

"Sounds like her," Aiden said with a grin, kneeling to help his brother unbox the television.

"You're lucky we waited this long," Ace called out from the kitchen, making both men laugh.

With the television freed from its packaging, Aiden and Shane worked together to mount it onto the stand. The process was mostly smooth, save for a moment when the edge of the box grazed a low-hanging ornament.

"Careful!" Aiden said sharply, steadying the box.

"Close call," Shane muttered, exhaling. "I'd rather not get banned from cookie privileges."

Once the television was securely in place, Shane grabbed the remote to power it on. "Looks good, right?" he asked, stepping back to admire their handiwork.

Aiden nodded. "It's perfect. Just in time for the Christmas-movie marathon."

Shane's face lit up. "Exactly what I was thinking. We're having some friends over later for hot chocolate and *It's a Wonderful Life*. You should stay."

Aiden shook his head with a smile. "Tempting, but I promised Mom that I'd help her finish the Christmas cards. She doesn't like sending them out this late."

Shane's expression softened at the mention of their mother. He sank into the sectional, motioning for Aiden to join him. "How's she really doing?"

Aiden hesitated before sitting. "You know Mom. She's always been strong. She keeps busy with the house and all her charity work, but…"

"But?" Shane prompted.

"I think she's putting on a brave face for us," Aiden admitted, his voice low. "She'll smile and talk about how Dad would want us to carry on, but sometimes I catch her staring at his chair or his picture on the mantle. It's like she's lost in another time."

Shane's gaze dropped to the floor, his fingers absently picking at the edge of a throw pillow. "I've noticed that too. It's been two years, but…it doesn't really get easier, does it?"

"No," Aiden said quietly. "It doesn't."

They sat in silence for a moment, the crackle of the fireplace filling the room. He felt the weight of his brother's grief mirroring his own.

"Do you think she's lonely?" Shane asked after a pause.

Aiden considered the question. "Maybe. But she'd never say it out loud. She's too focused on being there for us. That's Mom—always putting everyone else first."

Shane changed the subject by saying, "Plans for the staff luncheon is underway. Cia's going all out with the winter-wonderland theme. The employees are really excited about it."

"That's good," Aiden responded, although deep down he wasn't really looking forward to it.

"How's the engagement going?" Shane inquired. "Any dates yet?"

His stomach tightened. He forced a casual shrug. "Nothing set in stone. Tami and I are just... enjoying being engaged for now."

Shane's eyebrows lifted slightly, but he didn't press. "Fair enough. Ace and I took our time too. No rush when you know it's right."

He nodded, his throat dry. Aiden wanted to tell Shane the truth about the arrangement with Tami, about how it wasn't what it seemed. But the words wouldn't come.

"You're a good guy, Aiden," his brother said, his tone sincere. "Tami's lucky to have you."

Aiden's chest tightened further with secret he

was keeping there. He forced a smile, nodding in acknowledgment. "Thanks, man."

Shane slapped his shoulder lightly before standing. "Come on. Let's see if this thing streams Christmas music. Ace will be thrilled if it does."

Aiden followed his brother's lead, grateful for the distraction. As they fiddled with the new television, he couldn't help but glance at the tree again, its lights twinkling like tiny stars.

For all the warmth and joy surrounding him, he felt the weight of his own tangled emotions—about his family, about Tami, and about the future he hadn't yet figured out.

THE SOFT GLOW of Christmas lights reflected off the windows, and the familiar pine scent filled the air. Tami took a deep breath as she stepped into her mother's house, feeling instantly at home. The living room was aglow with holiday cheer, from the tree adorned with sparkling ornaments to the mantel draped with garlands and stockings. It was the same every year—this festive homecoming was a tradition that always made her feel like she was reconnecting with something timeless, something grounding.

Naomi and Samantha were busy icing cookies and setting up for the gingerbread house contest, while Summer was already knee-deep in candy sprinkles, gluing gumdrops onto her gingerbread house. The kitchen was a blur of activity and festive chatter as Tami's brothers-in-law, Jake and Randall, added their own touches to the decorations.

The smell of sugar cookies wafted through the house, and the competitive spirit of the gingerbread house contest was in full swing. This was one of Tami's favorite traditions—getting together with her family to see who could make the best house, or at least the most creative one. It was always fun, always loud, and always filled with laughter. And this year, she had a date for her partner.

As her eyes flickered over to Aiden, she caught him placing another candy cane on his gingerbread roof with surprising care. His plaid shirt sleeves were rolled up, his focus entirely on the task at hand. He was trying hard, she could tell—working so deliberately that Tami couldn't help but feel a pang of something unnameable. She was used to seeing him so capable at work, but seeing him here, in her family's home, in the middle of something so simple, so domestic, hit her in a way she wasn't prepared for.

"Everything okay?" he asked, his voice drawing her attention. He glanced up from the house, giving her a small, easy smile.

"Yeah," she said, pulling her thoughts back to the present. "Just thinking about how competitive this group is." She grinned. "You're going to have to up your game if you want to survive this."

Aiden grinned back, his hands still working carefully on his gingerbread house. "I'm ready for it. I didn't come here to lose." His eyes flickered toward her, and it make her heart skip a beat. She looked away quickly, her cheeks heating.

Samantha's laugh rang out from the kitchen. "If you want to survive the competition, Aiden, you better be ready to keep up with the pros."

Tami turned toward her sister, who was leaning against the counter, an amused grin on her face. She was holding a plate of freshly decorated cookies, watching them with an indulgent eye.

"We'll see who's still standing when the icing dries," Aiden said with a chuckle, his eyes still twinkling with that familiar mischievous glint.

Samantha gave him a wink. "You're about to meet your match."

Tami could hear the teasing in her sister's voice, but it didn't stop her from feeling a strange, unexpected sense of pride that Aiden was fitting in with her family. She didn't know if it was the pressure of the engagement lie or something else, but seeing Aiden so at ease in this setting, laughing with her family, had her chest tightening with emotions she didn't want to examine too closely.

Summer's bright voice interrupted her thoughts. "Aiden, look!" The little girl bounced up to him, her gingerbread house clutched in both hands like a prized possession. "I put the gumdrops like you showed me!"

Aiden smiled, kneeling to her level. "It looks amazing, Summer. You're going to win for sure."

She beamed, clearly proud of her work, her tiny fingers poking at the sprinkles still scattered around her table.

Tami watched Aiden with her niece, the way he encouraged Summer and the way her face lit up at his praise. He had a way with her. He was fitting into the role of uncle so easily, and it both warmed her heart and made her feel...conflicted.

Jake and Randall entered the room, both looking amused as they surveyed the gingerbread houses on display.

Jake clapped his hands together as he stepped toward Aiden. "All right, man, looks like you're giving us some stiff competition this year. Not bad for a rookie."

Aiden grinned, shaking his head. "Don't jinx me yet, Jake. I'm still in the running."

Tami smiled, watching her family interact with Aiden. The way they welcomed him into their circle made her feel a little lighter but also a little guilty. They were all so open, so warm toward him, and she couldn't help but feel the weight of the lie they were all participating in.

Samantha approached, a gleam in her eye. "Before we start judging, I've got some news." She smiled, drawing everyone's attention. "Jake and I... I'm pregnant."

Tami blinked in surprise. "Wait, what?" She

looked at Samantha, who was already glowing with excitement.

"I'm pregnant," her sister repeated with a grin, holding up her hands as though it was the greatest gift she could share.

There was a pause, and then Naomi's voice broke through the silence. "Are you serious? Oh my gosh, Sam, that's amazing!"

Jake wrapped his arm around Samantha, smiling widely. "It's true. We're going to need a bigger house soon."

Everyone in the room gathered around, their reactions a mix of excitement and surprise. Summer jumped up and down, clapping her hands. "I'm gonna be a big cousin!" she declared, clearly thrilled by the news.

The announcement had become the bright center of the night. Still, she couldn't shake the feeling of unease that had settled deep within her. Samantha's holiday news was real and so special, while Tami's was a lie.

Later, the gingerbread houses were put to the test and the judging began.

Aiden found himself once again on the receiving end of her family's good-natured teasing. Naomi handed him a small spoonful of icing, making him decorate her gingerbread house in exchange for her own judgment. "We need your opinion on what makes a *real* gingerbread house," she said with a sly grin.

As Aiden pretended to deliberate, making exaggerated faces over which candy to place where, Tami felt her chest tighten. Was this all an act? Or had their fake engagement already started to blur the lines between what was real and what wasn't? Would her family be hurt when they learned there'd be no wedding after all?

She tried to shake the thought off, focusing instead on how much fun they were having. But no matter how much she tried to push the questions from her mind, they lingered like a shadow she couldn't outrun.

As the evening wore on, laughter and joy filled the house, the sounds of family mingling with the occasional *whoops* of a gingerbread house collapsing.

She caught Aiden's eye from across the room, and he gave her a reassuring smile. How long could they keep pretending before the walls they'd built around themselves started to crack?

CHAPTER TEN

Monday afternoon, Rachel Rose adjusted her pearl necklace in the gilded mirror that hung near the entrance of the Southwinds restaurant at the Polk Island Hotel.

She spotted Madelyn Worthington already seated at a table near the windows, her salt-and-pepper hair catching the sunlight.

Madelyn looked up as she approached, a smile breaking across her face. "Rachel Rose! You're glowing. Let me guess—wedding excitement?"

Rachel Rose laughed softly, slipping into the chair across from her old friend. "What gave me away?"

"The sparkle in your eyes, for one," Madelyn said, her tone teasing but warm. "And the fact that you're already trying to orchestrate this wedding like it's the social event of the decade."

A waiter arrived to take their drink orders, and after a brief exchange, Rachel Rose folded her hands on the table, leaning forward slightly. "Well, it's not every day your youngest daughter gets engaged to her best friend. I want everything to be perfect. Don't tell me you haven't thought about it, too."

Madelyn sighed, a small, indulgent smile playing on her lips. "Of course I've thought about it. But Rachel Rose, they're adults. If Aiden and Tami want our help, they'll ask for it."

Rachel Rose's brow furrowed. "I know that. I just…want to be prepared. A perfect wedding takes time to plan. If I don't step in, who will?"

She shook her head, amusement and exasperation mingling in her expression. "You mean well, but you need to let them take the lead. This isn't your wedding."

The waiter returned with their drinks, setting down a delicate glass of iced tea for Madelyn and a flute of sparkling water for Rachel Rose. After placing their lunch orders, the two women settled into a more relaxed rhythm.

"You've always been like this," Madelyn said, her tone gentler now. "When we were kids, you couldn't sit still unless you were organizing something. A bake sale, a school dance, a church picnic…"

Rachel Rose chuckled, swirling her water. "Guilty as charged. But you have to admit things usually turned out better because of it."

"True," Madelyn conceded. "But this time, you're dealing with grown-ups. You need a hobby, Rachel Rose. Something to take your mind off your daughters and their lives."

"Oh, please," Rachel Rose said, rolling her eyes playfully. "As if you're not invested in Aiden's happiness."

"Of course I am," Madelyn said. "But I've learned the hard way that meddling doesn't always lead to the results you're hoping for."

A moment of silence passed, punctuated by the clinking of silverware and murmured conversations around them. Rachel Rose studied her friend, noting the way the light caught the faint lines around her eyes. "I've always admired your patience, Maddie. You make it look easy to sit back and let things unfold."

Madelyn's smile turned wistful. "It's not easy. Especially not after losing Angus. I think…when you go through something like that, you realize how little control you actually have."

Rachel Rose's chest tightened. She reached across the table, covering Madelyn's hand with her own. "I know what you mean. When Henry passed, I felt like the rug had been pulled out from under me. I wasn't prepared, financially or emotionally. I never want my girls to feel that kind of helplessness."

Madelyn squeezed her hand, her eyes soft with understanding. "And you've done an incredible job building a life for yourself and your daughters. Honestly, I've always admired your strength. You didn't just survive…you thrived."

Rachel Rose blinked, caught off guard by the

depth of her friend's words. It wasn't often people acknowledged her strength in such a quiet, understanding way. She'd always kept her emotions close, but Madelyn had a way of making her feel seen without asking for anything in return.

Taking a breath, she spoke softly. "It wasn't easy. There were days when I didn't think I'd make it. But I had to. For them." Her words slowed, carrying the weight of the past. "I couldn't give up, not with them to take care of."

Madelyn nodded. "I understand. But Rachel Rose, you have to trust them to figure it out. They're not kids anymore."

Their conversation paused as the waiter arrived with their lunch—a vibrant salad for Rachel Rose and a savory crab cake for Madelyn. The aromas of fresh herbs and spices filled the air, adding to the restaurant's cozy ambiance.

As they began to eat, Rachel Rose's mood lightened. "You know, I did tell you this would happen someday," she said, a hint of triumph in her voice. "Tami and Aiden becoming more than friends."

Madelyn chuckled, dabbing at her mouth with a napkin. "Yes, you did. And I'll admit I wasn't sure you'd be right. But now…seeing them together, I can't deny they make sense."

"They do," Rachel Rose said, her tone softening. "And I think that's why I'm so eager to help. I want this to be as beautiful as their connection deserves."

Madelyn reached across the table again, her eyes warm. "They're lucky to have you in their corner. Just remember, sometimes the best way to support them is to step back."

Rachel Rose sighed but nodded. "I'll try. No promises, though."

Madelyn laughed, and the sound was like a balm. As they finished their meal, the two women lingered over coffee, their conversation drifting to memories of their shared childhood, their late husbands, and the unique challenges of motherhood.

When they finally stood to leave, Rachel Rose felt a renewed sense of gratitude for the friendship that had seen them through so much. As they hugged goodbye, she promised herself she'd try to heed Madelyn's advice—at least for now.

THE COZY GLOW of the fire bathed Tami's living room in warm light, the soft crackle of burning logs a soothing accompaniment to the holiday music playing faintly in the background. She adjusted the throw pillow on the couch for the umpteenth time, her nerves a live wire as she glanced toward the kitchen where Aiden was pouring two mugs of hot cocoa. The air was thick with something unsaid, an undercurrent of tension she couldn't quite place—or, perhaps, didn't want to acknowledge.

"Extra marshmallows, just the way you like," Aiden said as he approached, his voice as familiar and comforting as the scent of cinnamon wafting from their drinks. He handed her a mug and took a seat beside her, his thigh brushing hers in a way that sent awareness up her spine.

"Thanks," Tami replied, her smile wobblier than she intended. She took a sip of the cocoa, the sweetness doing little to quell the storm inside her.

Aiden leaned back, his arm draping casually over the back of the couch. "So, what's the plan for tomorrow? Another round of cookie decorating with your mom, or are we braving the carolers?"

Tami laughed softly, grateful for the momentary distraction. "Mom's on a gingerbread-house kick. She's determined to win the neighborhood contest this year."

"I'm pretty sure your mom could out-decorate Santa's workshop if she put her mind to it."

"You're not wrong," Tami admitted, as the image of Rachel Rose meticulously piping royal icing onto gingerbread shingles brought a smile to her face.

He chuckled, his eyes crinkling in that way that always made her chest tighten. "Guess that means we'll be on gumdrop duty."

Their laughter faded into a comfortable silence, but the weight of their unspoken truths lingered. Tami set her mug on the coffee table and turned to face Aiden fully. "You've been…really good at this," she said softly.

"Good at what?" he asked, his brow furrowing slightly.

"This whole...engagement thing." The words felt foreign on her tongue, both a lie and a truth all at once. "You've made it...believable."

Aiden's gaze held hers, his expression unreadable. "That's the goal, right? To make it convincing?"

Tami nodded, but her heart sank at his response. *Convincing.* That was all this was supposed to be. And yet every stolen glance, every brush of their hands, every shared laugh felt more real than she dared to admit.

Because if she let herself believe it meant something—really meant something—and she was wrong? The fallout would wreck her. She'd been heartbroken before, but this...this would be worse. Because it wasn't just her heart on the line this time. It was her hope.

"You've been good at it too," Aiden added. His voice was quieter now, almost hesitant.

"Thanks," she said, her throat tight. She wanted to say more, to ask if he felt it too—the way their pretense was starting to feel less like an act and more like a fragile, tentative truth. But the words wouldn't come.

Instead, she reached for the small sprig of mistletoe that had fallen onto the couch earlier. "Mom's overdone it with these this year," she said, holding it up.

"That's kind of her thing, isn't it?" Aiden's smile was soft, his eyes flicking to the mistletoe in her hand. "Overdoing it?"

"Yeah," she agreed, her heart pounding as she noticed the way his gaze lingered on her lips for a split second too long. "It is."

Aiden shifted, his focus narrowing on her mouth, like he'd forgotten where they were for a heartbeat. Tami's breath caught.

For a moment, the world seemed to shrink, the distance between them closing as if drawn by some unseen force. Tami's breath caught as Aiden leaned in, his movements slow, deliberate. The kiss, when it came, was gentle, almost tentative, yet it sent a shockwave through her entire being.

When they pulled apart, neither of them spoke. The room was silent except for the crackle of the fire, the weight of what had just happened hanging heavy in the air.

"Tami..." Aiden began, his voice barely above a whisper.

"Don't," she interrupted, her eyes wide. "We don't have to...analyze this."

He hesitated, then nodded, but the flicker of uncertainty in his eyes didn't escape her notice. "Right. Part of the act."

But even as the words left his lips, Tami could feel the fragile line between pretense and reality beginning to blur. The kiss wasn't part of the script they'd written for themselves. It was something else entirely, something she wasn't ready to name.

The next day brought more holiday festivities, each one a test of their resolve. They attended a second tree-lighting ceremony, this time in the town square, the air filled with the scent of pine and the sound of carolers. Aiden held her hand as they navigated the crowd, his touch steady and grounding.

"You okay?" he asked, his breath visible in the crisp evening air.

"Yeah," Tami replied, her smile genuine this time. Being with him made it easier to forget the complexities of their arrangement, to lose herself in the magic of the season.

But the moments of simplicity were fleeting, overshadowed by the growing tension between them. Every moment since that kiss felt charged, as if the universe itself was conspiring to push them closer together.

The kiss still lingered in her thoughts, its warmth and weight carrying a meaning she wasn't ready to confront. How could she ignore it? Every time they touched or made eye contact, something sparked between them, and Tami had to look away, afraid of losing control.

She exhaled, realizing the line between their fake relationship and real emotions was blurring. The charade had always been manageable, but now it was more complicated. She didn't know how much longer she could pretend—or if she even wanted to.

Later that night, as they walked along the beach, the moonlight reflecting off the water, Tami felt all her tangled emotions pressing down on her. "Aiden, do you ever wonder what would happen if we weren't pretending?" she asked, her voice barely audible over the sound of the waves.

He stopped walking, turning to face her. "What do you mean?"

"I mean...if this wasn't just an act. If we were actually...you know." She trailed off, unable to say the words out loud.

Aiden's expression softened, a mixture of understanding and something else—something she couldn't quite name. "I think about it all the time," he admitted, his voice steady but low.

Her heart skipped a beat at his confession, but fear quickly followed. Fear of what it would mean to blur the lines even further, to risk their friendship for something that might not last. "But we can't," she said, her tone firm even as her resolve wavered. "This was supposed to be simple. A favor."

"Things change," Aiden said, his gaze unwavering. "Feelings change."

Tami looked away, the truth of his words cutting deeper than she wanted to admit. She had always been good at compartmentalizing, at keeping her emotions neatly boxed up. But Aiden had a way of breaking down her walls, of making her feel things she wasn't sure she was ready to feel.

"We should head back," she said finally, turning toward the distant glow of her town house. "It's getting late."

Aiden didn't argue, but as they walked back in silence, Tami couldn't shake the feeling that their carefully constructed facade was beginning to crumble.

RACHEL ROSE SETTLED into the small breakfast nook, the scent of freshly brewed coffee mingling with the delicate aroma of the tomato and basil tart she had sliced for lunch. Tami sat across from her, nibbling at a piece of tart but keeping her gaze trained on the plate, her posture unusually guarded.

Rachel Rose took a sip of her coffee, savoring the warmth, but her mind was already turning over the question she had been waiting to ask. "So, I've been meaning to ask," she began, her voice light, "who's going to be designing your rings? You and Aiden have a jeweler in mind?"

Tami paused mid-bite, her fork hovering over her plate. She finished chewing slowly, setting the fork down with deliberate care. "We haven't really talked about it. We're focused on getting through the holidays. This is a hard time for Aiden. He's still grieving."

Rachel Rose leaned forward slightly. "I understand, but designing a ring is one of those things that feels so...well, special. It's not just about the wedding. It's about what the ring will mean to you both. Are you sure you're not putting it off because of everything else going on?"

Tami reached for her water glass, sipping while clearly trying to gather her thoughts. Rachel Rose noted the nervous energy in the way her daughter adjusted her napkin, a habit she hadn't outgrown since childhood. Her smile was faint, more of a reflex than genuine warmth. "No, Mom. It's just been...busy, that's all."

Rachel Rose studied her daughter, trying to read between the lines. Something didn't feel right, but she wasn't sure what. Tami had always been the independent one, but this defensiveness felt different. She rested her hands on the table, her gaze steady. "Tami, is there something you're not telling me?"

She blinked, her smile faltering. "What? No, of course not. What would I have to hide?"

Rachel Rose raised an eyebrow. "I'm not sure. But something feels...off. You're not acting like someone who just got engaged. There's no sparkle in your eyes when you talk about it, no excitement...it doesn't add up."

Tami laughed lightly, but the sound didn't quite ring with good humor. "I guess I'm just tired. The holidays, the family stuff—it's a lot to take in all at once."

Rachel Rose studied her daughter's face for a long moment, her instincts tingling. Tami's explanations seemed plausible enough on the surface, but something didn't sit right.

She reached across the table, covering Tami's hand with her own. "You know you can tell me anything, don't you? Whatever it is, I'll understand."

Tami squeezed her hand briefly, offering a grateful smile. "Thanks, Mom. But really, there's nothing going on. Everything's fine."

Rachel Rose nodded, though she didn't believe it for a second. Her daughter had always been a terrible liar, and while she wasn't outright lying now, there was a guardedness in her demeanor that spoke volumes. Rachel Rose decided not to push further—yet. If something was amiss, she'd find out soon enough. Tami had never been good at keeping secrets for long.

They finished the meal in silence, and as Tami cleared the plates and moved to the sink, Rachel Rose sipped her coffee and made a mental note to speak with Aiden the next chance she got. Perhaps he could shed some light on what was really going on.

For now, Rachel Rose decided to bide her time. Whatever her daughter was hiding, it was only a matter of time before the truth came to light.

She glanced out the window, watching the sunlight dance over the garden as a gentle breeze swayed the trees. Aiden and Tami's engagement should have been a time of unrestrained joy, yet something about it felt shrouded in mystery.

She was determined to uncover what lay beneath the surface—if only for Tami's sake.

TAMI STOOD IN her kitchen, nervously wiping her hands on a dishtowel. She'd invited Aiden over for dinner—having her friend over shouldn't have felt like such a big deal, but she felt vulnerable in a way she hadn't anticipated.

She glanced at the clock. He would be there soon. The table was set, candles flickering warmly in the centerpiece she'd arranged with poinsettias and holly. Yet inside, her nerves buzzed like static, threatening to unravel her composure.

As if on cue, there was a knock at the door. Tami took a deep breath, plastered on a smile, and opened it. Aiden stood there, a bottle of wine in one hand and a lopsided grin on his face.

"Hey," he said, stepping inside and shaking snow off his coat. "It smells amazing in here. Did you make all this?"

She laughed softly, taking his coat. "Of course. You know I love to cook. Dinner's almost ready."

As they settled into the meal, it wasn't Tami's cooking or holiday cheer that occupied her mind—it was her mother's latest interrogation. It was part of the reason she'd invited him tonight, to warn him her mother was still on her about the ring.

Halfway through the meal, Tami put down her

fork and looked across the table at Aiden. "So, my mom cornered me today."

He glanced up, mid-bite. "Oh boy. What about this time? The wedding menu? Guest list?"

"No," Tami said, shaking her head. "She asked about the engagement ring. Specifically, why I'm not wearing one."

Aiden winced, leaning back in his chair. "I was wondering when that would come up."

Tami sighed, running a hand through her hair. "We need a story—a good one. And we need it, like, yesterday."

Aiden took a sip of wine, his brow furrowing before he chuckled softly.

Tami gave him a flat look, though her lips twitched. "This isn't funny. People are going to keep asking, especially with the holidays. They'll probably expect you to gift me a ring for Christmas."

He nodded slowly, his expression turning serious. "All right. How about this—we say you haven't decided on the kind of ring you want, so we're not going to design them together after the holidays. That way, it's not weird if I don't magically pull out a diamond under the tree."

"That could work." Tami tilted her head thoughtfully. "But if we say that, we'll have to act like we're seriously looking after Christmas."

"I can handle that. Can you?"

Her cheeks warmed as she imagined them in

a jewelry shop together, trying on rings, talking design ideas for a future that didn't actually exist. "Yeah," she murmured. "I can handle it."

Aiden studied her for a moment, his gaze softening. "It bothers you, doesn't it? Lying to everyone like this."

"Of course it does," she admitted, her voice low. "It's not just the ring or the proposal. It's everything. Keeping up this pretense feels like it's opening a door to questions we're not ready to answer. I hate feeling like I'm always two steps away from slipping up."

"Hey," he said gently, reaching across the table to touch her hand. "We're in this together, remember? We'll figure it out."

Tami managed a small smile. "Thanks. I just wish it didn't feel so…heavy sometimes."

"Fake engagement or not, we're a team," Aiden said, squeezing her hand. "If anyone asks, we'll stick to the story—we're designing our perfect rings after the holidays."

"Okay," she said, feeling a flicker of relief. "But you better keep that promise to look into it with me. If I have to go through this, you're suffering right alongside me."

He grinned. "Wouldn't dream of letting you do it alone. Besides, I have opinions. You're definitely not getting one of those rings with a massive stone that looks like it's weighing down your hand."

Tami chuckled, some of her tension easing. "Noted. No hand-weighing rocks."

They moved to the couch after dinner, and their conversation shifted easily to lighter topics, until another knock came at the door. It was her mother armed with a folder of wedding inspiration.

Tami exchanged a quick look with Aiden. "Ready to stick to the story?" she whispered.

"Born ready," he murmured with a wink.

As Rachel Rose swept inside with a stack of catalogs, her eyes immediately darted to Tami's bare hand. She held one out—it was a brochure on custom ring designs. "I thought we might look through these for inspiration."

"I already have an idea of how I want Tami's ring to look," Aiden interjected.

"Really?" Rachel Rose responded.

He nodded.

"Are you sure you don't want to take a peek at any of these—"

"We're good, Mama," Tami said with a smile. "I trust that whatever Aiden has in mind, I'm going to love it."

Her mother looked between them, then nodded, seemingly appeased—for now. But as the evening went on, Tami couldn't shake the feeling that keeping up the charade was only going to get harder.

Later, as she lay in bed, staring at the ceiling, she thought of Aiden's reassurance and his steady presence. Despite the complications, she realized how much she leaned on him. And that terrified her.

CHAPTER ELEVEN

AIDEN SAT ON HIS BED, his mind a whirlwind of thoughts—an endless loop of what-ifs, uncertainties, and fears. He knew he should call Tami, check on her after Rachel Rose ambushed them the other day. But he stared at the screen, hesitating.

When the phone rang, breaking the quiet tension, Aiden's heart jumped. It was his boss.

"Hey, Aiden. It's Blake."

Aiden sat up straighter, forcing a calm he didn't feel. "Hey, Blake. What's up?"

"Well, I've got some good news for you. I've been talking with the board, and we've decided to offer you a promotion. It's a big move for the company, and we think you're the right guy for it."

Aiden's pulse quickened. He'd known this moment could come, had worked for it for months, but hearing it finally spoken out loud hit him in waves—exhilaration, pride, and, strangely, fear. "Wow. That's...that's great news. Thanks, Blake. I appreciate the opportunity."

There was a pause on the line, as if Blake was

gauging his reaction. "There's more. The position would be in Charleston."

The word hit Aiden like a punch to the gut. Charleston. A city just across the bridge from Polk Island, where his father had lived—and died. Too close to the painful memories, too close to everything he had kept buried deep.

"Charleston?" he echoed, trying to keep his voice steady. "That's…that's quite a shift. I didn't know the job would be there."

"Yeah, it's a big change. We think it's the perfect spot to have you closer to the core of operations. We're hoping it's the right fit for you." Blake's voice softened slightly. "I know it's a lot to take in, but this could be a great move for you. You'd oversee a whole new department, getting in on the ground floor of something big."

Aiden's mind raced. On one hand, this was everything he'd worked for—a promotion, more responsibility, a chance to prove himself. But on the other hand, Charleston was too close to home. It would put him right back in the place he'd tried to escape—the city where his father had spent his last days.

Living in Charlotte had allowed Aiden some space to process the loss. He'd been far enough removed to focus on moving forward, to distance himself from the constant reminders of his dad. It was one thing to try to be present for his mother during the holiday season. But moving to Charleston? Charleston was just a stone's throw away from the place where everything had changed. Every day, every moment there would feel like a shadow looming over him, reminding him of the loss he had yet to fully face.

He shifted uncomfortably, glancing out the window at the place he had tried to call home, but the reality of Charleston being so close felt suffocating. "I... I need to think about it. It's a big decision."

Blake chuckled, clearly understanding. "Of course. Take your time, but I'd like to hear your thoughts soon. This is a big opportunity, Aiden. You've earned it."

The words echoed in Aiden's head as he hung up the phone. *You've earned it.* He had worked for years to get here, but at what cost?

He leaned back against the headboard, eyes closing, trying to clear his head. His thoughts centered back on Tami and his feelings for her. She deserved honesty—more than he had ever given her, more than he'd ever been capable of giving anyone, really. But there it was again, that suffocating knot of dread in his stomach. He wasn't sure what it was about Tami that made him want to protect her, not just from the world but from himself too.

His unspoken feelings for her weighed heavier than he could explain. It was so much more than the chemistry they shared, more than the gentle teasing and the late-night conversations where time felt like it bent around them.

There was something deeper there, something that scared him, something that told him it would ruin everything.

Tami was always steady, always so sure of herself. And Aiden? He was in pieces. Grief and loneliness had gnawed at the edges of him, pulling at the seams of his every thought, leaving him with nothing but the hollow echo of his past. Even now, he could feel his father's absence, that sharp sting of loss that never truly left him. He could still hear his voice, could still feel his presence in moments like this when everything seemed to close in.

He exhaled slowly, his fingers brushing across the screen of his phone, but he didn't press Send. He had done the math already, had weighed it all over and over in his head. He wanted to tell her that he was starting to fall for her, but what if that made him vulnerable?

What if she didn't feel the same way? What if everything changed? What if she looked at him and saw only the man who couldn't make it through the most basic parts of his own life, let alone navigate a relationship with someone else?

The thought of her stepping away, of losing what they had, was more than he could bear. He wasn't sure if his heart could survive that kind of break. And if he was honest, maybe that was the root of it—he didn't know if he could handle the fallout from any choice, and he had been avoiding making one for so long.

Aiden's gaze drifted over the room. There were reminders of Tami everywhere—her old oversize sweater he'd borrowed during the last rainy night they'd spent together. A small gift she'd given him years ago, sitting on the dresser. And her words—those quiet, sincere ones, offering him comfort and company without any expectation of more.

He could remember the way her voice softened when she asked him about his father, the way she had been there, letting him breathe through the grief, never pushing, never making him feel like he had to be anyone else.

But she deserved more than that. She deserved someone who could stand tall and steady for her, someone who didn't pull away when things got difficult.

Aiden's jaw tightened as he stood and paced across the room. He hated that he was still battling this war inside himself—one part of him wanting to take a step forward, to open up, to trust. The other part, the part that had been broken so many times before, demanding he keep his distance, protect himself, keep things casual.

But then there was the job offer he'd just received.

Senior project manager in Charleston. The role was a huge step forward in his career, one that he knew could change everything—bring stability and give him a fresh start.

Tami was always the first person he'd go to for advice, the one person he felt safe confiding in. But for the past few days, he'd been silent. Why? Because telling her meant opening up a whole new layer of uncertainty. The job opportunity in Charleston would bring him closer to home, closer to the family that had been a constant, chaotic force in his life, but it would also bring him closer to Tami.

And he wasn't sure if he was ready for that. Not yet.

Not with everything he was still processing. He ran a hand through his locs, pacing back and forth across the room, until he stopped in front of the window, staring out at the town that had been his home for so long. The skyline looked different tonight, like it was a place he barely recognized anymore. The lights glittered in the distance, mocking him with their clarity, while his mind remained clouded with indecision.

Aiden exhaled heavily, feeling the weight of his choices pressing against his chest, tighter than ever. He didn't know what to do. He didn't know how to move forward without losing everything in the process.

The doorbell rang, pulling him from his spiral. He was surprised that anyone was here. With a deep breath, he slipped downstairs to the foyer.

When he opened the door, Tami stood there, a soft smile on her face, but her eyes—those eyes—told him she was carrying a burden of her own. Aiden's stomach flipped, and he could feel his pulse quicken. She was here. And for some reason, that felt like a much bigger deal than it had any right to be.

"Hey," she said softly, her voice almost tentative, as if she wasn't sure how he was going to react.

Aiden stepped aside, his throat dry. He opened his mouth, but no words came out.

Tami, as if sensing the hesitation, stepped forward, glancing around with a knowing look. "I know something's going on, Aiden. You've been distant."

"I didn't mean to..." He struggled to find the right words, his voice faltering. "I just... I've got a lot on my mind, Tami."

"Talk to me," she urged, the kindness of her tone offering him an anchor in the storm. "Whatever it is, you don't have to carry it alone."

Aiden swallowed hard, stepping back and running a hand over his face. He wanted to tell her everything—everything about the job offer, his family, his grief. About the fears that consumed him whenever he thought about what could happen between them. But he couldn't bring himself to say it all. Not yet. Not when the fear of losing what they already had was so real.

"I'm… I'm not ready for this conversation yet," he admitted, the words slipping out before he could stop them.

Tami's gaze softened, and she stepped closer, her warmth enveloping him in a way that felt both comforting and terrifying. "I get it. I know being here on the island makes you miss your father even more. I know it's hard. Just know that I'm here."

He closed his eyes for a moment, battling the emotions inside him, the tug between wanting to lean on her and wanting to protect her from the mess of his life. He didn't know which way to turn. All he knew was that he was more afraid of losing her than anything else.

"I don't want to lose you," he whispered, barely louder than a breath, the words tumbling out without his permission.

Tami's hand reached up to touch his arm, her voice gentle but firm. "You won't."

He nodded, his heart heavy with the weight of everything he hadn't said.

Tami stood in the doorway of the Worthington house, her step faltering ever so slightly as she took in the stillness. The space, always so neat and orderly, seemed to hum with a different kind of quiet tonight—one that felt heavier, more distant. It wasn't just the silence of an empty house; it was something deeper, something that echoed the unspoken tension that had settled between her and Aiden over the past day or so.

She smiled at him, but the warmth behind it was tempered by a gnawing uncertainty. The words she had prepared felt heavy on her tongue, as if she had to be careful not to say too much, not to push too hard.

Tami wasn't sure when she'd started to notice the subtle shifts in him—small things, like how he seemed lost in his thoughts for longer stretches or how he was quieter than usual. She didn't need to ask; she knew Aiden well enough to see the signs. But how was she supposed to help him through this when she couldn't even help herself?

Her mind raced with the quiet anxiety that always simmered beneath the surface, the kind she had learned to keep hidden from the people closest to her. She didn't talk about it—never had, not even with Aiden. She had never been able to voice it, not even when it had nearly swallowed her whole during the worst of it.

Her fingers twitched at her sides, the nerves that always lingered just beneath the surface reminding her that she was never truly in control. That feeling of inadequacy had always followed her like a shadow, one she'd learned to keep in the background but had never quite shaken. She wanted to be the one who could be strong for him, the one who had the answers and could make things easier, but the truth was she often felt like she was barely holding on herself.

Tami took a deep breath and stepped further into the house, letting the door fall softly shut behind her. Aiden's eyes met hers, and she could see the tension in his posture, the way his jaw tightened as though he were bracing himself for something. He was holding something back, just like she was.

"You okay?" she asked, keeping her voice steady, though she felt anything but. It was one of those questions she asked often but never really expected an answer to. It was easier to mask her own feelings when she asked it, to focus on other things and pretend that she was fine even when she wasn't.

Aiden hesitated, the corners of his mouth twitching as though he might offer a smile but couldn't quite manage it. "I'm good."

He was her best friend—the one person who had always been there, the person who knew her better than anyone else. The thought of losing that connection, of him pushing her away when something was wrong, felt like a betrayal of everything they'd shared. But she didn't know how to help him if he didn't talk to her. Lately, she didn't know if she could even help herself.

There it was again. The anxiety. The ever-present, underlying hum of uncertainty that kept her from truly opening up. Every time she thought about saying the words out loud, the fear closed her throat, and the anxiety that accompanied it wrapped its tendrils tighter around her chest.

She wanted to tell him about what she'd been facing, of course. But she was afraid. Afraid that if she told him, Aiden would see her as weak or, worse, a burden.

Tami forced herself to sit down on the couch, crossing her legs beneath her. She folded her arms across her chest, trying to steady herself, but she could feel the unease stirring again—the tightness in her chest that only grew the longer she spent in this space, trying to hold everything together.

Aiden stood across from her, his hands shoved deep into the pockets of his jeans. He looked like he wanted to say something too, but he was holding back. The silence stretched out, thick and heavy, and Tami couldn't stand it anymore.

"You don't have to go through this alone, Aiden," she said, the words coming out more fragile than she intended. "I know... I know it's hard right now, and I just want to be here for you. Whatever you need."

He shifted slightly, his gaze never leaving her face, as though searching for something he wasn't sure he'd find. Tami could see the strain in his eyes—guilt, fear, the weight of everything he had been carrying for so long. He missed his dad, had thrown himself into work, and now he was back home, facing his family because of her. She wanted so badly to make it better for him, to ease his burden, but she didn't know how to fix something she wasn't sure she could even understand.

Aiden let out a quiet breath, the tension still tight in his shoulders. "I don't know if I'm ready to talk about it yet," he said softly, his voice almost apologetic.

Tami nodded, her throat tight. She wanted to say something else, to tell him that it was okay, that she didn't need him to have all the answers right now. But the words caught in her chest. Her father's death had been a while ago, yet there were days when the ache was still there, a quiet weight in her chest she hadn't quite shaken. How could she help him with his grief when she hadn't completely made peace with her own?

Tami could see the way he was wrestling with himself, the tightness in his jaw and the way his eyes flickered with a mixture of gratitude and something else. But then, just as quickly, the wall came back up.

"I don't want to drag you down," he admitted, his voice barely above a whisper. "I know how much you love this time of year."

"You're not dragging me down," she said quietly, her voice cracking slightly. "You came here for me. I know this isn't easy for you. Just don't shut me out. You're my best friend, Aiden."

The words hung in the air between them, and for a moment, neither of them moved.

Aiden's gaze softened, the edge of guilt still there, but something else was flickering in his eyes—recognition, maybe, or understanding. Tami wasn't sure.

"I'm sorry," he said finally, his voice low and steady. "I knew coming home wasn't going to be easy, but I didn't expect to miss him so much. I miss him more now than before. I guess it's all the memories. I just don't know what to do with all of this."

She smiled, though it felt bittersweet, the weight of her own unresolved grief pressing on her chest. "I don't know either," she admitted. "But we'll figure it out. Together. Grief doesn't come with a roadmap, but maybe we can help each other find our way through it."

Aiden looked at her then, really looked at her, and in that moment, Tami felt something shift. It wasn't a solution, but it was a beginning. A small step forward.

CHAPTER TWELVE

The Worthingtons' annual Christmas gathering was in full swing, the warm glow of twinkling lights reflecting off the garlands draped across Madelyn's home. Laughter and music blended with the rich scent of holiday spices, creating an atmosphere of easy joy.

Tami found herself nestled in the living room between Aiden's mother and his sister, London, cradling a glass of spiced wine. Her family, too, was mingling in the next room, laughing with familiar ease as they caught up with old friends, adding to the warmth in the house. It felt like a rare kind of togetherness, and for once, her worries seemed to ease.

The conversation was lighthearted, full of teasing and shared stories, but what struck her most was the way she felt—like she belonged.

At first, she had been an observer, careful not to overstep, but as the night wore on, the awkwardness faded. She wasn't just a guest anymore; she was part of the rhythm of the home. Tami imagined a future where she wasn't just Aiden's partner but fully woven into this family's traditions—holidays, vacations, the everyday moments that became cherished memories.

But the thought felt fragile, like glass in her hands. Because no matter how much she wanted this, it wasn't real.

As the clock struck just after midnight, the gathering began to wind down. Aiden's hand brushed hers, pulling her from her thoughts. His eyes were soft, full of understanding as he took her coat from the back of the chair where she had left it earlier. The evening was over, but there was still so much left unsaid between them—so much they needed to figure out. So much she needed to figure out.

"Could you get my coat please," Tami asked Aiden.

"You're leaving?" His voice was soft, but there was an edge to it, as if he didn't want the night to end. His eyes searched her face, as if gauging whether she felt the same.

Tami nodded, her heart suddenly feeling heavier than it had been moments ago. "Yeah, it's late. I should take Mama home." She forced a smile, trying to keep the sense of finality from creeping in. She hadn't wanted the evening to end either. The quiet moments, the subtle touch of his hand on her back, the shared laughter—she had wished, for a fleeting second, that this night could go on forever.

Aiden gave her a knowing look and helped her into her coat. The warmth of his touch lingered on her skin, even after his hand pulled away. She bit her lip, willing the flutter in her chest to settle.

The three of them—Tami, Aiden, and Rachel Rose—made their way out of the house. Aiden was just a step behind her, always close, always present. No matter what, he was her rock, her constant, and she couldn't deny that.

He walked them to the car. As they reached the vehicle, he turned to face her, his eyes lingering on her face in a way that made Tami's pulse race. The silence stretched between them for a moment too long, and then, without a word, Aiden cupped her face gently and pressed his lips to hers.

The kiss was soft—chaste, even—but it felt like it held everything unspoken between them. The warmth of his mouth on hers, the subtle pressure of his lips, left her breathless, and for a moment, it was as if the world had fallen away.

"I'll see you tomorrow," Aiden murmured, his voice a little hoarse, his gaze lingering on her with a tenderness that caught her off guard.

Tami smiled, her heart fluttering in her chest. She nodded, the words stuck in her throat. She wanted to say more, wanted to tell him how much that kiss had stirred something in her, but all she could do was offer a small smile.

Just as she turned to get into the car, her mother's voice cut through the quiet night air.

"I certainly hope your kisses are more passion-

JACQUELIN THOMAS 221

ate when you're alone," Rachel Rose said, her tone a teasing mix of curiosity and amusement.

Tami froze, the words sinking in before she could process them. She could feel the heat rush to her cheeks. She glanced at Aiden, who was looking down at his shoes, clearly trying to hide his own embarrassment. The air between them shifted, the easy camaraderie replaced by an awkward tension.

Tami opened her mouth to say something—anything—but the words caught in her throat.

She could feel Aiden's eyes on her, and the weight of the moment seemed to stretch forever. She wanted to laugh it off, to tell her mother to stop, but a part of her was stuck, unable to break free from the lingering emotions that kiss had stirred in her. It wasn't just a casual goodbye. It had felt like…more. And now, with her mother's teasing remark, everything she had tried to keep hidden suddenly felt exposed.

Tami didn't dare look at Aiden again as she slid into the car, her thoughts racing. She glanced at her mother, but the words she had prepared to say faded before they could leave her lips. Instead, she simply nodded, the silence growing between them like a thick fog.

The ride home was quiet. The familiar streets of Polk Island passed by in the night as the car hummed softly. She had always been good at hiding her feelings, but tonight, with Aiden, she wasn't sure she could keep them buried much longer.

Rachel Rose stood in front of the fireplace in her living room, her fingers brushing the edge of the Christmas-card display. The decorations had all been carefully arranged, a labor of love, to ensure that her space felt festive and welcoming. As she checked the clock on the wall, her gaze flickered to the front door.

She worked half-days on Saturdays, and earlier that morning, she'd had an unexpected visitor. Daniel Sterling had stopped by her office, his smile warm and genuine. His invitation had been simple yet earnest.

Would you have dinner with me tonight? Just the two of us—no pressure.

The idea of dating again felt foreign to Rachel Rose. She was older now, more cautious, and if she was honest with herself, more reluctant to open her heart. There was no underlying expectation, no veiled promise of romance or grand gestures—just the simple desire for companionship. That had been the part that unsettled her most. It wasn't that Daniel was unattractive—he was quite handsome, with kind eyes and a warm smile—but Rachel Rose found herself wondering if he was simply lonely. After all, he was around her age, perhaps a little younger, and had no significant other in sight. The possibility that he might just be seeking companionship was a thought that both flattered and concerned her.

She had almost said no, citing a thousand reasons why she was too busy. Her daughters, the ball, the never-ending responsibilities of being the matriarch of the Rose family—it all piled on top of her, demanding her attention. But something in her softened when she'd seen the sincerity in his eyes.

Okay, she'd heard herself say, surprising even herself. *Dinner sounds nice.*

Now, as she adjusted the collar of her sweater, she felt a mix of excitement and uncertainty. Was this a mistake? Was she simply stepping into something she wasn't ready for? After all, it had been years since she had been on a date. It was strange to think of herself in those terms, as a woman who might still be attractive or desirable, but Daniel's quiet confidence made her reconsider.

The sound of her doorbell echoed in the hallway, and Rachel froze for a moment. There was no turning back now. She smoothed her hair and took a deep breath before opening the door. Daniel stood there, looking effortlessly handsome in a dark jacket and a crisp white shirt. His smile was as warm as always, but tonight there was something different about the way he looked at her—a quiet appreciation that made her heart flutter ever so slightly.

"Good evening, Rachel Rose," he said with a soft chuckle.

She laughed nervously, brushing her hands down the front of her sweater. "I was just grabbing my coat."

She took it from the closet and put it on. Daniel's eyes crinkled at the corners as he extended his arm. "Shall we?"

She nodded and, for the first time in what felt like ages, let herself relax. It wasn't just the dinner that had her feeling this way—it was the fact that she was allowing herself a moment of something that wasn't about work, family, or obligations. For the first time in months, she felt like a woman, not just a mother, a wedding planner, or a host.

They walked to his car, and as they drove toward the restaurant, the streets lined with Christmas lights twinkling against the darkened sky, Rachel Rose couldn't help but feel a bit self-conscious. She hadn't been out with a man in so long. Her world had been so focused on her daughters, her business, and her community that she had forgotten what it felt like to just be with someone in that kind of setting. It felt almost like a new beginning, yet she was so acutely aware of the years that had passed, the experiences that had shaped her, and the heartaches she had left behind.

As they arrived at the restaurant, a charming little place tucked in a quiet corner of town, Rachel Rose allowed herself to be swept into the ease of it all. Daniel was a gentleman—he opened the door for her, guided her to their table, and settled across from her in a way that made her feel instantly comfortable. The restaurant was warm and intimate, filled with soft chatter and the comforting scent of freshly baked bread.

While they waited for their food, Rachel Rose's earlier concerns began melting away. Daniel had a way of making her feel heard—something that, at her age, was a rare gift. He spoke with genuine interest about her life, not just as a mother or an entrepreneur but as a woman with a rich history, dreams, and passions.

"So," Daniel said after a moment, leaning back in his chair and taking a sip of his wine. "What's something you've always wanted to do but never had the chance?"

Rachel Rose paused for a moment, considering the question. "That's a good question," she said, smiling. "I suppose there are things I've always wanted to do but… I put them off. There's always been something else that needed my attention."

He nodded, offering a look of understanding. "I get that. But what if now's the time? What if you gave yourself permission to explore those things?"

She laughed softly. "I'm not sure. It's hard to imagine. I've spent so many years focused on everyone else. My daughters, my business, my community. There's always something that needs doing."

"But what about you?" Daniel asked, his eyes sparkling with curiosity. "What about your dreams? What do you want?"

She felt a sense of quiet reflection come over her. She hadn't been asked that particular question in a very long time. She hadn't even thought about it. The truth was she didn't know. She didn't know what she wanted anymore, not for herself.

"I don't know," she admitted, her voice tinged with uncertainty. "Maybe I've forgotten how to want things for myself."

Daniel's gaze softened, and he leaned forward, his voice quiet but kind. "It's never too late to remember."

Rachel Rose smiled, his words sinking in. It felt comforting, the idea that it wasn't too late for her. That she wasn't too old to have dreams, or to rediscover herself. That maybe she wasn't just a mother, a businesswoman, a friend—she was still a woman, capable of growth and change.

The rest of the dinner flowed easily after that, with Daniel sharing stories about his own life—his work, his travels, and the things that mattered most to him. He spoke with a quiet passion about his volunteer work abroad, his eyes lighting up when he talked about the communities he'd helped and the ways he'd been changed by those experiences.

Rachel Rose found herself laughing more than she had in months, her worries fading away as she enjoyed the simple pleasure of someone else's company.

After dinner, they strolled along the quiet streets of the town, the air crisp and clear. Rachel Rose felt a sense of contentment she hadn't experienced in a long time, and for once, she wasn't thinking about the Christmas Ball, her daughters, or the responsibilities that loomed large in her mind. She was just here, in the moment, with someone who made her feel seen.

When they reached her front door, she hesitated for a moment, not wanting the evening to end. "Thank you, Daniel," she said quietly, her voice full of gratitude. "Tonight was…really lovely."

Daniel smiled, his eyes warm and genuine. "I'm glad you enjoyed it. I've been wanting to spend time with you, Rachel Rose. You're someone I admire."

She was flattered by his words, but there was also something else there—something deeper. "I'm glad we did this," she said softly.

As Daniel turned to leave, Rachel Rose stood in the doorway, watching him go with a mix of emotions swirling in her chest. She wasn't sure what the future held, but for the first time in a long time, she felt like it was okay to let herself enjoy the present. Tonight wasn't about weddings, family obligations, or being a perfect mother—it was simply about being Rachel Rose, a woman with her own life and desires.

Tami hadn't planned to stop by her mother's house that Sunday. With the Christmas Ball coming up on Friday, her mother was undoubtedly caught up in a whirlwind of preparations. Aiden had kept her at arm's length recently, and their unresolved tension since their last kiss made her heart heavy. She couldn't seem to focus on anything without thinking of him, and it was getting harder to ignore the connection between them.

Still, she found herself driving down to her mother's house, the familiar route to Rachel Rose's warm home somehow calling to her. Her mother's house was always a place of comfort, where Tami could escape from the demands of her busy life—where she once felt safe and understood. But lately, it had become a place where old wounds festered, and the comfort she longed for seemed just out of reach.

With everything that was going on in her own world, she needed that comfort more than ever, even if it felt complicated.

As she pulled into the driveway, Tami noticed that her mother's car was parked in its usual spot, the garden in front of the house was still filled with colorful winter flowers. The lights on the porch were glowing softly, adding a cozy charm to the late afternoon scene. Tami smiled to herself. There was something about her mother's home that never failed to ground her.

She walked up the steps and rang the doorbell.

A few moments later, the door opened, and Rachel Rose greeted her with a warm smile.

"Tami, sweetheart. It's so good to see you. Come on in."

She smiled back, stepping inside. The smell of freshly baked cookies and a hint of cinnamon greeted her, and she felt a wave of nostalgia wash over her.

"I wasn't expecting you today," Rachel Rose said as she closed the door behind her. "What brings you by?"

"I just needed to get out of my head for a bit," Tami admitted. "You know how it is, Mom. Even though I'm on a holiday break...it feels like there's always something more to do."

Her mother nodded sympathetically. "I need to finish a phone call, but sit down, relax, and have some tea. I'll be back shortly so that we can talk about whatever's on your mind."

Tami's gaze flickered around the house as they made their way to the kitchen. Everything was in its usual place—well-organized, warm, and inviting. It was always a little surreal to be here as an adult, standing in the same kitchen she had spent so many hours in as a child. But today something felt different. Her mother seemed...different.

Rachel Rose put her phone to her ear. "Sorry about that. My daughter is here for a visit..."

Tami peered around the corner, and her heart skipped a beat when she saw her mother cradling the phone, a smile playing on her lips as she talked.

"Mmm-hmm," Rachel Rose was saying. "That sounds wonderful."

Tami's eyes locked on her mother as she spoke again, her voice soft and pleasant.

"Absolutely, Daniel. I'm looking forward to it."

She froze.

Daniel? The name sent a ripple of unease through her, like a distant bell tolling in the back of her mind. She knew that name. But from where? Daniel?

Then it hit her. *Seaside Haven.* Her mother had looked into a venue for a wedding—Tami's wedding. And she had mentioned speaking to a Daniel Sterling about it.

A sharp, horrified thought gripped her. *Oh God. Did she actually meet with this man to plan my wedding?*

Tami's stomach lurched as she strained to listen. Rachel Rose's voice, uncharacteristically light, floated through the room.

"I'm glad you asked me out for dinner," she said. "It was really nice. I haven't enjoyed myself like that in a long time."

Tami blinked, her pulse pounding in her ears. *Dinner?*

The tension in her chest loosened just a fraction, enough for a wave of shock to take its place. Her mother, always so composed, so focused on the family and everyone else's lives, had gone out to dinner with a man.

Tami couldn't stop herself. As soon as her mother hung up, she asked, "Who is Daniel?" The words came out sharper than she intended.

Rachel Rose turned, clearly surprised. She set her phone on the counter and let out a soft laugh, a faint flush coloring her cheeks. "Oh, Tami," she murmured, smiling. "I didn't realize you'd be so curious."

Tami folded her arms across her chest. "Well, you're talking about him like you've known him for a while. Are you two…dating?"

For a moment, her mother hesitated, her gaze flickering downward before meeting Tami's eyes again. There was something softer in her expression than Tami was used to, something almost… vulnerable.

"Dating?" Rachel Rose echoed, shaking her head. "Oh, no, sweetheart, it's not like that. Daniel's just…someone I've been getting to know. He owns Seaside Haven. Remember? I told you about it—it's perfect for a wedding."

Tami stared at her, still trying to process the sudden shift in her reality.

Her mother continued, almost offhandedly, "I've agreed to have dinner with him again tonight. But there's nothing romantic going on, if that's what you're wondering."

Tami narrowed her eyes. "You're having dinner with him *again*, but it's not romantic? Then what is it, Mom?"

Rachel Rose sighed, turning toward the kitchen to pour herself some tea. "Tami, I know this probably seems out of the blue, but sometimes people find companionship in unexpected places." She glanced over her shoulder, her voice softer now. "Daniel and I are becoming good friends. That's all."

Tami's lips curved into a small smile, her heart warming in spite of herself. Maybe it was time for Rachel Rose to find joy in her own life again. The thought of her mother not being alone, of possibly rediscovering happiness, eased a weight Tami hadn't realized she'd been carrying.

CHAPTER THIRTEEN

THE NIGHT OF the Christmas Ball had finally arrived. Aiden stood in the living room, adjusting the silver cufflinks on his crisp white shirt. His mother moved with her usual blend of elegance and purpose, a vision in her stunning red gown. She flitted around him, her practiced hands fussing over his collar, smoothing out invisible creases in his tuxedo, and ensuring not a single detail was out of place.

Aiden had never been a fan of fancy events, but his mother loved them—loved the glitz and glamour that came with hosting family celebrations—and she would never let anyone in the family show up looking anything less than impeccable.

"I swear, Aiden, you're always so difficult about the bow tie," Madelyn teased, her voice light as she moved behind him.

Aiden let out a short laugh, but it was laced with tension he couldn't shake. He wasn't worried about the bow tie. He wasn't worried about the tuxedo or his appearance. What gnawed at him, what weighed on him, was the feeling of being a fraud, of having pretended for so long to be something he wasn't, especially in front of the people he loved most.

"Mom, I've told you I don't even know why we still do this whole 'bow tie' thing," Aiden said, trying to keep his voice light, but the undertone of guilt was unmistakable. "You've got to admit it's a little outdated."

His mother laughed, a soft, genuine sound that made Aiden's chest tighten. "I'll never understand how you manage to look so put together, yet you complain about things like bow ties," Madelyn said, reaching around him to adjust the knot of his bow tie. "It's one of those things I can never get you to change, isn't it?"

She was a woman of elegance, someone who loved the traditions of the family, even when they sometimes felt like burdens to him. But his mother had been his anchor through so many of life's storms, and her ability to turn anything into a cherished tradition, no matter how small or trivial, was something Aiden admired deeply—even if he didn't always show it.

"I'm not trying to pressure you, but like Rachel Rose, I am wondering if you and Tami plan on setting a wedding date soon?" Madelyn asked, a casual question that felt like a thunderclap in the middle of the quiet room.

Aiden didn't respond. What could he say? Tami was supposed to be his partner—his equal—but the weight of everything that had transpired over the past few weeks kept him from being completely honest with her, with himself, or with his family.

Aiden had never been a man of many words. He preferred action to conversation, but there were things he had been keeping from Tami, and the guilt gnawed at him. He wanted to tell her the truth. He wanted to tell her about the job offer and his growing feelings for her, but something inside him held him back. And now, with their families watching, the truth felt like it would crumble everything he had worked so hard to build. The lie they had created was now so tangled that he wasn't sure how to undo it.

Aiden's heart sank. The question hit him harder than he'd anticipated, and for a moment, he felt as though the air in the room had been sucked out. He turned to face his mother, trying to hold it together, trying not to let the panic rise in his chest.

His mother was looking at him expectantly, her gaze soft, but her smile was one of those smiles that conveyed so much more. She wasn't asking out of casual curiosity—this was the kind of question a mother asked because she cared, because she wanted answers, because she was watching her son make a life with someone she loved and respected.

But for Aiden, that question felt like a chain, tightening around his neck.

"I—uh..." He cleared his throat, trying to find the right words, but his mind scrambled to form an answer. The truth was too complex, too messy to put into words right now. "We haven't talked about a date yet," he said, his voice hoarse. He tried to keep it neutral, tried to make it sound like it was no big deal, but it was a lie. He knew that he was dancing around the truth, trying to avoid the inevitable question that was waiting to be asked.

"It's clear how much you care for each other. I was curious to see if you were thinking short or long engagement period. It's fine if you haven't figured that much out yet."

He could hear the unspoken hope in his mother's voice—the belief that he and Tami were building a future together, that they would take the next step in their relationship and start planning for a life that would make his family proud. Aiden forced a tight smile. "We'll let you know something soon."

Aiden swallowed hard, trying to shake the feeling that his world was unraveling. She stepped back and admired him for a moment.

"You look handsome, Aiden," she said with a smile.

He nodded at his mother's words, his smile thin. "Thanks, Mom."

But the words didn't feel real—not when he was lying to himself, lying to Tami, and lying to his family. The truth had become a labyrinth, a maze that he couldn't find his way out of.

Madelyn tilted her head slightly, her gaze lingering on him for a moment longer. "Is everything okay?" she asked softly, her concern evident in her eyes.

"I'm fine," he said, his voice husky.

Madelyn didn't push any further. She smiled, adjusting his collar once more, and gave him a quick kiss on the cheek. "Let's try and have a wonderful time tonight."

Aiden nodded again.

He looked at his reflection in the mirror. But all he could see was a man who wasn't sure if he was ready to open up, to take that next step with the woman he was starting to fall for. And the thought of losing her—the thought of losing everything because of his own fears—was more than he could bear.

It was too late to change anything now. All he could do was walk into the ball, pretending everything was fine. But in the back of his mind, he knew that the longer he waited to be honest, the more it would hurt when the truth finally came crashing down.

TAMI STOOD IN front of the full-length mirror in her bedroom, her reflection staring back at her like a stranger. The soft glow of the LED floor lamp in the corner reflected off the golden silk of her dress, the fabric glimmering like starlight as it cascaded down in delicate folds. She had to admit she looked beautiful, but her mind was somewhere else entirely. It was a quiet, suffocating space in her head where self-doubt lived, where her body felt like it was betraying her, and where the weight of every tiny imperfection loomed large.

In previous years, the annual Christmas Ball was an event that Tami dreaded. But tonight, it was a whole new level of stress. She wasn't just trying to avoid unwanted advances from Rachel Rose's chosen dates. Tonight, she was pretending to be someone's fiancée. Someone's future wife. The thought alone caused her chest to tighten with anxiety.

She had been doing well recently, or at least, she had convinced herself she was. She had a handle on her social anxiety most days—she could make it through work without too much trouble, she could smile and engage with people without feeling like her heart was about to beat out of her chest. But tonight, with the added pressure of her engagement to Aiden and the impending ball, everything felt like it was spiraling out of control.

The expectations, the eyes on her, the idea that tonight was supposed to be perfect. That, somehow, she should be the embodiment of grace and beauty. Someone who could hold her own among the Worthington family, who would seamlessly slip into their polished world.

But Tami didn't feel polished. She didn't feel graceful. She didn't feel like she belonged. Instead, she felt like a nervous wreck.

Her heart thudded in her chest, its rhythm picking up speed as the thoughts in her head came faster and faster. The sound of the soft jazz music playing in the background, which usually calmed her nerves, felt distant and far away, muffled by the noise in her mind. Her breathing was shallow, like she couldn't catch enough air, and the heat of the room seemed to be closing in on her. Her reflection in the mirror flickered, distorted, and for a moment, she couldn't recognize the woman staring back at her.

I'm going to embarrass myself.
What if I say the wrong thing?
What if I look stupid in front of his family?
What if Aiden regrets this? Maybe that's why he's been so distant lately.

Her thoughts were a whirlwind of anxious chatter, each one more urgent and consuming than the last. Tami's stomach twisted into tight knots, the acid from her nerves creeping up her throat.

She tried to take deep breaths, but they came in sharp, jagged bursts, making her dizzy. The familiar feeling of being trapped in her own body was overwhelming. She wanted to run, to hide, to stay in the comforting shell of her town house and let the world pass by. She could picture herself on the couch with a book in her lap, Aiden sitting beside her, both in the quiet safety of their shared space.

A Christmas celebration was supposed to be full of light, joy, and magic. And yet all Tami could feel was the fear creeping in like a shadow, draping itself over everything.

She looked at her phone, wondering if she could somehow avoid going altogether. Maybe she could fake being sick, stay home and let Aiden go without her.

But she couldn't do that. Not tonight. Not with everything hanging between them. She couldn't be the one to pull away now, especially when she knew how much this night meant to him.

Just breathe.

Tami's hands gripped the edge of the vanity, and she squeezed her eyes shut for a moment, trying to slow her racing thoughts.

I can do this.

She let out a shaky breath and then tried to steady her pulse, the beating of her heart like a drum inside her chest. She had to pull it together. There was no choice. She wasn't going to let this disorder win tonight. She wasn't going to let her anxiety control her life, control the moments she shared with the people she loved or with Aiden, who had shown her so much patience and support.

Tami straightened her back, lifting her chin slightly as if she were trying to hold on to some semblance of control. She was an adult. She was a woman who had worked hard to get where she was. She could handle a night out, a night in a room full of people she knew, including Aiden's family. Yes, her heart was racing, and yes, she felt like she might burst into a million little pieces at any moment, but she wasn't going to back down.

She took another slow, deep breath, letting it out as steadily as she could, forcing her mind to quiet. The anxiety was still there, a constant hum beneath her thoughts, but it wasn't going to win.

Her eyes shifted to the dresser, where her small bottle of lavender essential oil sat. It was a tool she'd found helpful when she had the space to pause and work through her anxiety. She reached for it and unscrewed the cap and inhaled the soothing scent. Lavender was calming. She closed her eyes and held the bottle under her nose, taking in a few deep breaths. The fragrance, familiar and grounding, helped her start to reset. She could feel her body slowly begin to release some of its tension. It was only a little bit, but it was something.

She opened her eyes, her reflection more composed than it had been a few moments ago. Tami smoothed her hands over her dress again, taking another long breath and letting the oils settle her before stepping away from the mirror. She was going to do this. She was going to walk into that ballroom, stand tall, and smile.

The next few minutes were a blur of movement—putting on her shoes, making sure her makeup was just right, trying not to feel the panic rise back up as the clock ticked closer to the time when Aiden would arrive. Each step forward felt like a small victory, but the doubt still clung to the edges of her mind, just out of reach.

She was scared. She feared how her anxiety might sabotage everything. But she wasn't going to give in to it. Not tonight.

When the knock on her front door came twenty minutes later, Tami took a deep breath, gathering all the courage she had, and opened the door.

Aiden stood there, looking as handsome as ever in his tuxedo, his warm smile immediately grounding her. He held out his hand, and the warmth of his touch as she placed her hand in his was the last thing she needed to push through the tightness in her chest.

"You look stunning," Aiden said softly, his voice filled with the warmth that she had come to crave.

Tami offered him a shaky smile, her hands still slightly trembling, but she didn't pull away. She wasn't going to give into her anxiety tonight, not when she had him by her side.

"Thank you," she said, her voice surprisingly steady. "You look very handsome. If Mama was giving out prizes for the best dressed couple—we'd win."

Aiden grinned. "We'd definitely win."

Tami wasn't sure what the night would hold, and she still felt that tightening in her chest.

But as she walked beside Aiden, his presence a steady anchor to reality, she felt something shift inside her. The night was just beginning.

The ball, the chaos, the nerves—everything that felt so overwhelming was still ahead. But Tami felt like she had the strength to face it.

She would push past the anxiety. She would make it through the night.

One step at a time.

THE ROAD TO the venue was lined with tall, towering trees adorned with sparkling white lights, their delicate branches glistening with a thin sheen of frost. Though snow hadn't fallen on the island, the crisp chill in the air and the festive glow of the decorations gave everything a serene and magical quality.

The Polk Island Hotel loomed ahead, its grand facade a perfect mix of classical charm and modern sophistication. Lights shimmered from every corner of the building, a warm glow spilling out from its high windows. Outside, a fountain graced the front courtyard, and the sound of gently cascading water was a soothing contrast to the hum of excitement inside.

Tami's stomach fluttered as Aiden parked the car under the awning. She took a steadying breath.

He was already around to the passenger side to open the door for her.

"You really look beautiful," Aiden said softly, reaching for her hand as she stepped out of the car.

She gave him a shaky smile, trying to push down the nervous flutter in her chest. His presence was the one constant that anchored her, his steady hand in hers offering reassurance as they approached the entrance together.

Inside, the lobby of the hotel was breathtaking. Rich marble floors gleamed under the low, ambient lighting, and the walls were adorned with lush greenery and wreaths of red holly. The scent of pine mixed with the delicate aromas of spiced wine and fresh pastries weaved through the space like a warm invitation.

The Grand Ballroom where the event was being held was even more magnificent. It was a sprawling ballroom with high, vaulted ceilings and crystal chandeliers that sparkled like stars suspended in midair. The soft clink of silverware and the murmur of low conversation filled the air as guests mingled, over the low hum of an orchestra playing classical holiday music in the background.

Tables were draped in white silk linens, ornate gold chargers and flickering candles in elegant holders.

The buffet stretched across one side of the room, the spread a feast for the eyes and stomach: glistening roasted meats, platters of delicate smoked salmon, a selection of cheeses that looked almost too beautiful to touch, and a rich variety of roasted vegetables.

The dessert table was a masterpiece of chocolate fondue fountains, sparkling sugar cookies, and elaborate cakes, their layers visible in soft shades of deep red, green, and gold.

Tami took in the scene with wide eyes, the grandeur of the room almost overwhelming. She had attended similar events before, but tonight it felt like she was stepping into a fairy tale.

"Wow," Tami breathed, barely above a whisper as they made their way further into the room. "Mama and Cia really outdid themselves this year." She knew it was her mother's vision, and she'd entrusted Cia to bring it to life.

Aiden agreed.

As they moved further into the space, she spotted several members of Aiden's family, mingling with the other guests. Shane, his tall frame instantly recognizable, stood near a corner, laughing with his wife, Ace, who wore a sparkling green gown that accentuated her warm brown hair. London, Micah, and Kenyon were gathered around a small table, their smiles bright and welcoming as they talked in low voices.

London looked Tami up and down and smiled. "You look incredible. I love that dress on you."

Tami smiled back, feeling the tension in her shoulders ease just a little. The support from

Aiden's family and the warmth of their welcome settled the constant flicker of nerves. She found herself more grounded than she had been earlier in the evening.

The night stretched on in a blur of laughter and conversation. She caught glimpses of Cia, looking stunning as always in a black gown that shimmered like the night sky.

Her gaze flickered briefly toward the door, where Naomi appeared with her husband, followed by Samantha. She noticed Tami and waved enthusiastically.

As Tami walked with Aiden through the crowd, she saw her mother, the hostess of the night, standing near the center of the room. Rachel Rose had always been an elegant figure, but tonight she practically glowed with excitement. Her red sequined dress caught the light in every angle, and the radiant smile on her face couldn't be mistaken for anything other than pure joy.

Tami's heart swelled at the sight of her mother, her unshakable poise, and the pride she had in hosting the night's festivities. Rachel Rose had always been a woman who knew how to throw an unforgettable event, but it was clear from the way she spoke to the guests that she took as much pride in the connections and relationships that were formed as she did in the event itself.

"Mom, you look absolutely beautiful," Tami

said, walking over to where her mother was greeting guests.

Rachel Rose's smile widened. "Thank you, darling. You look exquisite, I must say. That gown was a great choice for you."

Tami hesitated for only a moment, feeling a flicker of doubt but quickly pushing it away. "You were the one who chose it," she said, forcing a bright smile.

Rachel Rose raised an eyebrow knowingly before giving her a brief hug. "This is going to be unforgettable evening."

Tami nodded.

As the night progressed, Tami found herself participating in conversations and navigating through the crowd with a slightly calmer heart. There were moments where she stumbled over her words or her hands trembled, but Aiden was always there as her support.

The music shifted from holiday classics to jazz, and the soft sound of a saxophone filling the room, carrying with it an easy elegance that made Tami's chest feel a little lighter. The atmosphere shifted too, becoming more relaxed as people began to gather in smaller clusters, conversing freely and occasionally laughing over shared stories.

Tami stood with Aiden near the edge of the room, her heart still fluttering but not nearly as tightly bound by anxiety. She leaned toward him, feeling the solid warmth of his presence, and his hand brushed over hers. He smiled down at her, his eyes filled with an understanding she didn't always have the words for.

"Having a good time?" he asked.

Tami smiled back, feeling the last of her unease begin to lift. "I am."

"I'm having a great time as well. Thanks to you..."

Aiden's words, soft and sincere, helped push past the remaining walls inside her. Despite the nerves, despite the overwhelming sensations, she realized something in that moment. This wasn't just about fitting in or meeting expectations. It was about being fully present with him.

For tonight, she would simply be here. With Aiden.

CHAPTER FOURTEEN

TAMI DAZZLED IN her stunning gold gown, capturing the attention of everyone in the room. Aiden found himself lost in the enchanting atmosphere of the evening, but he couldn't shake off the feeling that something was off about her. Despite Tami's charming interactions and cheerful smile, there was a subtle shift in her usual demeanor that he couldn't quite pinpoint.

He had known her long enough to pick up on even the smallest changes. Tonight, Tami's usual vivacity was slightly muted, her energy more restrained than usual. She wore a smile, but it didn't quite reach her eyes. She'd seemed so relaxed earlier, but now it was as if she was battling a quiet storm within herself, and Aiden couldn't shake the feeling that something was wrong.

As they stood near the buffet table, she balanced a plate of hors d'oeuvres in one hand, her other hand loosely cradling a half-filled wineglass. Always measured, Tami seemed even more meticulous tonight, as though controlling the little things would keep the evening from unraveling. Aiden's chest tightened at the sight. He hated seeing her like this—guarded and distant in a way she rarely was with him.

"I'm going to check on my mom," he said casually as they returned to their table. "I'll be right back."

Tami nodded with a calmness that appeared practiced. "Okay, I'll be right here."

Aiden found his mother chatting happily with a group of guests and made sure she had everything she needed before excusing himself. As he made his way back to the table, he saw Tami sitting alone, her hands resting on the tablecloth, her wineglass untouched. The sight of her, so poised and yet so distant, stirred something protective in him.

"Did you miss me?" he teased gently as he slid into his seat.

She let out a short laugh, her lips curving into a playful smirk. "Always."

Aiden studied her for a moment, and his usual instinct to tease back gave way to something more serious. "Come on," he said softly, his voice edged with concern. "Let's take a walk. Just for a minute."

Her posture shifted ever so slightly, a hesitation he wouldn't have noticed if he didn't know her so well. Tami's eyes flicked to the crowded ballroom, scanning the clusters of guests, and for a moment, he thought she might decline. But then she nodded, setting her plate down with deliberate care.

Without another word, he offered her his arm, and she slipped her hand into the crook of his elbow. Aiden led her past the bustling room, weaving through clusters of laughter and conversation. The music and chatter began to fade as they exited the room.

Tami exhaled softly, her shoulders relaxing as they walked side by side in comfortable silence.

"Better?" he asked after a moment, glancing at her out of the corner of his eye.

She nodded, offering him a small, genuine smile. "Yeah. Much better."

Once they reached a small sitting area off to the side, Aiden pulled a chair out for her, guiding her to sit down before taking a seat next to her.

Tami fiddled with the delicate tennis bracelet around her wrist, her fingers trembling slightly. She wasn't doing it intentionally, but Aiden could see signs of anxiety all too clearly. The way her breathing was just a touch too shallow. The tightness in her jaw, the way she kept glancing around like she was preparing to leave at any second.

"There's something bothering you," he said softly, his gaze never leaving hers. "Tami. I can see it."

She blinked, her lips pressing together as if she wanted to argue but couldn't find the words. For a moment, she sat there in silence, clearly wrestling with whatever she was holding back.

"I'm fine," she said finally. "I had some concerns earlier, but I meant it when I said I was enjoying myself."

Aiden smiled, pulling her a little closer, pressing a soft kiss to her forehead. "I guess we should go back inside."

"Not just yet," Tami murmured. "Five more minutes please."

Her words made him chuckle. "I remember saying that all the time when we were younger."

"I know, right..."

"I'm glad I came home for Christmas," he said softly, his hand still holding hers. "I have you to thank for that. I wouldn't have come otherwise."

A small smile tugged at the corners of Tami's lips, a mix of relief and happiness evident in her expression. She seemed to lean into his touch, appearing to take comfort in his presence.

The moment lingered between them, an unspoken understanding passing silently in the shared quiet of the hallway. For a heartbeat, time seemed to stand still, wrapped in the warmth of their connection.

Finally, with a shared glance, they rose from their seats, ready to return to the lively party awaiting them. As they walked back toward the ballroom, Tami tucked her arm through Aiden's, their steps in sync as they moved forward together.

As soon as they entered the ballroom, as if on cue, her mother took center stage, the clink of her glass drawing the attention of the room. She beamed, her smile so wide it could light up the entire house. Tami could almost see the announcement coming before Rachel Rose even spoke the words.

"Everyone," her mother said, raising her glass. The room quieted as all eyes turned to her. "It is my greatest pleasure to announce that my daughter, Tami, and her handsome fiancé, Aiden Worthington, will be getting married next Christmas. What better way to celebrate the season than with the joining of two hearts?"

The air in the room seemed to shift. Tami felt her pulse spike, her chest tightening, her breath catching in her throat. Her mouth went dry. The words, the announcement—*their* engagement— felt like a cold wave crashing over her. She wanted to speak, to stop it, to tell everyone that this wasn't real. But she couldn't.

Instead, she turned to Aiden, her hand gripping his arm harder than she intended. His chuckle next to her was more out of place than anything else in the room.

As Rachel Rose continued to gush about the upcoming wedding festivities, Tami's mind raced with thoughts of how to escape this situation.

It was clear that her mother would never change and that she believed her daughter was incapable of living life without her help. Tami's stomach twisted into knots.

The pressure in the room was suffocating, and she had to escape. But before she could even move, the applause erupted around her as everyone congratulated them on their *wedding* and showered them with enthusiastic compliments.

Aiden seemed to thrive in the attention, but Tami felt herself withdrawing deeper into herself. "I'll be right back," she whispered to him, her voice barely audible as she made a beeline for the restroom.

"Tami, hey..." Aiden's voice followed her, concern laced in his tone.

He took a few steps after her, but she didn't stop. She couldn't.

The bathroom door closed softly behind her as she leaned against the sink, staring at her reflection in the mirror. The carefully applied makeup now felt like a mask that couldn't conceal the turmoil inside her. Her eyes were wide and frantic, nothing like the composed woman who had arrived at the hotel just hours ago.

She ran a trembling hand through her hair and let out a slow, shaky breath. *This isn't real*, she thought again, the words echoing in her mind. The sounds of laughter and celebration from guests who believed they were celebrating her engagement—one that wasn't even real—only heightened her sense that everything she had built and planned for was slipping further away from her grasp.

Her phone buzzed in her clutch, interrupting

the dark spiral of her thoughts. She pulled it out quickly, hoping for some distraction.

It was Naomi.

You okay?

Tami bit her lip, her fingers hovering over the keys. She wanted to be honest with her sister, to tell her that everything was falling apart, but she didn't. Not here, not now. Not with so many people around. So, instead, she typed back: Didn't expect the news to come out like that, but I'll be fine.

She slipped the phone back into her purse and leaned over the sink, staring into the mirror again. Her reflection seemed to mock her—perfect makeup, beautiful dress, all shattered by a single announcement.

As Tami stepped out into the hallway, she saw Aiden waiting by the door, his brow furrowed with concern. His voice carried an edge of worry as he spoke her name softly.

"Tami, what happened back there?" he asked.

"I'm fine now," she replied, the words coming automatically, but this time they felt like a lie. She gave him a tight smile, knowing it didn't reach her eyes. "I just needed a minute."

Aiden didn't seem convinced. He moved closer to her, his hand brushing hers to comfort her.

"You don't seem fine," he stated, searching her face.

"I truly thought pretending to be engaged would

finally make my mother stop trying to control my life," she confessed. "But I was wrong." Shaking her head, she looked up at him. "I can't go back in there. I don't want to see her right now."

"I'll get a key to one of the family suites. We can go there," Aiden suggested. "Or we can go to your place."

Tami shook her head. "No, she'll just come over there. It's best she doesn't know where I go because I need space. I'm absolutely furious with her."

THE NOISE FROM the ballroom seemed to linger in the back of Aiden's mind even as the door to the Worthington suite clicked shut behind them. The music, the laughter, the clinking of glasses—everything that had filled the grand space just moments ago now felt miles away. They had retreated here, to the suite overlooking the water, for some quiet.

Tami had needed space to process the whirlwind of emotions that had followed Rachel Rose's unexpected announcement. He was trying to process his own feelings, though the storm inside him was likely no less chaotic.

Aiden watched as Tami stood by the window, the city lights stretching out before her like stars against the horizon, but her posture was stiff, her gaze distant. There was no joy in her face as she looked out over the water, no sparkle in her eyes.

She had slipped into a stillness, a kind of quiet that worried him more than words ever could.

He couldn't help but wonder what had caused this shift. From everything he knew of Rachel Rose, what had just happened didn't seem like something that should bring Tami to this point.

"Why are you so upset?" he wanted to know, his voice soft with concern, trying to break through whatever wall had suddenly gone up between them.

Tami didn't turn around immediately, as if she needed a moment to collect herself before facing him. When she did, her expression was unreadable, her lips pressed together in a tight line.

"Did you really just ask me that?" she asked, the sharpness in her voice catching him off guard.

Aiden winced, stepping farther into the room. The tension between them was heavier now than it had ever been. "I didn't mean it like that, Tami. It's just—what your mom did tonight…it's not a huge deal. We're calling off the engagement after Christmas anyway." He hesitated, his voice softening with understanding. "I know this wasn't supposed to play out in front of the whole town. You're probably feeling like you have to orchestrate a public breakup now, and that's a lot. I get that. But we're in this together, okay? No matter how messy it feels, we'll handle it, just like we always do."

She let out a small, humorless laugh, but it

didn't reach her eyes. "It's more than that, Aiden. She's still at it…trying to control my life. She had no right to make that announcement." Her voice cracked slightly at the end, betraying her deeper frustration.

He took a step closer, his gaze softening as he saw the hurt in her eyes. He hated that she was hurting, but he also understood why she was. "You're right. She shouldn't have said anything without consulting us, but that's nothing new for your mother."

Tami's eyes locked onto his, the hardness in her gaze softening just slightly. "You didn't try to stop her. You didn't even try to fix any of this. You could've gone to her and made her retract her words. Instead, you just went along with it." Her voice shook a little, though there was an edge of accusation as she continued, "Why did you laugh along like it was some sort of joke? You were good-natured about it, like nothing was wrong. I don't get it."

Her words struck him like a punch. "Honestly, it didn't matter to me because I know it isn't real, Tami."

"You're right and when we break up… I'll be the one left looking like a failure to the entire island. This thing has already spiraled out of control." Aiden's heart squeezed at her words. He reached for her, but she stepped back, shaking her head once more, though there was a slight tremble in her hands.

"Please don't," she murmured. "I need space right now."

"I know it feels like we've crossed some line that we can't come back from. I'm sorry, Tami. I didn't mean for this to hurt you."

She took a deep breath. "This is on me. It's not your fault. You went along with this to help me with my mama drama."

Aiden wanted to reach out, to hold her, but he held himself back, not wanting to push too far, too fast. "I don't know how to fix this. I don't know what to do."

Her shoulders slumped as she exhaled sharply, her breath heavy. "I don't know what to do either." Her voice cracked, and she wiped a hand over her eyes quickly. "But we can't keep doing this. I can't keep doing this. It's tearing me apart."

The admission broke something inside him. The guilt, the fear, the endless parade of lies. He'd been so consumed with maintaining the charade, with keeping up appearances, that he had ignored how deeply it was draining her. And how much he hated lying to his mother. The weight of it all settled heavily on him, and for the first time, he wondered if the cost was too high.

"I'm sorry," Aiden whispered, his voice cracking. "I never should have let it go this far. But I—"

He stopped, swallowing the lump in his throat. "I don't know how to make it right."

Tami finally turned to face him, her eyes shining with unshed tears. The vulnerability in her gaze was a punch to the gut, and Aiden felt the sting of it deep within himself.

"You can't make it right," she said quietly. "Not anymore. I just... I just need to figure out how to move forward. I can't keep living this lie."

Her words settled in the room like a heavy silence, and for a moment, neither of them spoke. The sound of their breathing was the only noise between them, thick with the weight of everything they hadn't said before.

Aiden reached for her then, but this time she didn't pull away. His hand found hers, and she allowed it, the touch a fragile bridge between them. She didn't smile, didn't say anything more, but the tension between them felt lighter, at least for now.

"I never wanted to hurt you," he said softly. "And I don't want to lose you."

Tami squeezed his hand, looking up at him with the same mixture of frustration and tenderness he had seen so many times. "You haven't lost me. But we've got to stop pretending. I can't live in this fantasy. It's hard to know what's real anymore."

Aiden nodded slowly, his chest heavy with the truth of her words. "We'll figure it out," he promised, his voice barely a whisper. "I swear we will."

The promise hung in the air between them.

CHAPTER FIFTEEN

A FESTIVE ATMOSPHERE of joy and warmth filled the space, with the soft murmur of laughter and clinking glasses drifting through the air. But Rachel Rose stood at the edge of the dance floor, her champagne glass trembling slightly in her hand, her heart heavier than it should have been on such a beautiful night.

She had poured her heart into planning this Christmas Ball, wanting it to be perfect—not just for the holiday but for her youngest daughter. This was supposed to be a celebration of Tami's engagement to Aiden, the man Rachel Rose was certain would give Tami the stability and happiness she deserved.

When Rachel Rose raised her glass to announce the engagement earlier, she'd been bursting with pride. With a gleam in her eye, she'd added a casual yet unmistakable suggestion to the crowd that they get married at Christmas. She hoped they'd take the hint.

But the moment she caught Tami's expression, her elation had faltered. The room had been alive with applause and congratulations, yet Rachel Rose could only see her daughter's tight smile, the way her eyes darted to Aiden and back again, avoiding her mother's gaze. Tami's shoulders had stiffened, her energy retreating into a shell that Rachel Rose recognized too well. Something was wrong, and she couldn't understand why.

Her intentions had been pure. She wanted her daughter to feel celebrated, loved, and surrounded by family and friends. But Rachel Rose also had her own quiet agenda. She had hoped the announcement would force Tami and Aiden to commit to a date, and she couldn't deny she wanted that date to be the following Christmas. After all, it seemed fitting—a beautiful, festive wedding to match their joyous engagement.

Rachel Rose's gaze wandered across the room, searching for her daughter. She could see Samantha and Naomi, her two older daughters, mingling with ease, their laughter echoing above the soft hum of conversation. They were so self-assured, so confident. Rachel Rose never worried about them. They had always taken charge of their own lives, making decisions without hesitation. But with Tami, it was different.

Her youngest had always been more reserved, more cautious. Rachel Rose couldn't help but feel protective of her, as if Tami needed that extra care and guidance. That protectiveness had turned into a quiet anxiety over the years—a fear that Tami might let life pass her by if someone didn't step in to nudge her along. And so, Rachel Rose had done what she thought was best. Yet now, seeing Tami's reaction, she couldn't help but wonder if she had overstepped.

"Rachel Rose?"

Daniel's voice pulled her from her thoughts. She turned to see him approaching, his brow furrowed with concern. He had a way of reading her, even when she thought she was hiding her feelings.

"How are you?" he asked softly, his steady presence grounding her.

"I'm fine," she said, though her voice sounded far from convincing. She offered a distracted smile, her eyes darting back to the crowd. "It's just…Tami."

Daniel's head tilted slightly, encouraging her to continue.

Rachel Rose sighed, her words slow and uncertain. "I thought she'd be happy, excited even. But when I made the announcement, she…she looked so upset, Daniel. Like I'd done something wrong."

"Maybe she didn't expect you to announce it tonight," he suggested gently.

She frowned, his words striking a nerve. "But I'm her mother. I just wanted to share her happiness with everyone. Why would she be upset about that?"

Daniel's expression softened, and he stepped closer. "It's not that you did something wrong. But

Tami's an adult now. Maybe she wanted to share the news her way, on her terms."

Rachel Rose blinked, his words landing uncomfortably, a tight knot forming in her chest. Her back straightened, and she folded her arms, as if physically shielding herself from the implication. "I've *always* been there for her," she said, the words coming out sharper than she intended. "I've supported her through everything. Every achievement, every setback—I've *been* there."

Her pulse quickened, and she felt the heat rising in her face. Why was this even a question? *Why wouldn't Tami want her to be part of this moment?*

She scoffed, shaking her head. "That doesn't just disappear overnight." But even as she said it, a flicker of doubt crept in, gnawing at the edges of her certainty.

"Sometimes being part of the moment means stepping back and letting her take the lead," Daniel said carefully. "Especially with something as personal as her engagement and wedding plans."

Rachel's chest tightened. She had never thought of it that way. She had always seen herself as her daughters' greatest advocate and protector. Was it possible she had crossed a line she hadn't even seen?

"I just... I wanted to help," she murmured, her voice faltering. "Tami's always needed a little push."

Daniel gave her a small, understanding smile.

"Maybe this time, she needs you to trust that she can push herself."

Rachel Rose stood there for a moment, her thoughts swirling. Had her well-meaning intentions unintentionally hurt her daughter? The shimmer of the ballroom suddenly felt muted, the festive glow dimmed by the weight of her thoughts.

Her heart ached at the thought of Tami being hurt by her actions, and yet, a small, stubborn voice inside her insisted that she had only done what any mother would do—what any mother should do. She had been proud, and that pride had spilled over into the announcement.

"I don't understand," Rachel Rose said softly, her gaze distant. "Why would she be upset? I wasn't trying to take anything away from her. I just wanted to share in her happiness."

Daniel studied her quietly for a moment before speaking again. "Rachel Rose, I think you're missing the point. It's not about you taking anything away. It's about her wanting to take control of that moment. She's not a little girl anymore, and maybe she wants to do things her own way."

Rachel Rose opened her mouth to respond but closed it when she saw the truth in Daniel's eyes. Maybe he was right. A feeling of discomfort settled in her chest, a mixture of confusion and vulnerability she wasn't used to. It wasn't easy to admit that perhaps she had been too involved, too eager, and now her daughter was upset with her for it.

Daniel's voice was calm, but it carried weight. "Sometimes, you have to let go, Rachel Rose. You can't hold onto everything. Let Tami make her own choices, even if that means stepping back. She's an adult. She needs to be the one to share her life, not you."

Rachel swallowed hard, her heart sinking as his words resonated with her. She had always thought of herself as the one who would take care of things, the one who could fix everything. But maybe, just maybe, this time she had gotten it wrong. The realization stung, but the more she thought about it, the more she saw the truth in it.

"I don't know if I can just...step back," she whispered, the words barely audible, more to herself than to him.

Daniel gave her a soft, sympathetic look, but before he could respond, Rachel stood a little straighter, wiping away the moment of vulnerability. She wasn't ready for this conversation. Not now.

"I don't have time to think about this right now," she said, her voice firming up, her pride returning.

Daniel nodded, though his expression didn't hide the concern in his eyes. "I understand. But just remember, Tami loves you. This isn't about love. It's about letting her have her own space."

Without responding to him, Rachel Rose turned

away and walked toward the balcony doors, needing some air. Her thoughts were a tangled mess, but one thing was certain: she had to figure out how to fix things with Tami and Aiden.

TAMI'S EYES WERE DOWNCAST, her lips pursed, her face pale. Aiden had tried to read her, but whatever was going on in her head, she wasn't letting him in.

He had always prided himself on being a good observer, on knowing when something was wrong with her, even if she wasn't saying it. And tonight, more than ever, he felt the distance growing between them—a distance that had nothing to do with the engagement charade, or the pressure of keeping up appearances for their families. This felt deeper, like an undercurrent of something bigger, something he had yet to understand.

"Tami," he said gently. "Talk to me please."

She gave a faint nod but didn't meet his eyes. "I'm fine," she replied, her voice quieter than usual, like she was trying to convince herself as much as him.

Aiden had never been good at just letting things go, especially when it came to her. He could see the tightness in her shoulders, the way she moved as if something were weighing her down. It was much more than the stress of their fake engagement.

"You don't look fine," he said, taking a step

closer. He watched her shift uncomfortably, her fingers tugging at the hem of her dress in a way that made his chest tighten.

"You're not fine. What's really going on here?"

She exhaled slowly, her face flushing with frustration, but it wasn't anger at him. He knew that much. Perhaps, she was frustrated with herself; with the way things had spiraled out of control.

"I… I don't know," she murmured, but then, as though the weight of it all was finally too much to bear, she froze. Her hand moved instinctively to her neck, and she winced, the skin beneath her fingertips rippling in a way that made Aiden's heart skip a beat.

"Tami…" His voice cracked slightly, a mix of concern and fear creeping in as he watched her eyes widen. "Are you okay?"

She turned her face away, but he could see the red patches already starting to form across her neck and down to her chest. Her breath quickened, and Aiden could feel a chill settle in the pit of his stomach.

He moved to her side in a few strides and gently grasped her wrist, his fingers tracing the angry welts of hives that were spreading across her skin. "Tami, you're breaking out in hives. I should take you to the hospital."

"It's…it's nothing. This happens sometimes when I'm under a lot of stress," she said quickly, trying to pull away, but Aiden didn't let her. His heart was racing now, and a sudden clarity hit him with force.

She winced again, trying to hide her discomfort, but Aiden could tell that this wasn't just about her skin. This was about everything. The pressure of their lie, the weight of pretending, the way her body was reacting to everything she had kept inside. He had never seen her like this—vulnerable, exposed, as if the facade she'd been holding up was crumbling in front of him.

"Do you want me to have one of your sisters come up here?" Aiden's voice was low and urgent as he gently led Tami to the couch, his hand never leaving hers. Tears welled in her eyes, and she shook her head, trying to hold back her emotions. But Aiden could see right through her facade, he knew her too well. Her shoulders trembled and her composure was hanging by a thread.

"No... I can't," Tami whispered, her voice breaking. "I just... I can't right now." She closed her eyes, letting the tears fall freely now as she buried her face in her hands and sobbed quietly.

Aiden's heart ached for her, torn between wanting to be strong for her and scared of what this meant. He could feel the weight of her burden bearing down on her, breaking her down.

Kneeling in front of her, he placed a hand on her knee with gentle firmness. "Sweetheart, I don't understand," he said, his voice filled with emotion. "What can I do for you?"

Tami pulled out a tissue from her clutch purse and dabbed at her face. "There's nothing you or anyone can do, Aiden. I... I have social anxiety disorder," she admitted softly. "I've been dealing with it since college."

While he had noticed that she seemed anxious at times, he had no idea that it had developed into a full-blown disorder. "Why didn't you tell me? Why didn't you tell me sooner?"

Tami's gaze flickered to him, her face flushed with shame and sorrow. She opened her mouth to speak, but the words didn't come right away. She took a deep breath, her hands gripping the edges of the couch as she collected herself.

"I never wanted you to see me this way," she finally said, her voice barely above a whisper. "I didn't want you to look at me like I was...broken. Like I'm not enough. I just couldn't bear it. My mother already makes me feel that way."

Aiden felt his heart shatter at her words. His throat tightened, and he struggled to find the right thing to say. He hadn't realized how deep her fears ran, how much she had been hiding from him, even when she had seemed so strong.

"It's not true," he whispered fiercely, cupping her face gently in his hands. "You are more than enough, Tami. You always have been. But you don't have to carry this alone. You don't have to hide from me. I'm not going anywhere."

Tami quivered, but she remained in his embrace. She leaned into him, resting her forehead against his chest as she let the tears flow freely. Her body shook with sobs.

Aiden held her tightly, hoping to shield her from the weight of her own thoughts.

"I've been struggling with this for a long time," she said, her voice breaking as she clung to him. "And each time it gets worse, I think maybe this time, maybe I'll be okay. But I can't catch my breath, Aiden. I can barely function, and everything is getting worse because of what's going on."

He swallowed hard, trying to process what she had just revealed.

Social anxiety disorder. She had been carrying this burden alone, hiding it not only from him, but from everyone else too. And he never even knew. Aiden couldn't believe it. She had put on such a brave face, pretending to be strong for him and everyone else, while he was completely clueless.

"This is my fault," he murmured, pulling her closer. "I should have noticed that something was bothering you. I've been so consumed with maintaining this…this lie that I didn't see how much it was hurting you."

"No," she hissed under her breath, shaking her head as she pulled back slightly to look up at him through teary eyes. "Aiden, this isn't your fault. I… I didn't want to burden you. You were dealing with your own grief. I was supposed to be your support system. I failed you."

He shook his head adamantly. "No, you didn't. You've been exactly what I needed," Aiden spoke softly, gently brushing a strand of hair out of her face. "But I'm trying to understand, Tami. You know my secrets and I know yours... Why did you keep this from me? Did you really think I would judge you?"

Tami paused for a moment, nervously wringing her hands together as she looked down at the floor. "I care about what you think of me, Aiden. I didn't want to seem...weak in your eyes."

Aiden's heart ached at her words. The vulnerability in her voice, the fear that she had been carrying all this time—it tore him apart. But in that moment, he finally understood. He understood the true depths of loving her. It wasn't just about supporting her when things were easy. It was about staying by her side, even when she felt like a burden or not enough.

"I'm not going anywhere, Tami," he repeated firmly, filled with quiet determination. "You are not weak. You are the strongest person I know. And we will get through this. Together."

Tami sniffed, her eyes red from crying, but there was a glimmer of hope in her expression—something that told him she was starting to believe him. That maybe, just maybe, he could help shoulder this burden with her.

But even as Aiden held her, as he promised her

that everything would be okay, the reality of their situation hung heavily between them.

"You should stay the night here," he said softly, after a long pause, his hand still gently resting on her knee. "I'll sleep here on the sofa. You need time to rest. To breathe."

Tami shook her head weakly, her voice barely audible as she spoke. "I just want to go home, Aiden."

His heart twisted at the rawness of her words. He had never wanted anything more than to make her feel safe, but he also knew that for the first time, she needed space to process everything. To think.

"Okay," he said, his voice gentle but firm. "I'll take you home. I promise you, I'll be right here with you, every step of the way."

Tami nodded, though her eyes were distant, lost in thought.

The cool night air nipped at Aiden's face as he opened the passenger-side door for Tami, her slender form brushing past him with a muttered "thanks" before she slipped into the car.

He paused, studying her for a moment. Her profile was lit by the soft glow of the dashboard lights, her expression unreadable, her fingers clasped tightly in her lap. The silence stretched between them, heavy and brittle, as he closed the door and walked around to the driver's side.

When he slid into the seat and started the engine, Aiden's chest tightened. He'd seen Tami upset before, but tonight—tonight felt different. She seemed locked within herself, a fortress he couldn't breach. The grand announcement of their engagement had struck a nerve he hadn't anticipated.

Aiden shifted the car into Drive and pulled away from the hotel, glancing at Tami as she stared out the window. He wanted to say something, to reach out to her, but the tension rolling off her made him hesitate. She clearly needed space, and he would respect that—even though it went against every instinct he had.

The roads were quiet, the festive lights lining the streets casting soft patterns of gold and red onto the pavement. The hum of the engine was the only sound, broken occasionally by the faint rustle of Tami shifting in her seat. Aiden tightened his grip on the steering wheel, forcing himself to focus on the road instead of the turmoil brewing inside him. She hadn't said much since they left the ballroom. Not about the announcement, not about her mother, and certainly not about the sudden withdrawal he'd seen in her.

When they arrived at Tami's town house, Aiden barely had time to shift into park before she reached for the door handle. The subtle rebuff landed like a punch, but before he could process it, she turned to face him, her expression steeled.

"This isn't working," she said, her voice too even, too controlled.

Aiden frowned. "Tami—"

"I mean it." Her fingers curled into fists in her lap. "We don't have to wait until New Year's. The engagement is off. As of tonight."

A cold knot formed in his stomach. "You're upset. Let's talk about this tomorrow—"

"No, Aiden. There's nothing to talk about." Her voice wavered, but she pressed on. "I shouldn't have let you see me like that. I shouldn't have told you." She exhaled shakily. "This was supposed to be pretend. And it got too real."

His pulse pounded in his ears. "Too real for who?"

She shook her head, looking away. "For both of us."

Aiden swallowed hard, searching for the right words, but the weight of hers crushed his chest. He'd thought they were past pretending, that what had started as a ruse had evolved into something real—something worth holding on to. But she was shutting the door on it. On him.

"Tami—"

"I need space." Her hand finally landed on the door handle. "And I need you to let me have it."

There it was. The final nail in whatever fragile thing they had been building.

His throat tightened, but he nodded. "Okay."

She hesitated only a second before stepping out,

closing the door behind her with quiet finality. Aiden sat motionless, watching her disappear inside, the ache in his chest growing sharper with every passing second.

By the time he reached his mother's house, the silence felt unbearable. He parked in the driveway but didn't move, gripping the steering wheel as if it could anchor him. The warm glow of the porch light offered no comfort. Everything was slipping through his fingers.

He dropped onto the couch, elbows braced on his knees, face buried in his hands.

Tami hadn't trusted him. She'd let him in—then pushed him away harder than ever. And the worst part? He wasn't sure if she'd just ended their fake engagement…or their friendship.

It was a very really possibility that he'd already lost the chance for anything more.

He ran a hand through his locs, the frustration bubbling to the surface. Tami's reluctance to share her struggles with him felt like a confirmation of his deepest fear: that she didn't trust him, didn't see him as someone she could lean on. And yet, he couldn't shake the memory of her smile, the way her eyes lit up when they were together, the quiet moments that felt like they were building something real.

Aiden's gaze drifted to the Christmas tree in the corner of the room, its twinkling lights casting soft shadows on the walls. He thought about going to Rachel Rose, about telling her the truth—that they were only pretending to be engaged and the reason why. But he dismissed the idea almost as quickly as it came. It wasn't his place. If Tami wanted her mother to know, it had to come from her.

Still, the thought of leaving her to face this alone gnawed at him. He'd always prided himself on being there for the people he cared about, on being someone they could count on. But tonight, he'd felt powerless, unable to bridge the gap between them.

Aiden sighed, leaning forward and resting his elbows on his knees. He hated leaving Tami alone in her distress, but he had to respect her wishes. She'd asked for space, and he would give it to her. But he couldn't shake the feeling that they were standing on the edge of something fragile, something that could break if they weren't careful.

And as much as he wanted to protect her, to shield her from the things that hurt her, he couldn't do that if she didn't let him in. The realization settled heavily on his shoulders, a sobering reminder that love—the kind of love he wanted with Tami—required more than just good intentions. It required trust, vulnerability, and the courage to face the difficult truths together.

Aiden closed his eyes, the flickering light of the Christmas tree painting patterns on the inside of his eyelids. Tomorrow, he'd talk to her. He'd tell her about the job offer, about the choice he was facing. Then they could start to untangle the mess between them.

THE NEXT MORNING, the kitchen felt warm and inviting as Tami sat at the breakfast table, her untouched coffee growing cold. Her stomach churned with anxiety over the lie she carried. Today was the day she would tell her mother the truth.

Taking a deep breath, she grabbed her keys and coat before stepping outside into the cool morning air.

The short drive to her mother's house felt longer than usual, the streets seeming foreign under the weight of what lay ahead.

When she pulled into the driveway, Tami's heart pounded so hard she thought it might drown out the sound of the engine. She killed the ignition and sat in silence, gripping the steering wheel as if it were her lifeline.

I can do this. I have to do this.

With a deep breath, she stepped out of the car and walked up the familiar path to the front door. The house, with its cheerful white shutters, seemed almost mocking in its serenity.

Inside, Rachel Rose was already bustling around the kitchen. Her velvet loungewear swished as she moved between the counter and the stove, humming an old gospel tune. The sound was comforting, grounding, but it also made Tami's throat tighten with unshed tears.

When her mother noticed her standing in the doorway, she smiled warmly. "Well, good morning, sweetheart. You're up bright and early."

Tami forced a smile, stepping inside and hanging her coat over the back of a chair. "Morning, Mama."

Rachel Rose tilted her head, her sharp eyes narrowing slightly. "You okay? You look like you didn't sleep a wink."

Tami's laugh was hollow. "I didn't."

"Want some tea?

"Mama, can we talk?" Her voice sounded foreign to her own ears, trembling and thin.

Rachel Rose turned fully, her brow furrowing, likely at the uncharacteristic tone. "Of course, baby. What's on your mind?"

Tami's heart raced as she clasped her hands together to still their shaking. "I... I have to tell you something. About me and Aiden."

Her mother's face lit up. "Oh, is this about the wedding date?"

Tami's chest tightened. This was it. No turning back. She took a deep breath and forced herself to meet her mother's expectant gaze. "Mama, there isn't going to be a wedding."

Rachel Rose froze, her hands gripping the counter. "What do you mean there's not going to be a wedding? Tami...?"

"There...there never was going to be one," she admitted, her voice cracking under the impact of her confession.

Rachel Rose's face shifted from confusion to shock. "What are you saying?"

Tami swallowed hard, tears welling in her eyes. "Aiden and I weren't really engaged. We made it up. I did it to get you to stop your matchmaking, but it spiraled out of control. I'm so sorry for lying to you."

Her mother's face went pale, and she sank into the chair across from Tami.

Silence filled the room, heavy and suffocating. When Rachel Rose finally spoke, her voice was laced with disbelief. "You lied to me? To Aiden's family? What were you and Aiden thinking?"

"This wasn't Aiden's idea. I asked him to go along with the ruse," she said quickly.

Rachel Rose's gaze pierced her. "Tami, how could you?"

Her tears spilled over as she reached across the table, desperate to bridge the growing chasm between them. "Mama, I thought if I pretended, maybe it would give me some space to figure things out. I just didn't want you up to your usual antics. But then you started telling everyone that Aiden and I were engaged... I felt so trapped, like I couldn't live up to what you wanted for me."

Rachel Rose pulled her hand back, her hurt evident. "Trapped? Tami, all I've ever wanted is for you to be happy. To find someone who loves you as much as you deserve. How could you think this would solve anything?"

"Because I was s-scared." Tami's voice broke. "Scared of disappointing you, of being alone, of not knowing what I want. And then, when Aiden agreed to help, it seemed like a way to make everything easier. But it's only made things worse."

Rachel Rose's expression softened slightly as she listened, though the pain lingered in her eyes. "Worse how?"

"I did exactly what I wanted to avoid—I've disappointed you. And I think I... I might have ruined my friendship with Aiden," Tami admitted, her voice barely above a whisper. "He's been so kind through all of this, but now I don't know if things will ever be the same between us. And it hurts, Mama. It hurts more than I thought it would."

Rachel Rose's gaze held hers for a long moment before she sighed and reached for Tami's hand. "I'm disappointed, Tami. I'm disappointed that you felt you had to do something like this because of my actions. Honey, I can see how much this has been eating you up inside, and I'm so sorry. You're my daughter, and I love you. Nothing will change that."

The words were a balm to Tami's raw emotions, but her guilt remained. "I never wanted to hurt you, Mama. I... I think part of me did it because

I didn't know how to tell you about my struggles. About why I find it so hard to…to be the person you want me to be."

Rachel Rose frowned, her concern evidently deepening. "What struggles, baby?"

Tami hesitated but knew it was time to be fully honest. "I've been dealing with social anxiety. It's not just shyness, Mama. It's this overwhelming fear of being judged or not measuring up. Sometimes it feels like I can't breathe when I'm around too many people or when I feel like I'm not good enough."

Her mother's hand tightened around hers. "Oh honey…why didn't you tell me?"

"Because I… I thought you wouldn't understand. You've always been so strong, so sure of yourself. I didn't want you to think I was weak."

Rachel Rose's eyes glistened with unshed tears as she stood up and walked over to where her daughter sat. "Tami, my strength doesn't mean I've never struggled. And you're not weak for feeling this way. You're human. And if you're dealing with something like this, I want to help you—but I promise not to overstep."

Tami let out a shaky breath, the weight of years pressing down on her. "It's not just the wedding." Her voice wavered, but she forced herself to continue. "It's everything. You've always had a plan for me—for all of us. The schools we went to, the jobs we took, the kind of men we should marry.

You love us so much, but sometimes…it feels like you don't trust us to figure things out on our own."

Rachel Rose flinched, as if the words had struck her. "Tami, that's not—" She hesitated, then sighed. "I never meant… I just wanted to make sure you had everything you needed, every opportunity. I—I've always felt like I had something to prove, raising three daughters on my own. I wanted to give you the kind of life where you never had to struggle the way I did."

Tami swallowed past the lump in her throat. "I know, Mama. But sometimes, it feels like you don't believe I can stand on my own two feet." Her voice trembled. "And after last night, I'm not sure I can either."

Rachel Rose reached for her, and Tami didn't resist. A sob broke free as she leaned into her mother's embrace, her mother's arms strong and warm around her. The weight of the lie she had carried was finally gone, replaced by the tentative hope of healing.

Yet, as she clung to her mother, a new fear lodged itself deep in her chest. The way she had pushed Aiden away last night—the finality in her words, the hurt in his eyes—she hadn't just ended their fake engagement.

She might have ended them.

Their friendship. Their late-night record store hunts. The easy way he could make her laugh even on her worst days.

She had told herself she was protecting them both. That it was better to cut things off before she got in too deep. But now, with the cold reality settling in, she wondered if she had made the worst mistake of all.

Maybe she had lost Aiden forever.

CHAPTER SIXTEEN

AIDEN GLANCED AT the door, half-expecting his mother to walk in and tell him breakfast was ready, just like she used to. Instead, he had called her into the room, hoping for something he wasn't sure he deserved: understanding.

When Madelyn stepped inside, her presence was as steadying as it had always been. She was a woman of quiet strength, her calm demeanor a contrast to the storm inside him.

She closed the door softly behind her and settled down at the edge of his bed. "What's going on, son?" she asked, her voice laced with concern.

Aiden exhaled sharply, dragging a hand through his locs. "I...need to tell you something. And it's not easy."

Madelyn tilted her head, her brow furrowing. "Take your time."

He stood abruptly, his nerves a live wire under his skin. He paced to the window, shoving his hands into his pockets as if to keep them from trembling. The street below was quiet, the kind of stillness that felt mocking when your world was anything but. The words he needed to say churned in his chest, too tangled and too big to force out all at once.

Finally, he turned to his mother. "Tami and I… we've been pretending to be engaged."

The admission landed in the room like a blow, and Aiden braced himself. His mother's eyes widened slightly, the flicker of surprise passing quickly. But she didn't say a word, wouldn't interrupt, and that quiet patience somehow made it harder to continue.

He exhaled sharply, dragging a hand through his hair. "It started as a favor to her. She was feeling pressured by her mom, and she asked me to help her. It seemed harmless at first, like something we'd laugh about later. But it's not harmless. Not anymore. We never wanted anyone to get hurt, least of all you." His words had sped up, tumbling over each other in his rush to explain. "The plan was to get through the holidays and then call it off. Things would just…go back to normal. At least, that's what we told ourselves. But now I don't believe that anymore."

Madelyn leaned forward, her hands clasped tightly in her lap. "Anymore?" she repeated, her voice gentle but steady. "What do you mean when you say that?"

Aiden turned away from her probing gaze, dropping back onto the couch as if his legs could no longer hold him up. He pressed his hands to his face, wishing he could hide from the truth of it all. "Because somewhere along the way, it stopped feeling fake to me," he admitted, his voice barely above a whisper. The words burned as they left him, raw and unforgiving. "I've fallen in love with her, Mom."

Saying it out loud should have felt like a relief, but instead, it left Aiden hollow, exposed. His hands fell from his face, and he looked at her feeling weighed down with his emotions. "I texted her earlier. She was on her way to her mom's house. I assume she's telling her the truth right now. I'm terrified of how it's going to turn out—for her, for me, for us. I think I might have ruined everything."

Madelyn's expression softened, but she remained quiet, letting him pour out what he'd been holding inside for far too long.

"Our friendship…the trust we had…" His voice cracked, and he shook his head. "There's something she's been dealing with for years—something big—and she didn't trust me enough to tell me. And there's something I've been keeping from her, too." His throat tightened, and he swallowed hard, the vulnerability of his own shortcomings clawing at him. "What does that say about us? About me? How can I love her this much and still feel like I've failed her?"

Madelyn reached out, placing a hand on his arm. "It says you're human, Aiden. It says you care so much about her that you're scared of making mistakes. That's not failure—that's love. Messy, complicated, and imperfect love."

Her words were a balm, but they couldn't chase away all his doubts. Aiden shook his head, his jaw tight. "But what if it's not enough?"

Madelyn's grip on his arm tightened slightly, a quiet reassurance. "You won't know until you try. Love isn't about getting it all right from the start. It's about being willing to fight for it, to learn from your mistakes, and to show up even when it's hard."

He turned to look at her, his eyes glassy with unshed tears. "And what if she doesn't feel the same?"

Her gaze held his, unwavering and steady. "Then you'll know you were honest about your feelings. You can't control how Tami will respond, but you owe it to yourself—and to her—to be truthful. If you love her, don't let fear keep you from saying so. If anything, honesty is what strengthens real relationships."

Her words settled deep within him, stirring something fragile but determined. He nodded, though his heart still felt heavy. He didn't know what the future held, but for the first time in days, a small spark of hope flickered in the chaos of his emotions.

Madelyn gave his hand a gentle squeeze. "You've known Tami for years? That kind of bond doesn't just disappear. It's okay to be afraid, but don't let that fear stop you from telling her how you feel. You deserve to be happy. And she deserves to know the truth."

"I don't know if she feels the same way," he admitted. "There were times I thought she might, but I could be wrong."

"And if she doesn't return your feelings…" Madelyn said gently. "Then you'll know, and you'll deal with it. But if you don't take the chance, you'll always wonder. And that's a different kind of pain."

Aiden nodded slowly, her words sinking in. He still felt raw, exposed, but also a little lighter. His mother's unwavering support gave him the courage to think about what he needed to do next.

As they sat in the quiet room, he leaned into her embrace, grateful for her wisdom and love. He didn't know how things with Tami would turn out. But whatever happened, he wouldn't let fear hold him back any longer.

THAT EVENING, THE soft glow of the restaurant's chandeliers cast a warm light across the table, reflecting off the delicate china and polished silverware. Rachel Rose took a small sip of her wine, its crispness grounding her in the present moment.

Across from her sat Daniel, his salt-and-pepper hair neatly combed, his smile easy and genuine. His dark suit fit him impeccably, a testament to his understated elegance. She caught herself smiling at his story about a mishap with his dog, Barkley, and she leaned in just slightly, feeling the pull of his charm.

"So, there I was," Daniel said, chuckling, "chasing a muddy golden retriever through the neighborhood in my socks. It was like something out of a sitcom."

Rachel Rose laughed, the sound surprising her with its lightness. It had been years since she'd felt this comfortable, this entertained in someone else's company.

"And did you catch him?" she asked, her voice teasing.

"Eventually," Daniel admitted, raising his glass. "But not before I gave the neighbors a good show."

She clinked her glass lightly against his, feeling the gentle warmth of the wine spreading through her chest. But as the laughter faded, a quiet ache settled in. A part of her remained elsewhere, stuck in the events of the past twenty-four hours.

She had lost a future she'd already started dreaming about.

Not just the fake engagement—that was a small part of it. But Aiden. The way he looked at Tami when he thought no one was watching. The way Tami had softened around him, the way they fit together so seamlessly. The quiet hope she hadn't even realized she'd been holding on to had shattered with Tami's confession. It was a lie. All of it. And worse—her daughter had felt the need to lie to her in the first place.

Had she pushed Tami too hard? Had she made Tami feel like she had something to prove? Like she couldn't come to her mother, couldn't be honest with her?

She took another sip of wine, ignoring the tightness in her chest.

"Rachel Rose," Daniel said, his tone gentle, "I hope I'm not overstepping by saying this, but it's really nice to see you laugh."

Her heart gave a small, unexpected flutter. She glanced down at her hands, suddenly feeling vulnerable under his kind gaze. "Thank you," she murmured, her voice quieter now. "It's been a long time since…" She let the sentence trail off, unwilling to bring the past into this moment.

Daniel seemed to understand. "Since you let yourself enjoy something?" he offered gently.

She nodded, meeting his eyes again. There was no pity there, only understanding. Daniel, too, had lost his spouse—a fact that both drew her to him and made her wary. Falling for someone again felt like treading on sacred ground, a betrayal of what she'd shared with Henry. But as she looked at Daniel, she wondered: Was it possible to honor her past while opening her heart to the future?

Their conversation flowed easily as dinner progressed. He spoke about his late wife, Lydia, with a reverence that mirrored her own memories of

Henry. It comforted her, knowing he understood the delicate balance between cherishing what was and embracing what could be.

And yet, even as she laughed and sipped her wine, her mind drifted back to Tami. To Aiden. To what could have been.

As they finished their meal, Daniel glanced at his watch. "We should head out soon if we don't want to miss the opening act."

Rachel Rose nodded, a small spark of excitement breaking through her trepidation. "I haven't seen *The Nutcracker* in years. It used to be a family tradition."

"Same here," Daniel said as he stood and helped her with her coat. His touch was light, respectful, but it lingered just long enough to make her pulse quicken.

"My late wife, Lydia, loved it," he continued, adjusting his own coat. "Every December, we'd take our son to see it—no matter where we were, no matter how busy life got. He'd pretend to be bored, of course, but I know he secretly enjoyed it."

Rachel Rose smiled at the warmth in his voice. "And where is he now?"

"San Francisco. He's a cardiologist—married with twins who keep them on their toes. With his hectic schedule and family life, they don't make it back east as often as I'd like."

Daniel's expression softened, a quiet longing

flickering in his eyes—one Rachel Rose recognized all too well. "But they're happy, and that's what matters. This year, they're spending Christmas with the in-laws, but we had Thanksgiving together, which was nice."

She nodded, understanding that mix of pride and distance all too well. "You must miss them."

"I do," he admitted, then turned to her with an easy smile. "But that's what visits—and video calls filled with toddler chaos—are for."

Rachel Rose chuckled, letting the warmth of the moment settle around her.

The theater was alive with the hum of anticipation when they arrived, the ornate hall decorated with garlands and ribbons. Rachel Rose allowed herself to be swept up in the festive atmosphere, the scent of pine and the sound of a string quartet tuning their instruments pulling her further from her doubts.

As the lights dimmed and the overture began, Rachel Rose stole a glance at Daniel. His profile was illuminated by the soft glow of the stage, his expression one of quiet contentment. She felt a pang of longing—not just for what she'd lost, but for what she might find again.

Through the first act, her emotions swirled. The dancers' graceful movements and the familiar strains of Tchaikovsky's score stirred memories of past Decembers, of Henry holding her hand in the very same theater.

Yet tonight, Daniel's presence beside her was a comforting anchor. When he leaned over during intermission to whisper a witty observation about the Mouse King's oversized crown, she found herself laughing again.

By the time the final curtain fell, Rachel Rose's heart felt lighter, though her mind remained a maze of conflicting emotions.

As they exited the theater, Daniel turned to her. "Care for a walk?"

The air outside was crisp but not biting, and she nodded.

They strolled through the historic streets of Charleston, the cobblestones uneven beneath their feet. The city's charm enveloped them, gas lamps casting a warm glow and wreaths adorning the doors of centuries-old homes.

"This was wonderful," Rachel Rose said, breaking the comfortable silence. "Thank you for inviting me."

"Thank you for saying yes," Daniel replied, his tone sincere. "I know this isn't easy for either of us."

She stopped walking and turned to face him. "No, it's not," she admitted. "I keep wondering if it's even fair…to you, to my daughters, to Henry."

Daniel stepped closer, his expression earnest. "Rachel Rose, loving someone new doesn't erase the love you had. It doesn't diminish it. If anything, it honors it by showing how much you've learned about what matters."

His words struck a chord, echoing thoughts she'd been too afraid to fully articulate. Could she allow herself this chance? Could she trust her heart again, knowing the risks?

As they resumed walking, Rachel Rose felt the stirrings of hope. Daniel's hand brushed hers briefly, and though he didn't take it, the gesture lingered like a promise. For the first time in years, she wondered if it was possible to find joy, not as a replacement for what she'd lost, but as a testament to the resilience of the human heart.

SUNDAY MORNING, AIDEN parked his car in front of Tami's condo, his heart pounding so hard he swore it echoed in the silence of the car. The drive over had been a blur, his mind consumed by what he was about to do. For the past couple of days, he'd avoided this moment—the one where he would lay his heart bare, with no idea if she would accept it or break it.

The text from Tami had come just as he was summoning the courage to call her. Seeing her name light up his screen had sent a jolt through him. She wanted to talk. Face-to-face. There was something in her message—a vulnerability that mirrored his own turmoil—that told him this wasn't just about mending their friendship. It was about something more.

Taking a deep breath, Aiden stepped out of the car and walked up to her door. The condo, with its cheerful pots of flowers on the porch and the wreath she always hung out front, felt like a second home. He hesitated for a moment before knocking, his fist hovering over the wood. When the door opened, Tami stood there, her expression a mixture of anxiety and hope.

"Hey," she said softly, stepping aside to let him in.

"Hey," he replied, his voice equally quiet. The scent of fresh bread and herbs wafted through the air, but the table set with sandwiches and salad felt like an afterthought to the charged atmosphere between them.

"I made lunch," she said, gesturing to the table. "But honestly, I don't think either of us is here for the food."

Aiden chuckled, the tension easing slightly. "You're probably right."

They moved to the couch instead, sitting close but not touching. For a moment, neither of them spoke, the weight of unspoken words filling the space between them. Finally, Tami broke the silence.

"I've been doing a lot of thinking," she began, her voice trembling slightly. "About everything. About us. And I... I just want to say I'm sorry. For the argument, for dragging you into the fake engagement, for everything. I hate the thought that I might have ruined our friendship."

Aiden's chest tightened. "Tami, you didn't ruin anything," he said firmly. "If anything, I'm the one who should apologize. I wasn't honest with you. With myself."

She looked at him, her eyes wide with curiosity and a hint of fear. "What do you mean?"

This was it. The moment he'd been dreading and longing for in equal measure. He took a deep breath, running a hand through his hair before meeting her gaze.

"When we started this whole fake engagement thing, I thought I was just helping out a friend," he said. "But somewhere along the way, it stopped feeling fake for me. I… I've fallen for you, Tami. Completely. And it's been tearing me apart, not knowing how you feel or if I've ruined everything by keeping this to myself."

Tami's breath hitched, her hands clenching the fabric of her jeans. "Aiden…"

He held up a hand. "Let me finish. I know this might change everything. And if you don't feel the same way, I'll respect that. But I couldn't keep it to myself anymore. I had to tell you."

For a moment, the room was silent except for the faint ticking of the clock on the wall. Then Tami reached out, placing a trembling hand on his.

"I'm glad you told me," she said softly. "Because I've been feeling the same way. I just didn't know how to say it. Or if I should."

Aiden held her gaze. "Tami, you can tell me anything. And I want you to know that you could've told me about the social anxiety."

She let out a slow breath. "I thought I could just push through, but I'm realizing I need help. I'm going to start therapy."

Aiden brushed a curl from her cheek. "You don't have to do this alone. Just so we're clear—you're not weak. Not to me."

Tami squeezed his hand. "Thank you."

He hesitated, then exhaled. "I got a promotion at work. However, the position will relocate me to Charleston."

Tami tensed. "And?"

"I haven't accepted it." His eyes searched hers. "I don't want to make this decision without thinking it through—without considering what I'd be leaving behind…and what I'd be coming back to."

She tightened her grip on his hand. The mess between them wasn't fully untangled, but for the first time in weeks, it felt like they were moving toward something real.

"Okay," she said. "Then let's talk about it, but first… Aiden, I have to be completely honest with you. You've been my best friend for so long. And this fake engagement…it made me realize how much more you mean to me. How much I care about you. I think I've been in love with you for a while, but I was too scared to admit it. To you or to myself."

Aiden's hand tightened around hers, the weight of his fear lifting as joy filled its place. "Tami..."

Before he could say anything more, she leaned forward, her lips brushing against his in a tentative kiss. It was soft, hesitant, but it carried all the emotions they'd been holding back. When they pulled apart, Aiden rested his forehead against hers, a smile spreading across his face.

"So, where do we go from here?" he asked, his voice filled with hope.

Tami smiled, her hand still in his. "I guess we'll figure that part out together."

Aiden finally felt like everything was exactly the way it was meant to be.

CHAPTER SEVENTEEN

TAMI STIRRED AWAKE, the soft warmth of the morning settling around her as she lay in bed, the quiet stillness of the room enveloping her. She blinked a few times, letting the memory of the previous day wash over her. Aiden's words echoed in her mind: *This isn't fake for me anymore, Tami.* She pressed a hand to her chest, as if to steady the fluttering that began there. For so long, she had tried to convince herself that her feelings for Aiden were manageable, containable. But now, she didn't have to. He felt the same way.

The realization brought a giddy sort of disbelief, like the kind she'd felt as a child waking up on Christmas morning. Yet beneath the joy lurked a quiet hum of anxiety. Could they truly navigate this shift in their relationship without jeopardizing the deep friendship that had been their foundation?

She slipped out of bed and padded to the kitchen, brewing a pot of coffee as she replayed their conversation from the day before. She could still see the earnestness in Aiden's eyes, hear the vulnerability in his voice as he admitted his feelings. It had been both exhilarating and terrifying to hear him say the words she'd secretly longed for. But what if they were wrong? What if stepping into this uncharted territory ended up hurting them both?

"Stop overthinking," she muttered to herself, pouring coffee into her favorite mug. She took a sip, savoring the warmth, and resolved to focus on the present. For the first time in years, she was looking forward to Christmas, and she wouldn't let her fears overshadow that.

Later that afternoon, Tami arrived at her mother's house for their planned lunch.

Rachel Rose greeted her at the door with a warm smile and an even warmer hug. "You look radiant, darling," her mother said, stepping back to study her face. "Is there something you're not telling me?"

Tami laughed lightly, brushing past her mother into the cozy kitchen that smelled of rosemary and baked bread. "Let's just say it's been an eventful couple of days."

Rachel Rose arched an eyebrow but didn't press further as she finished setting the table. The two women sat down to a simple but elegant spread of roasted chicken, salad, and fresh rolls. They chatted about the usual things—work, family, and Christmas—before Rachel Rose leaned forward, her expression tinged with curiosity.

"So, are you going to ask me about my date with Daniel, or do I have to volunteer the information?"

Tami's eyes sparkled with amusement. "I didn't want to pry. But since you brought it up...how did it go?"

Rachel Rose's cheeks flushed ever so slightly, a telltale sign that the date had gone well. "It was lovely," she admitted. "He's a wonderful man. Thoughtful, kind, and..." She hesitated, searching for the right words. "He makes me feel something I didn't think I'd feel again after your father."

Tami reached across the table to squeeze her mother's hand. "I'm so happy for you, Mom. You deserve this."

Rachel Rose's gaze softened. "Thank you, sweetheart. But enough about me. What about you? How are things with Aiden?"

Tami's heart skipped a beat. She hadn't anticipated this moment so soon, but there was no reason to hold back now. "We..." She paused, choosing her words carefully. "We've decided to explore our feelings for each other. It's still new, but I think... I think it could be something really special."

Rachel Rose's smile was immediate and genuine. "Oh, Tami, that's wonderful. I've always known you and Aiden belonged together. I've seen the way he looks at you. You two have something rare."

Tami's cheeks warmed at her mother's words.

"I'm just...trying to take it one day at a time. But for the first time in a long time, I'm actually excited for Christmas."

Rachel Rose's smile deepened, and she reached for her daughter's hand again. "I'm proud of you, Tami. For being brave enough to follow your heart."

As they finished eating, Tami felt a sense of peace settle over her. The tangled web of emotions and uncertainties that had consumed her for weeks now seemed a little less daunting.

With her mother's blessing and Aiden's confession still fresh in her mind, she allowed herself to hope—for love, for happiness, and for a future she hadn't dared to dream of until now.

AIDEN ADJUSTED THE lapel of his jacket as he strode through the polished halls of the Polk Island Hotel, his footsteps echoing softly against the marble floors. Overhead, a grand chandelier glittered like a cascade of stars, bathing the richly adorned lobby in a warm, golden light. With Christmas just two days away, the hotel radiated holiday cheer—from the towering tree in the corner adorned with red and gold ornaments to the intricately crafted gingerbread village proudly displayed near the reception desk.

For as long as Aiden could remember, his family's Christmas luncheon had been a cherished tradition, bringing together the hotel staff, their families, and close friends. This year, though, it felt more significant, more personal.

He turned a corner and stepped into the private dining room where preparations were underway. The long tables were already covered with crisp white linens, and an assortment of red and green floral centerpieces dotted the room.

Servers bustled about, arranging silverware and lighting candles, their chatter blending with the faint strains of holiday music filtering through the speakers. This would be the perfect setting to bring Tami and her family into his world.

Aiden pulled out his phone, his thumb hovering over Tami's name in his call log. They'd been in such a good place since their heartfelt conversation. Her willingness to explore their feelings for one another had buoyed his spirits in a way he hadn't felt in years. Still, a faint sliver of nervousness crept in as he tapped her number and held the phone to his ear.

"Hey, Aiden," Tami's voice came through, warm and familiar, and it eased some of the tension knotting his shoulders.

"Hey yourself," he said, a grin spreading across his face. "How's your day going?"

"Not bad," she replied. "Just finished up some errands. What about you?"

"Well," he began, leaning casually against a chair, "I have a proposition for you."

There was a pause on the other end of the line,

followed by a light laugh. "Okay, now I'm curious. What's this about?"

"The luncheon for the employees," he said. "I want you and your family to join us this year."

Tami was silent for a moment, and Aiden wondered if she might decline.

Then she spoke, her tone tinged with both surprise and warmth. "You want us to come to a staff dinner?"

"I do," he said earnestly. "It's a big event, but it's also about community and family. Plus," he added with a playful lilt, "I happen to know Santa's making a special appearance."

Tami laughed, and the sound was like a melody in his ears. "Well, how can I say no to Santa?"

"Exactly," Aiden said, chuckling. "But seriously, Tami, it would mean a lot to me to have you there."

"I'll talk to my mom and sisters," she promised. "It sounds wonderful. Thank you for inviting us."

They chatted for a few more minutes before hanging up, and Aiden slid his phone back into his pocket, his heart lighter than it had been all day. He glanced around the room, imagining Tami and her family here among the warmth and laughter, and for the first time, he felt a genuine sense of anticipation for Christmas Eve.

CHRISTMAS EVE ARRIVED, draped in the enchantment that only the holiday season could bring. It was an evening steeped in cherished traditions, yet alive with the quiet anticipation of fresh starts and unspoken possibilities.

Aiden stood near the entrance, his posture relaxed but purposeful as he greeted guests, offering his signature grin and quick words of welcome. His family had always made a big deal of this dinner—an annual tradition that brought together those who were most important to them: friends, colleagues, and, tonight, the people who filled the voids in his life in ways he'd never expected.

His mother, Madelyn, was already inside, her ever-present energy alive as she chatted animatedly with some of the staff's children. She wasn't just his mother tonight; she was the heartbeat of the event, ensuring everything went smoothly with a sharp eye for detail and a soft touch of love.

The scent of roasted turkey, honey-glazed ham, and spiced cider hung in the air, a welcoming embrace for anyone stepping into the space. It was the kind of warm, homey smell that made him think of his childhood—the kind of scents that felt like safety, love, and everything good about home.

The sound of carolers performing in the lobby added another layer to the atmosphere, their soft harmonies floating toward him, mingling with the voices of arriving guests. Each note seemed to remind him of everything that was good about this night: peace, joy, connection.

But when the doors opened again, and Tami

walked in with her family, everything else seemed to fade into the background.

Aiden's breath caught, an involuntary reaction to her presence. She looked like something out of a dream. Radiant in a deep green dress that seemed to catch the light in all the right ways, it highlighted the warmth of her skin. Her short hair lay in soft waves, effortlessly framing her face. She had the kind of beauty that made him feel like he couldn't breathe—like the world had tilted ever so slightly, and he was seeing everything for the first time.

Behind her, her mother, Rachel Rose, and her sisters, Samantha and Naomi, followed closely, their bright smiles lighting up the room in a way that only a close-knit family could.

Aiden felt his heart skip a beat at the sight of Tami and her family—how they carried themselves with grace, how they laughed so freely, how they fit into this moment as though they had always belonged. He couldn't help but step forward, a smile spreading across his face as he caught her eye.

"You made it," he said, his voice thick with relief, joy, and something deeper he couldn't quite name yet.

Tami's response was instant, her eyes sparkling with that infectious energy he couldn't resist. "We wouldn't miss it."

Her voice was a melody of warmth, and as she

spoke, he realized how much he had missed hearing it, how much he had missed her presence in his life. She was more than just a part of the evening now. She was an integral part of everything that made this night so perfect.

Aiden greeted her family warmly, his mind still reeling from the moment of seeing her walk through the door. Tami had a way of making everything seem effortless. She wasn't just here as his date; she was here as someone who belonged in his life, someone who brought with her a new sense of possibility.

He ushered them into the room, his hand resting gently on Tami's lower back as they navigated through the bustling crowd. The lively chatter and infectious laughter created a vibrant energy, weaving through the air like a familiar melody. Her family mingled seamlessly with his family and the hotel staff, while children darted around with treats and drinks in hand, their joy lighting up the room.

The warmth of familial love wrapped around Aiden like a comforting embrace, yet there was something else—a presence he couldn't ignore. He felt it in the way the laughter resonated, in the faint smell of spiced cider that seemed to hang near the fireplace, and in the glimmer of light reflecting off the ornaments on the tree. It was as though his father's spirit lingered in the room. The connection and belonging Aiden always felt at these gatherings now pulsed with an unspoken depth, stirring something new and achingly familiar in his heart.

As the evening wore on, Aiden found his eyes continually drawn to Tami. She was radiant. He watched as she made the rounds, greeting people with her usual kindness, and even helping a group of children build marshmallow snowmen near the hot cocoa station. It was a simple thing, but watching her, seeing the joy in the kids' faces as they crowded around her, made something inside him tighten in an entirely unfamiliar way. She wasn't just beautiful. She was nurturing, warm, and full of life. It made his heart swell with a yearning he hadn't realized was there.

Seeing her like this—happy, entirely herself—made him feel like he was watching someone who was meant to be part of his life. There was a quiet certainty in that moment, a voice inside him that whispered that this could be something real, something lasting.

When dinner was served, Aiden guided Tami and her family to a table near the center of the room, his fingers brushing against hers as they walked. The closeness felt natural, but it also made his heart race in a way he couldn't ignore. He settled them in, his hands moving to arrange the napkins just so, a nervous energy buzzing just beneath the surface.

Plates were passed, glasses clinked in toasts,

and he found himself stealing glances at her throughout the evening. The conversation around them felt like a blur, a hum of voices that faded in and out. All he could focus on was her—the way she looked across the table at him, her smile soft and knowing, the way her eyes sparkled when they caught his. It was as though they were the only two people in the room, as though everything else had fallen away.

The staff gathered in the corner, a slight buzz of excitement filling the air as children lined up to sit on Santa's lap. Aiden and Tami exchanged a look, their shared smile a silent understanding. As Santa handed them their sack of gifts to distribute, Tami leaned in. "Let's do this," she said, her voice low but full of energy.

They were Santa's helpers tonight, giving out presents to the staff and their children. Aiden had imagined this part of the evening as one of the highlights—this small act of generosity felt like it wrapped everything the Worthington family stood for into one gesture. There was something deeply fulfilling about watching the children's faces light up as they received their presents, and Aiden couldn't help but look at Tami as they handed out gifts, watching the joy on her face mirror that of the children.

When the last gift was handed out, Aiden felt a surge of warmth in his chest—more than just from the laughter and the holiday cheer, more than the joy of giving. It was the feeling of a future taking root, and as they finished their duties, Tami turned to him, her eyes alight with the same quiet certainty he felt. She smiled that soft, knowing smile again.

In that moment, Aiden realized this was the start of something bigger. Something real. Something with Tami. And for the first time in a long while, he could see the future stretching out before him—clear, bright, and full of possibilities. With her by his side, he was ready to take every step.

CHAPTER EIGHTEEN

THE GRAND BALLROOM shimmered with holiday cheer, its high ceilings draped with sparkling garlands and twinkling lights, casting a soft golden glow over the bustling room. Children's excited chatter and the rustling of wrapping paper filled the air as the kids tore into their gifts from Santa, their faces alight with the kind of joy only the magic of Christmas could bring.

Tami smiled at the sight, her heart warmed by the laughter and merriment that seemed to spread through the room like a contagious spark.

But despite the festive scene unfolding around her, Tami's attention was fixed elsewhere.

Across the room, near the tall Christmas tree with its glowing ornaments, she saw him.

Aiden.

Tami stood quietly by the edge of the room, her gaze fixed on Aiden as he crouched beside his niece, Bella, patiently guiding her small hands through the intricate steps of assembling her toy. His deep, calming voice carried a steady rhythm, filled with encouragement and warmth. There was a confidence to him, an unshakable steadiness that seemed to radiate from the core of who he was. Watching him in this unguarded moment, Tami felt a surge of emotion she wasn't entirely prepared for.

He had always been good with people—kind, reliable, a steady hand in a storm—but this was different. This was Aiden in a light she hadn't fully allowed herself to see before. The way he interacted with his niece wasn't just playful or dutiful. It was deeply intentional, as though he understood how much every word, every gesture, meant to her. And Tami felt it too—felt the way he saw people, really saw them.

Her heart tightened as an ache rose in her chest, one she couldn't quite ignore anymore.

She'd spent so much of their friendship holding herself back, pushing away what was growing between them. Even during their fake engagement, she'd told herself it was temporary, a convenient arrangement for the holidays. But now? Now, they weren't pretending anymore. Somewhere along the way, their story had shifted, and now they were officially a couple—a thought that left her both exhilarated and quietly terrified.

Their transition from friendship to romance felt natural, like something inevitable finally falling into place. And yet, it was also new, fragile in its early days. The foundation they'd built over years of shared laughter, mutual trust, and unspoken support felt solid, but the leap into this new chapter was still tinged with uncertainty. Would it last? Could they grow into something that was as real and enduring as she hoped?

As if sensing her thoughts, London appeared at her side, her presence as calm and assured as ever. "He's great with her," she said softly, her gaze fixed on her brother.

Tami followed London's eyes, watching as Aiden stood, lifting his niece into his arms. The little girl giggled, her tiny arms wrapped tightly around his neck.

The sight tugged at her heart, a bittersweet mixture of joy and longing. "Yes, he is," she said, her voice quiet.

London turned to her, a small knowing smile playing on her lips. "He's always been great with kids. Always had a way of making them feel safe." She paused, her expression shifting to something gentler. "He has a way of making you feel that too, doesn't he?"

Tami met London's gaze, feeling her cheeks warm. "He does," she admitted, her voice barely above a whisper. "You should see him with my niece, Summer. She adores him."

"I've always thought you and Aiden were perfect for each other," London said, her tone both teasing and earnest. "I could never figure out why it took you so long to see it too."

Tami laughed softly, though the sound was

tinged with nervousness. "It's funny, isn't it? How things just...happen when they're meant to."

"Exactly," London agreed, her smile widening. "And I'm glad you're finally here—together. You make him happy, Tami. Really happy."

The words settled into Tami's heart, warming her in a way she couldn't quite explain. "I hope so," she said softly. "Because he makes me happy too."

London reached out, giving her arm a light squeeze. "You're good for each other. And whatever comes next, I know the two of you will figure it out."

As London stepped away to join the rest of the family, Tami turned her attention back to Aiden. He was spinning his niece in a playful circle now, her laughter ringing through the room. The sound seemed to dissolve the last of Tami's hesitation, leaving only a quiet, certain hope.

Whatever uncertainties lay ahead, she believed in what they had—believed in the foundation their friendship had built. And now, as they stood on the edge of something new, she let herself imagine the future she'd once been too afraid to hope for. Her future. Their future. Together.

The night was alive with the sounds of carols and laughter. The air inside the venue felt like it had been plucked from a holiday postcard—twinkling lights and decorations that reminded Aiden of every Christmas he had ever known, but with a twist. The glow of the room wasn't just from the soft golden bulbs strung across the ceiling or the trees adorned with ornaments that sparkled with every passing moment. The real light in the room came from something deeper—something he had been afraid to acknowledge for so long.

Aiden's breath caught as his eyes found Tami across the room. She was chatting with his mother, Madelyn, laughter spilling from her lips, the kind of laugh that made you feel like you were in on a joke, even if you didn't know the punchline. He watched as she tipped her head back, her hair cascading around her shoulders like a wave of warmth, and it hit him all over again. He loved her.

There was no question about it anymore. He had spent so much time convincing himself that they were just friends, that their connection could be explained away, but the truth had slipped in without him even realizing it. It wasn't just the way she made him laugh or how she could finish his sentences. It wasn't the way she knew exactly how to calm him when his stress spiraled out of control, or how her touch made his heart race, even when it was just a simple hand on his arm. It was everything—the way she made him feel like he could finally be himself, like he was enough just as he was.

And tonight, with the room full of people who meant everything to him, with the soft hum of holiday cheer all around them, he knew it was time. It was time for him to stop pretending that he wasn't terrified of this next step, of making this real. Time for him to take the leap and show her that he wasn't afraid anymore. That he knew what he wanted, and it was her.

He glanced over at the table where the children were gathering, their excited chatter echoing in the room. He could hear Santa's jolly voice booming from the stage as he greeted the kids, spreading holiday magic like only he could. Aiden smiled to himself, his heart swelling.

This wasn't just a holiday dinner. This was the moment that would change everything for him and Tami.

Tami had come into his life like a sudden gust of wind, sweeping him off his feet, shaking everything up. He had fought it for so long, tried to tell himself that their fake engagement—something they'd come up with in a moment of silliness—was just a passing phase. That it didn't mean anything. But as time passed, and as they grew closer, that temporary plan had blossomed into something undeniable.

Aiden decided that here, amidst the glow of twinkling string lights and the hum of laughter that rippled through the room, surrounded by the people who had shaped their lives, this was it—the perfect moment. The warmth of the season enveloped everything; the kind of atmosphere that made everything feel possible. This wasn't just another holiday gathering; it was their gathering, their families united under one roof for a night that already felt steeped in magic. And Aiden knew he couldn't let this moment slip away.

He stood near the edge of the room, his gaze flickering to Tami as she mingled effortlessly with her family. She looked radiant tonight, her laughter ringing out like music, her cheeks flushed with joy. The way she tilted her head as she listened intently to her sister's story—it was a little thing, but it sent a pang through his chest. She didn't know what he had planned. Not yet.

"Hey, you good?" The familiar voice cut through his thoughts, and Aiden turned to find his younger sister, Cia, at his side. Her face was lit with an easy smile, as it always was, her energy bright enough to pull anyone out of their thoughts. But she wasn't fooled by his forced calm.

"Yeah," he replied after a beat too long, forcing a smile that didn't quite reach his eyes. "Just...a lot to take in tonight."

Cia arched an eyebrow and studied him. She'd always had this uncanny ability to see right through him, peeling back layers he tried to keep hidden. "Aiden," she said softly, tilting her head in that way that made him feel like he was being studied. "What's going on? I can tell that you're up to something."

He glanced away briefly. "It's nothing," he murmured, though the words sounded hollow even to him. "Just nerves, I guess."

"Nerves?" she echoed, folding her arms and leaning slightly closer. Her voice dropped just enough so no one else could hear them over the conversations in the room. "You've never been nervous about anything in your life. Come on, spill it."

There was no point in hiding it from her—not Cia. He sighed and rubbed the back of his neck, feeling the tension there like a coiled spring. "It's Tami," he admitted finally, his voice barely above a whisper.

Her expression softened instantly, and something tender flickered in her eyes. "I knew it," she said with a grin that held both amusement and affection. "You're going to formally propose, are you?"

He nodded slowly, his throat tightening again as if even admitting it aloud made the whole thing more real. "I have the ring," he confessed, his hand instinctively brushing against his pocket where the small box rested like an anchor.

Cia's smile widened into something brighter—almost proud—and she reached out to squeeze his arm reassuringly. "You've got this," she said firmly, her voice brimming with conviction. "We all knew she was the perfect woman for you. You just had to realize it for yourself. I'm so happy for you."

Aiden swallowed hard as her words sank in. His gaze drifted back toward Tami across the room. God, she was beautiful. And Cia was right—somewhere deep down, he'd always known what he wanted.

"I don't know what I'd do without her," he admitted quietly, almost as though saying it aloud could make it less terrifying to think about. His chest constricted at the thought—at the idea that there could be a future where she wasn't by his side. "I don't think I've ever told her that."

"You don't have to tell her," Cia replied softly but firmly. "Tami knows already." She paused for a moment before adding with a teasing glint in her eye, "But maybe tonight's your chance to remind her anyway."

Aiden let out a shaky laugh at that, feeling some of the tension begin to ebb away under his sister's unwavering support. He met her gaze again and nodded resolutely this time. "You're right," he said simply but with newfound determination.

Aiden's eyes instinctively sought out Tami once more, as though some magnetic pull drew him toward her. And when they found her again, everything else seemed to fade away. The noise of the party dulled into background static; the only thing that mattered was her. The way she moved through the room effortlessly, the way everyone around her seemed brighter just by being near her—it took his breath away.

The moment had come, and he was prepared. Every detail, every word, every movement had been carefully planned.

AIDEN GUIDED TAMI through the doors of the conference room, which had been transformed just for them. The soft glow of fairy lights twinkled overhead, casting a warm, intimate ambiance. Their parents followed closely behind, a comforting presence that brought some steadiness to his nerves.

"What are we doing in here?" Rachel Rose asked.

"Tonight, surrounded by the twinkling lights and the warmth of our mothers," Aiden began, his voice steady despite the whirlwind of emotions inside him, "I want to take this moment to share something important with all of you."

He paused, his heart racing in his chest as he felt Tami's gaze. The connection between them felt electric, as if time slowed, and the rest of the room faded into the background.

"Tami, from the moment I met you...back in the sixth grade, my world shifted. You brought light into my life when all I saw was darkness. Your laughter became the melody that filled my days, and your kindness showed me beauty in even the simplest moments."

His voice wavered slightly, but he pressed on. Tami's eyes shimmered with unshed tears, and her hand unconsciously reached out toward him. Seeing that small gesture made his heart swell with love.

Just then, Summer appeared at Tami's side, holding a bouquet of red roses. She handed them to her with a bright, innocent smile, the flowers blooming with symbolism. As Tami's fingers brushed the petals, the little girl then handed her a medium-sized box tied with a red ribbon.

Aiden smiled as Tami opened it, revealing her favorite peppermint bark.

"I know how much you love peppermint bark," he said, his voice thick with emotion. "It's a small thing, but it's something that reminds me of you—of everything you are."

Tami's lips curled into a soft, tearful smile as she looked up at him. Aiden knew he had her full attention, her heart open to what was to come next.

"You are my best friend, my confidante, and my greatest love," Aiden continued, his voice strong now, filled with all the emotion he had been holding back. "I want to spend every moment by your side, facing whatever challenges may come our way, together."

Madelyn and Rachel Rose both seemed to hold their breath as Aiden dropped to one knee.

He took Tami's hand in his, his gaze never wavering from hers.

"So, in front of our mothers and Summer," he

said, his heart pounding, "I ask you, Tami...will you marry me?"

The silence that followed felt endless, every heartbeat echoing in Aiden's ears as he waited for her answer. Time seemed to stretch, but the only thing that mattered in that moment was Tami's response.

"Yes..." she said. "Yes, I'll marry you, Aiden Worthington."

EPILOGUE

Six months later

THE DRESSING ROOM was filled with an electric sense of joy and anticipation. The air was warm, with a soft glow from the chandelier above creating a gentle ambiance. It felt like stepping into a dream, the kind of fairytale moment that Tami had always imagined for her mother. Today was Rachel Rose's wedding day—the woman who had been her rock, her heart, and her constant.

Tami stood in front of the mirror, adjusting the strapless bodice of her dress, her eyes briefly meeting her own reflection. The blush pink fabric shimmered slightly, soft and ethereal. The dress hugged her curves in just the right way, the lace bodice delicate and intricate with floral patterns that seemed to bloom as she moved. It was a flattering contrast to her deep, dark skin, and she couldn't help but feel beautiful in it. As Rachel Rose would say: a bridesmaid's dress was never just a dress—it was a symbol of the occasion, and this one, with its understated elegance, seemed to capture the essence of her mother's taste.

Tami reached for her engagement ring absentmindedly, her thumb gently brushing over the one carat diamond. A soft smile tugged at her lips as she thought of Aiden. He'd had the ring reset in a custom-designed band, a beautiful blend of rose gold and platinum, with delicate filigree detailing. It felt like a promise on her finger, the matching wedding band still to come.

At the end of the year, she and Aiden would have their own wedding on New Year's Eve. She could picture it—the soft music, the warm smiles, the moment when Aiden would stand at the altar, waiting for her to walk down the aisle to him. The thought made her heart flutter, as it always did when she imagined their future together. But today, it wasn't about her and Aiden. Today was about Rachel Rose—her mother. Tami felt the weight of the day, the joy and emotions that came with watching the woman who had given so much of herself finally find the love and happiness she deserved. Her mother had been so much better about respecting Tami's space and boundaries, and it meant the world to her that, this time, Tami could trust her with the wedding planning.

"Are you ready, Tami?" Naomi's voice interrupted her thoughts, pulling her back into the present.

Tami turned toward her sister, who was adjusting the mint green fabric of her own dress. Naomi looked radiant, her warm brown hair curled to perfection, her smile wide and full of excitement.

Naomi had been married for several years now, and Tami was sure that her sister's joy today wasn't just for their mother—it was a reminder of the love she had built with her own husband, and the joy of witnessing her mother's happiness reflected in her own.

"I'm ready, I think," Tami said softly, meeting Naomi's eyes in the mirror. "It's just... I've never seen Mom like this."

Naomi grinned and came over to stand beside her, her hand resting on Tami's shoulder. "I know. She's going to look beautiful, don't you think?"

Tami nodded, her eyes softening. "She always does. But today...there's something different about it."

"I can't wait to see the look on her face when she walks down the aisle," Naomi said, her voice filled with warmth. "I think this is going to be one of the happiest days of her life. She's blessed to have found love *twice*."

Tami agreed, but a part of her couldn't help but feel the weight of the day. Rachel Rose had been through so much in her life, so much pain and sacrifice. The years of raising them as a widowed mother, of pouring every bit of love she had into her children, had shaped her into the incredible woman Tami had always admired. Seeing her now, about to marry Daniel, made Tami's heart swell with emotion. It was a moment Rachel Rose never thought would come a second time, but here it was. And Tami couldn't be happier for her.

Samantha stepped into the room then, her presence a calming one. There was still a soft glow about her whenever she spoke of her own husband.

"You both look stunning," she said, her voice full of pride. She adjusted the lacy sleeves of her own dress, a soft lavender color that looked perfect against her skin. She was always the practical one, the steady one, but today even she couldn't hide the emotion in her voice.

"Thanks," Tami said, trying to keep the tears at bay as she smiled at Samantha through the mirror. "I keep thinking about how this is the moment Mom's been waiting for."

"I know," Samantha agreed, her smile softening. "She deserves this. After everything, she deserves a love like this."

"I don't think I'll ever be ready for this moment," Naomi said, her voice teasing but full of affection. "I mean, I know she's been through a lot, but it still feels surreal that she's actually about to marry Daniel."

Tami looked at Naomi and nodded. "It feels that way for me, too. Like I'm dreaming. But she's really going to do it. She's going to walk down that aisle today and make it official."

Samantha smiled warmly. "And she's going to be the most stunning bride we've ever seen."

Tami's heart swelled with pride. Her mother had always been stunning in her eyes. But today, she could feel something extra—a kind of glow, a light that had been dimmed for too long. She had always seen her mother as the epitome of strength and grace. Rachel Rose had never needed anything from anyone, always giving so much of herself to her children. But today, it was as if the world was giving her something back.

"I can't wait to see her," Tami said quietly, the words carrying a weight that she hadn't anticipated. She felt a rush of emotion surge within her, and she blinked back the tears that threatened to spill. She was proud of her mother, proud of the woman Rachel Rose had become—she was no longer interfering or trying to control Tami's life.

Naomi noticed the shift in her expression and nudged her gently with a smile. "Are you okay?" she asked softly.

Tami nodded, her lips curving into a tender smile. "I'm more than okay. I'm just…emotional. It's hard to believe that this day is finally here."

"I get it," Samantha said, her tone soft with understanding. "I think we all do."

They shared a quiet moment, each of them lost in their thoughts, in the shared bond of love and family that had shaped them all. It was in moments like this that Tami truly understood the depth of their connection. Her family—her mother, her sisters—were everything to her.

Tami's gaze fell again on the engagement ring glinting on her finger, and her heart seemed to pause.

She looked forward to wearing a wedding dress, to walk down the aisle and make promises of her own. Aiden had been patient with her, always steady, always sure, and every day she found herself falling a little deeper in love with him. She loved him in a way she hadn't known was possible.

Her thoughts were interrupted as the sound of soft footsteps echoed from the hallway, signaling that the time had come. A quiet knock at the door followed, and Tami's heart leapt. It was time.

"Are we ready?" Samantha asked, looking from Tami to Naomi. "Mama wants to see us."

"I think so," Tami replied softly, blinking away the moisture that had gathered in her eyes.

Naomi smiled, her eyes shining. "Let's go. She's waiting for us."

They stood together, taking one last look at themselves in the mirror before they walked out to support Rachel Rose as she stepped into the next chapter of her life.

As Tami watched her mother, beautiful and radiant in her wedding dress, preparing to walk down the aisle, a fresh wave of emotion washed over her. The sight was breathtaking—so full of love, commitment, and the promise of a new chapter.

Her thoughts were interrupted by another soft knock at the door. When she turned, Aiden stood there, his eyes filled with warmth.

"Hey, beautiful," he murmured, stepping into the room. "I just wanted a moment with you before everything begins."

Tami's heart swelled at the sight of him. "I'm glad you did," she whispered.

He reached for her hand, giving it a gentle squeeze. "I can't wait for our turn," he said, brushing a soft kiss against her lips. "This winter, it'll be you and me, standing together, ready to start our life as husband and wife."

A soft smile spread across her lips. "I can't wait either."

They lingered for just a moment, savoring the quiet intimacy between them before Samantha's voice broke through. "Come on, lovebirds, it's time."

Laughing softly, Tami gave Aiden's hand one last squeeze before following her sisters out into the venue. She took a deep breath, stepping forward to precede her mother down the aisle, the future bright ahead of her.

And just across the bridge in Charleston, where Aiden would soon be working, their future awaited—a life built on love, commitment, and the promise of all the tomorrows to come. They would make their home on the island, where their hearts belonged, creating a life together surrounded by family and the familiar comforts of home.

* * * * *

If you enjoyed
Fiancé Under the Mistletoe

Be sure to check out Shane and Ace's story,

His Carolina Redemption

*And more from the Polk Island series
by Jacquelin Thomas!*

Available now from Harlequin Heartwarming.

Discover more at Harlequin.com.

Get up to 4 Free Books!

We'll send you 2 free books from each series you try PLUS a free Mystery Gift.

FREE Value Over **$25**

Both the **Harlequin® Special Edition** and **Harlequin® Heartwarming**™ series feature compelling novels filled with stories of love and strength where the bonds of friendship, family and community unite.

YES! Please send me 2 FREE novels from the Harlequin Special Edition or Harlequin Heartwarming series and my FREE Gift (gift is worth about $10 retail). After receiving them, if I don't wish to receive any more books, I can return the shipping statement marked "cancel." If I don't cancel, I will receive 6 brand-new Harlequin Special Edition books every month and be billed just $6.39 each in the U.S. or $7.19 each in Canada, or 4 brand-new Harlequin Heartwarming Larger-Print books every month and be billed just $7.19 each in the U.S. or $7.99 each in Canada, a savings of 20% off the cover price. It's quite a bargain! Shipping and handling is just 50¢ per book in the U.S. and $1.25 per book in Canada.* I understand that accepting the 2 free books and gift places me under no obligation to buy anything. I can always return a shipment and cancel at any time by calling the number below. The free books and gift are mine to keep no matter what I decide.

Choose one:
- ☐ **Harlequin Special Edition** (235/335 BPA G36Y)
- ☐ **Harlequin Heartwarming Larger-Print** (161/361 BPA G36Y)
- ☐ **Or Try Both!** (235/335 & 161/361 BPA G36Z)

Name (please print)

Address   Apt. #

City   State/Province   Zip/Postal Code

Email: Please check this box ☐ if you would like to receive newsletters and promotional emails from Harlequin Enterprises ULC and its affiliates. You can unsubscribe anytime.

Mail to the Harlequin Reader Service:
IN U.S.A.: P.O. Box 1341, Buffalo, NY 14240-8531
IN CANADA: P.O. Box 603, Fort Erie, Ontario L2A 5X3

Want to explore our other series or interested in ebooks? Visit www.ReaderService.com or call 1-800-873-8635.

---

*Terms and prices subject to change without notice. Prices do not include sales taxes, which will be charged (if applicable) based on your state or country of residence. Canadian residents will be charged applicable taxes. Offer not valid in Quebec. This offer is limited to one order per household. Books received may not be as shown. Not valid for current subscribers to the Harlequin Special Edition or Harlequin Heartwarming series. All orders subject to approval. Credit or debit balances in a customer's account(s) may be offset by any other outstanding balance owed by or to the customer. Please allow 4 to 6 weeks for delivery. Offer available while quantities last.

Your Privacy—Your information is being collected by Harlequin Enterprises ULC, operating as Harlequin Reader Service. For a complete summary of the information we collect, how we use this information and to whom it is disclosed, please visit our privacy notice located at https://corporate.harlequin.com/privacy-notice. Notice to California Residents – Under California law, you have specific rights to control and access your data. For more information on these rights and how to exercise them, visit https://corporate.harlequin.com/california-privacy. For additional information for residents of other U.S. states that provide their residents with certain rights with respect to personal data, visit https://corporate.harlequin.com/other-state-residents-privacy-rights/.

HSEHW25